How to Buy Fine Wines

How to Buy Fine Wines

Practical Advice for the Investor and Connoisseur

STEVEN SPURRIER

AND

JOSEPH WARD

STEPHEN GREENE PRESS
Lexington, Massachusetts

FOR CANDY AND BELLA

The views expressed in this Christie's Collectors Guide are those of the authors. They do not necessarily reflect the views of Christie, Manson & Woods Ltd.

Acknowledgements
In preparing this book we spoke with dozens of people in the wine trade, in vineyards and in retail shops, and at points in between. Everywhere we met with lively interest and encouragement. Indeed one of the great pleasures in writing such a book is the company one keeps. To all those who helped our sincere thanks. We would also like to thank individually the following: John Avery, John Casson, Ian Jamieson, David Peppercorn, Serena Sutcliffe, and Helen Thomson.

We are also grateful to James Ward for the computer analysis of auction results, and to Jazz Wilson who transcribed hours of interviews and typed the final manuscript.

First published in Great Britain in 1986 by Phaidon · Christie's Limited
First published in the United States of America in 1987 by
The Stephen Greene Press, Inc.
Distributed by Viking Penguin Inc., 40 West 23rd Street, New York, NY 10010

Library of Congress Cataloging-in-Publication Data

Spurrier, Steven
    How to buy fine wines.
    (Christie's collectors guides)
    Includes index.
    1. Wine as an investment.   2. Wine industry.
I. Ward, Joseph.   II. Title.   III. Series.
HD9370.5.S68 1987   332.63   86–14870
ISBN 0-8289-0601-7

Printed in Great Britain by Butler & Tanner Limited, Frome, Somerset
Typeset in Apollo by MS Filmsetting Limited, Frome, Somerset

Contents

Preface

Here, I am happy to say, is an entirely practical book which should prove of great value to anyone seriously interested, or about to take an interest, in wine. Beginners can take heart: there are tips 'from the horse's mouth'. The authors, both highly experienced, name names. They outline the best areas, recommend specific types of wine and, perhaps most important of all, the major growers, shippers and merchants. Stick to these names—and to the best vintages— and even the newcomer to wine cannot go wrong. The more experienced will be reassured, and even old hands in the trade will be made more fully aware of important trends, the up-and-coming growers and châteaux, the best vintage bargains.

The rather unpleasant wine boom and slump of the mid-1970s highlighted the disastrous mistakes made not only by totally ignorant newcomers to the beat-inflation-commodity-market, but by some really big trade American and United Kingdom buyers. There were old-established merchants and large brewers who bought the graceless 1972 red Bordeaux in vast quantities, and at ridiculously high prices. They not only burnt their fingers badly, but depressed the market further when they were forced to unload at a loss. I cannot help feeling that had they had a sensible book like this in their hands, they would not have made such awesome mistakes.

But wine, sooner or later, is for drinking; for pleasurable and civilized drinking. And the main reason for people to take an intelligent interest *and* invest some spare cash in wine is to enable them to buy prudently, early and well, so that they have a supply of their favourite wines, well cellared and ready for them when the time comes for drinking—and at opening prices. The alternative is to live from hand to mouth, hoping to find the right wine and vintage and, of course, paying its full maturity— possibly scarcity—value.

One other thing I must stress is that buying for laying down must not just be a one-off investment but a continuous process, so that a succession of mature wines is planned. And at any one time, one's cellar should contain newly purchased young wine, maturing wine, and fully mature wine, some of which can then be drunk at its peak of perfection, some sold at its full maturity value for re-investment in the new young vintages.

There are additional bonuses. Getting to know wine not only awakens the senses of sight, smell and taste, it quite literally opens doors. Keen wine buffs meet other enthusiasts, and all are welcomed warmly by grower and merchant. Wine enthusiasts have a built-in passport not only to earthly delights, to beautiful vineyard areas, but to a variety of delightfully hospitable people.

This book will enable you to become a fine wine passport holder.

Michael Broadbent
Christie's, London, 1986

The Four Seasons Restaurant in New York's Seagram's building is known as much for its wines as for its cuisine. A feature is the temperature-controlled glass display case in the foyer.

A NOTE ABOUT PRICES
Conversions from dollars to sterling are given at the rates in force at the time.

Introduction

These are exciting times for wine drinkers. Never before has there been such widespread interest in and enthusiasm for fine wine, nor, thankfully, such widespread expertise in producing it. The traditional European leaders, France and Germany, seek to maintain positions won through centuries of experience with the finest grape varieties grown on the most propitious soils. Italy and Spain, having adapted new technology to their traditional ways, are now challenging, and the New World, first to embrace that technology, has allied it to a passion to equal or surpass Old World archetypes. Everyone is competing to produce the bottle that ends up on the dinner table.

The same spirit of competition is evident in the wine trade, and the consumer is now spoiled for choice. In both the United States and Great Britain more wines than ever before are available, and marketing techniques have improved dramatically. Consumers have become more sophisticated about wine, and merchants more sophisticated about selling it.

California's emergence as a fine wine region has been crucial in generating interest in the United States, which does not have the wine-drinking tradition of many European nations. The trade in America is also handicapped by tight Federal, and, often, State regulations that treat wine as the equivalent of spirits. None the less, American wine consumption increased dramatically during the 1960s and 1970s, and though it has now levelled off, fine wine's share of the market is increasing.

Sam Aaron of New York's Sherry-Lehmann remembers early attempts to sell Bordeaux futures. 'We started selling futures just after the war,' he said. 'We were the first, and it was very difficult. It wasn't until the 1959 vintage that there was any great interest.' Now futures are an integral part of Bordeaux sales, and the United States is the most important market for the top Crus Classés. While Bordeaux, Burgundy, and California are the leaders in the American fine wine market, they now face increasing competition. Today American wine drinkers are among the most sophisticated in the world and, being refreshingly free of chauvinism, are among the most catholic in their tastes.

In these circumstances buying wine should be easy, and, above all, it should not be a chore. The consumer, however, is confronted by two potentially off-putting facts when shopping for wine: the large and growing range of wines available, and the startlingly high prices of a small selection of them. Are these wines too expensive? Are the cheaper ones no good? Can you only get quality by paying a great deal of money? This book hopes to show that the answer to all three questions is 'No'.

Wine buying can be an everyday affair. Wine collecting turns this into a hobby which needs a little more time, effort and money, but which will return much more in pleasure, and, sometimes, in profit. It is open to everyone, not just the wealthy connoisseur, and it is a skill that can be acquired gradually, beginning with the first bottle. One of the most interesting cellars in Paris belongs to a retired dustman who began his collection by trading the empty bottles he picked up on his rounds for a single full one. The labels fired his enthusiasm; the facts he learned from his local wine merchant.

This brings us to the first rule concerning fine wine: find a merchant you can trust. There are so many wines and so many merchants; the aim of this book is to show you which ones are good and why. Throughout we shall draw on comparisons between the American and British markets.

We shall also be discussing wine as an investment, and because the secondary market is in Britain that is where our emphasis will be. In most American states it is very difficult for a private individual to re-sell wine, while in some states it is positively illegal. London auctioneers, mainly Christie's and Sotheby's, provide the principal secondary market for fine wine. There are about sixty auctions per year in London, and a constant turnover of stock from trade and private cellars. This compares to the 1985 figure of auctions held in Chicago, the only important centre for such sales in America. If you are planning to buy wine solely for re-sale, consider doing so on the British market. Shrewd investments can cut costs, but the primary purpose of wine, both fine and everyday, is to give pleasure. This book should help you get the maximum satisfaction and greatest pleasure from your wine buying.

Guidelines for Buying Fine Wine

There are two rules to keep in mind when buying fine wine: buy according to your tastes, and buy well in advance of use. The first is no more than common sense, but is not intended to discourage curiosity. Bordeaux is a splendid drink but there are other red wines. Those from America and Australia get better every year, and if after trying a few Californian Cabernets, you find them too big and alcoholic, you can always go back to Bordeaux. Trust your own tastes, but give the competition a try.

The second rule will force you to buy more knowledgeably, and should

Tokay is probably the least well-known of all fine wines. The best examples of this sweet white wine from northern Hungary have an extraordinary lifespan.

save you money, while ensuring that you enjoy wines at their best. There are some wines that can be bought and consumed straightaway, but generally wines are better with a few days' rest. When it comes to buying Bordeaux and port, planning ahead may be the only way to ensure a supply at reasonable prices. Recent experience shows that fine wines increase in value faster than the rate of inflation. Buying a case of 1985 Pichon-Lalande at $350 ex cellars is an investment; a case of 1961 at $1,800 is an extravagance although it could have been bought for $40 a case in 1964. Furthermore, if you get into the habit of buying wines at your leisure, you will not only save money, but also be sure of having the right bottle for any occasion.

Merchants' Lists

The first task is to collect as much information as possible from merchants and other sources. You cannot take Hugh Johnson or Michael Broadbent along to the liquor store, but you can certainly consult their books before making decisions. The wine merchants recommended in this book publish regular lists, some with tasting notes, and, in addition, most supplement the list with seasonal offers and special value sale items.

Compare the lists for range, prices, and services. If you do not have a cellar, it is wise to choose a merchant who offers storage. Find out about delivery and whether you can return items you find unsatisfactory. Then, talk with the merchants. Tell them your requirements, and ask their advice. Do not be shy. Very few people buy Château Lafite, and most merchants are glad to talk about the range of eight-to-ten dollar a bottle wines which they had to seek out specially.

Seize every opportunity to try the wines. Good merchants arrange tastings (the law permitting), both vertical and horizontal. A vertical tasting is one that compares wines of the same château from a number of vintages, while a horizontal tasting compares several wines of one region or commune in a particular vintage. You can arrange such tastings yourself; it helps if you find like-minded friends to share the costs.

Magazines and Wineletters

To learn more about individual wines, *Decanter Magazine* and *Wine Magazine* are the best sources of general information in Britain, though the latter's comparative tastings concentrate on everyday wines. In America *The Wine Spectator*, a twice monthly publication, is of comparable standing; there are also several newsletters devoted entirely to tasting notes.

The Wine Advocate is the work of one man, Robert M. Parker, Jr, and is the best guide to what is going on vintage by vintage that there is. It is published six times a year. *The Underground Wineletter*, a monthly publication from California, is another reliable source. Unlike *The Wine Advocate*, it is compiled from several people's judgements.

Clive Coates, a former wine merchant, began a newsletter in Britain in 1985. Called *The Vine*, it concentrates on fine wine, and mixes vineyard profiles with its assessments of new releases and classic vintages. From the very first it has been informative and well written.

The Consumers' Association publish, the *Which? Wine Guide* yearly. It is especially helpful for identifying Britain's best wine merchants and good value wines. Such publications can act as a pointer to the right wines and vintages, but they are no substitute for tasting the wines yourself.

Berry Bros. & Rudd Ltd., one of London's most distinguished fine wine merchants. Their shop at 3 St James's has remained virtually unchanged since the early eighteenth century.

1　Styles and Types of Fine Wine

Wine is the result of a combination of three main factors: the soil and climate, the grape varieties used, and the type of vinification and ageing. Paramount, of course, is the human factor, which is the dominant influence on whether a wine is good or not. This can be seen with precision in Burgundy, where the system of 'métayage' allows the vigneron who tends vines for an absentee landlord to receive half the grapes in payment and make the wine himself. Identical grapes, vinified by two different winemakers will not produce the same wine. On big estates in Bordeaux, the 'chef de culture', who looks after the agricultural side and everything to do with the vines, and the winemaker are of equal importance, for the French consider that a good vintage is made in the vineyards. In California, where buying in grapes under contract is more common than owning vineyards, it is the winemaker who is the star. All fine wine has a personalized quality about it: it may be made in large amounts, but it is rarely mass-produced. This being so, it is still possible to isolate specific types and styles of wine, which are based, more or less, on the grapes from which they are made.

It is undeniable that French wines are the benchmark for the majority of the wines throughout the world. Only one of the 'cépages nobles', the noble grape varieties that either singly or blended with each other produce the finest wines, finds its highest expression outside France, and that, the Riesling, is planted in France as well. The red grapes—Cabernet Sauvignon, Cabernet Franc, Merlot, Pinot Noir, Syrah and Grenache— and the whites—Chardonnay, Sauvignon, Sémillon and Chenin Blanc— produce wines that other countries may not wish to copy, or cannot, due to their soil or climate, but which are nevertheless viewed as models to be referred to. For this reason, we have separated the French varietals into their natural families, not because other wines have to resemble them, but because France was where the style began. 'Non-French' styles of wine are referred to under their own country.

The Bordeaux Family

Red

The Cabernet Sauvignon is the world's most important single grape variety. In France, the Pinot Noir is its rival, but not world-wide. The home of Cabernet Sauvignon is in the Médoc and Graves appellations in

Bordeaux, where—blended with a little Merlot and Cabernet Franc—it can account for up to 80 per cent of wines such as Ch. Mouton Rothschild, Ch. Léoville-Las-Cases and Ch. Latour. It is a late-ripening varietal with small, very dark berries that produce a wine of intense colour, of striking blackcurrant, bell-pepper aroma, and of hard, even austere tannin-backed flavour with great depth and ageing potential. Only in years when the Merlot fails in Bordeaux, such as 1961 and 1984, are wines made of 100 per cent Cabernet Sauvignon, for it needs the soft fruit of the other grape for balance. Cabernet Sauvignon has crept up from Bordeaux to the Loire Valley, the home of the Cabernet Franc, and across into le Midi and Provence, where it has helped to upgrade quality from the south, but its greatest successes outside Bordeaux have been outside France. In Europe, Piero Antinori and other Italian vintners have used the Cabernet with remarkable results either 100 per cent, as in the famous and rare Sassacaia, or blended in with the Sangiovese grape to produce Antinori's Tignanello. In Spain, it has added to the complexity of the superb Gran Coronas Black Label from Torrés, and allowed Jean Léon to produce a Médoc-styled Cabernet Sauvignon that is surpassed in reputation only by his Chardonnay.

Yet it is outside Europe that the Cabernet Sauvignon leads other red grape varieties. The warm climates of California, South Africa and Australia suit the Cabernet and produce a wine even more dark in colour and intense. After some years of making block-busting 100 per cent Cabernets, most wineries now accept a little Merlot in the blend, or vinify to extract less tannin. Nevertheless, such wines require long ageing to show the same complexity as a Médoc, although in their youth they possess a warm, plummy fruitiness that the slightly austere Médocs lack. The Cabernet Sauvignon also flourishes in New Zealand, whose cool climate produces a wine more French in style. These New World Cabernets are without question very fine wines indeed, and in blind tastings are often placed ahead of the wines from Bordeaux.

By contrast, the Cabernet Franc is very much a younger brother, yet one whose charm is a perfect foil to the other's intensity. The Cabernet Franc is at its best in the Loire—Chinon, Bourgueil, Saumur Champigny and all those delightful rosés—while in Bordeaux it is most planted in the Graves, St-Emilion and Fronsadais appellations. With a deep carmine colour, an aroma of raspberries or violets, and a firm but not hard finish, wines based on the Cabernet Franc mature relatively early. Outside France, it is notable for some delicious wines in Italy, especially from the Veneto and Friuli regions.

Cabernet Sauvignon's partner, and to some extent rival, in Bordeaux is the Merlot. This is a dark grape, which ripens early, but which is subject to rot in wet years. Its rich, plummy fruit provides the perfect foil for the Cabernet Sauvignon in the Médoc, and the dominant flavours in St-Emilion and Pomerol. Merlot is less tannic that the Cabernet family, and the wines open up after three to five years. One of the greatest wines in the world (and certainly the most expensive red wine) is virtually 100 per cent Merlot: Ch. Pétrus. Outside Bordeaux, the Merlot is successful in the south-west of France, and particularly fine in northern Italy. In California

Soil is an important element in shaping the character of fine wines, which thrive in poor soil. Châteauneuf-du-Pape is an illustration of this.

it has been much experimented with, but it is difficult to grow. However, it is used as a blender grape to produce very fine Cabernets, and with Stag's Leap and Sterling, who are two of the few wineries to make a 100 per cent Merlot, its quality is spectacular.

White

Bordeaux has two principal white grapes, the Sémillon and the Sauvignon, the latter of which it shares with the Loire Valley. The Sauvignon ripens early to make a crisp, fruity, dry wine with an attractive acidity. In the right conditions, in the Sauternes and adjoining regions of Bordeaux, and in certain parts of California and Australia, it can take on the 'pourriture noble' condition, to produce an intensely sweet wine. 'Sauvignon Blanc Sec' is a new style of wine in Bordeaux, unheard of before modern methods of vinification arrived in the early 1970s. It is now the principal white grape planted in the Graves, and the Sauvignon Blancs from California that make a Bordeaux-style wine—Sterling Vineyards, Iron Horse—will bottle their wine in the clear upright Bordeaux bottle, while those making a Loire style—Robert Mondavi, Dry Creek—will use the dark green Burgundy bottle. The Sauvignon also makes dry but flowery whites in Chile, in northern Italy and especially in New Zealand.

The Sémillon is a more noble grape than the Sauvignon, but less versatile. In the Graves region, it adds roundness and flavour to a crisp, slightly uncomplex Sauvignon. In Sauternes it comes into its own when the year is propitious for 'pourriture noble', for it is the major varietal in all the sweet wines of Bordeaux and the south-west, with the exception of Jurançon. Here it is always blended with a little Sauvignon to add acidity (and sometimes a tiny amount of Muscadelle). Ch. d'Yquem, for instance, is 80 per cent Sémillon, 20 per cent Sauvignon, while in the Graves, Domaine de Chevalier is almost the reverse with 70 per cent Sauvignon and 30 per cent Sémillon. Outside France, notable success for the Sémillon is found only in Australia, particularly in the Hunter Valley.

The Loire Family

Red

The only major grape planted in the Loire is Cabernet Franc, which makes the delicious, raspberry-scented red wines of Touraine, already mentioned above. The Gamay is also widely planted, for its popular, easy fruit, but the origin and style of this grape belongs under Burgundy.

White

The two major white varieties in the Loire are the Sauvignon and the Chenin Blanc. The Sauvignon is at its best and most typical in the Central

Work in the vineyard goes on throughout the year. Winter is the time for pruning and preparing the vines for the following season.

Loire, particularly at Sancerre and Pouilly-sur-Loire. In contrast to Bordeaux, where the wine has a certain leanness due to the soil, here the Sauvignon is dry, but packed with fruit, even to the point of aggressiveness. It is also always 100 per cent varietal, so these wines are used to denote benchmark Sauvignon style. It is not by coincidence that, beginning with Robert Mondavi, many New World wineries use the term Fumé Blanc to describe their Sauvignons, taken from the appellation Pouilly-Fumé. Although the Loire is a cool climate, the Sauvignon flourishes in warmer climates like California and Australia, where it has become extremely popular.

The Chenin Blanc, like the Sémillon, is falling from fashion due to the demand for dry fruity wines to be drunk young. The Chenin is an underrated 'cépage noble' that can produce a range of wines from very dry to very sweet, as well as being an excellent base for a méthode Champenoise. In the Loire, its finest expression is found in the wines, both dry, demi-sec, and fully sweet of Vouvray, and in the splendid, historically famous wines of Anjou, now justly coming back in reputation. In common with the Sémillon, the richness and complexity of these wines comes from overripeness in the form of noble rot. The Chenin Blanc is hardly planted outside the Loire, but is well respected in South Africa, where it is known as the Steen, and is popular for its off-dry flavours in California. As yet, the Chenin is perhaps the only one of France's 'cépages nobles' that has not reached the same stature abroad as it has at home. Perhaps the luminous, soft climate of the Loire Valley has something to do with this.

The Burgundy Family

Red

Burgundy is made from the Pinot Noir, whose capriciousness as a fragile, late-ripening grape is not helped by the vagaries of the northern climate. Moreover, while Bordeaux may benefit from at least three grape varieties, Burgundy relies solely on the Pinot Noir. Attempts to blend Pinot in the fermenting vat, as in the Pinot Noir-Gamay Bourgogne Passetoutgrains, are not very exciting, and while the South African hybrid Pinotage, a Pinot-Cinsault grape, has its own character, it cannot be described as a 'cépage noble'. The charm of Burgundy, its pure class, is found in elegance and finesse and definition of 'terroir'. Its wines are not full-bodied, dark-coloured robust wines, and therein lie many of the problems surrounding this region. A fine Burgundy, Clos de Vougeot, Volnay for instance, from a good year may well have a deep colour and a firm, fruity finish, even a certain earthiness, but it should not be heavy. If anything, it should be 'spirituel'. There are enough confusing and contradictory wines coming out of Burgundy (which has the poor luck to have fewer good vintages than Bordeaux, and then to have some of its successes—1972, 1980—damned by the failure of those in Aquitaine) to make it difficult to establish a Burgundy style, and so different is the climate on the Côte d'Or from any other vineyard, with the possible exception of Champagne, that the 'Burgundy' type is difficult to ascertain, and the Pinot Noir world-wide does not represent it. In northern Spain, the Torrés family have made some fine, oak-aged Pinots, Italy and Alsace produce fruity, not excessively varietal wines, but Australia, South Africa and California are too hot, and Germany too cold. Exceptions are notable in the excellent Pinots from Oregon and Washington State, and from vineyards either of high elevation such as the Pinnacles, south of San Francisco (Chalone, Calera), or of very cool climate north of San Francisco (Carneros Creek). In New Zealand, the Brajkovitch family make a lovely, Côte-Chalonnaise style wine from Kumeu River grapes.

Another red grape from Burgundy, or more exactly from the Beaujolais, 60 miles to the south, is the Gamay. This is an early ripening varietal, which is vinified quickly to capture the fruit. It is best in the Beaujolais, and transports well to cool climates such as the Loire. Careful vinification of the Gamay-Beaujolais in the USA has produced a similar style of wine.

White

The Burgundy grape is the Chardonnay, the varietal that makes the greatest dry white wines in France and throughout the world. Its only rival is the Riesling, yet the finest Riesling wines are not wholly dry. Burgundy is in the north-east of France (no matter how far south it may look to the British), and it is not surprising to rediscover the principal Burgundy grapes, Chardonnay and Pinot Noir, in Champagne, only 90 miles to the north. The Chardonnay grape is remarkably adaptable, for although it prefers a coolish climate and a lightish soil, it produces extremely stylish wines even in hot countries. In Burgundy, style ranges from the flinty, long-lasting Chablis to the fatter, more buttery wines of Meursault and the Montrachet family, and the fresh, fruity wines of the Mâconnais. Much influence is attributed to 'terroir' for a Meursault will always be very different from a Puligny, even though the villages are next door to each other, but methods of vinification and ageing play an equal part in determining the final taste. A Meursault that is cool-fermented and aged in tanks will be quite different from one that is barrel-fermented and kept in oak. Chardonnay is one of the least obvious wines, very difficult to put into words, but with a definitive style, and the way it is handled is almost as important as where it is grown.

The Chardonnay is also the most successful grape around the world, alongside the Cabernet Sauvignon. There is hardly a wine-growing country, on a latitude south of Champagne, where it is not grown successfully. Individual wines are too numerous to mention, but notable bottlings come from Spain (Jean Léon), Italy (Lungarotti, Gaja), California, Australia and, for cool-climate French style wines, New Zealand. It is a tribute to the vignerons of the Côte d'Or that their few hundred acres of vines have encouraged so many brilliant wines to be made.

The Rhône Family

Red

The Rhône Valley produces unabashedly full-bodied wines, but wines that do not lack elegance.

The grape which has made Rhône wines famous across the world is the Syrah, the varietal that is responsible for wines such as Cornas, St-Joseph and Hermitage, to the extent that the Hermitage name is much used to denote the Syrah style. The style is as unmistakable as the Cabernet Sauvignon, and magnified by the extra ripeness and body from warmer climates: it is very dark in colour, almost black when young, with a rich, fruity bouquet, in which spices and blackcurrants predominate. Although it is a big wine, it is rarely more than 13 per cent alcohol, and so goes well with food. If ever there were a benchmark wine, it is Hermitage, since the few growers who cultivate the 120 hectares produce a uniformly high quality. Italy and Spain have not taken to the Syrah, nor has South America, but California, and especially South Africa and Australia, have used its adaptability to hot climates to great effect. Two decades ago Hermitage was a forgotten wine, and ten years ago it was still underrated. It is now in the forefront of French wines, alongside the Pauillacs and the Pommards, and 'Hermitages' around the world can only benefit.

The other great wine from the Rhône Valley is Châteauneuf-du-Pape, which is made principally from the Grenache. This is originally a Spanish grape, the Garnarcho, as is the other fine varietal from the south, the Mourvèdre. Grenache makes a fat, fleshy wine, full of fruit and always high in alcohol (the famous Vin Doux Naturel of Banyuls and Rivesaltes, a rival to port for the French, is made from the Grenache), but with a tendency to oxidization. Thus, unless there is sufficient Mourvèdre, Cinsault or Syrah in the blend, as there should be in a good Châteauneuf-du-Pape, these wines are to be drunk young. The Grenache is planted in California and Australia, and usually ends up in a 'jug' wine.

White

The white wines are enjoying the popularity of all dry white wines and the considerable increase in price of white Burgundies. With few exceptions they are made from a mixture of grapes: Roussanne and Marsanne in the north, Grenache Blanc, Clairette, Bourboulenc and Ugni Blanc in the south. These are not major grape varieties, and seldom find their way on to a wine label, although Chateau Tahbilk in Australia makes some 100 per cent Marsanne.

The German Family

The king of the German family of grape varieties is the Riesling. This is one of the finest of the white wine grapes, with the range of the Chenin Blanc

Gewürztraminer: this spicy, fruity variety is a native of Italy but it is most closely identified with Alsace, where it produces wines that rival the great Rieslings.

and the complexity of the Chardonnay. It has a distinctive clean fruit, purity of style and lemony acidity (even at its most sweet), that transcend differences in region and climate. It reaches perfection in the northern slate-based terraced vineyards of Germany, where it almost defies nature to ripen slowly and late to produce wines of incredible richness that are never cloying. The Riesling is also the king of Alsace where, with the exception of great vintages when the style may be more Germanic, it is vinified as a dry wine.

It is perhaps the Riesling more than any other grape variety that is most recognizable outside its native country. Winemakers in South Africa, on both coasts of the USA, and in Chile, Australia and New Zealand have pushed their experiments with Riesling further than with any other varietal, and with more success, both in the dry and the late-picked styles.

Other grape varieties that are found across the world, but which are at their most typical in Alsace rather than Germany, include the Gewürz-traminer, Muscat and Tokay (Pinot Gris). The Gewürztraminer has a heavily perfumed, slightly spicy aroma with explosive, almost exotic fruit flavours. The Muscat possesses a 'musky', grapey aroma with a dry finish, and the Tokay a rich, mouth-filling fruit, but low acidity. All three transport favourably from this north-east corner of France to northern Italy, where the style is lighter and less aromatic, and across to the New World, where the wines are correspondingly richer due to the warmer climate. Only in New Zealand, with its cool climate, do these German–Alsace grapes lack this extra sweetness.

Other Important Varieties

These, then, are the truly international grape varieties. Each country has fine varietals of its own, and new strains are being developed. The wines of the major wine-producing countries are covered at length elsewhere in the book, but one could perhaps single out four red grape varieties which, although they are not seen outside their country of origin, have a distinctive style and character. They are the Nebbiolo from Piedmont, responsible for Barolo and Barbaresco, dark-coloured, hugely concentrated wines with a high level of tannin; the Sangiovese from Tuscany, the principal grape of the noble Chianti Classicos; the Tempranillo from Rioja, with more finesse than the Garnarcho (Grenache); and the Zinfandel from California, whose origins are blurred, but which is the only truly American varietal.

It has been said that the grape variety gives a wine its character while the terroir gives it its soul. Both are at the heart of all fine wine, yet in the hands of a skilled vigneron and winemaker, neither should dominate in an harmonious rendition.

Muscat: an important varietal in Alsace characterized by its sweet, fruity, grapey nose, though the wines are invariably vinified dry.

Tokay: a white grape with pink-coloured berries, more correctly known as Pinot Gris in France, Pinot Grigio in Italy and Rulander in Germany. Not to be confused with Tokay, a very sweet white wine from Hungary, the Pinot Gris produces flowery wines, full of flavour but lacking in acidity.

2 Buying the Wine

Great Britain

The British wine drinker is in a fortunate position. Only the United States can match the range of fine wines, but, there, because of state-by-state regulation, they are not available to all. Geography and history account for Britain's bounty.

Though not a major wine producer, Britain belongs to a trading community dominated by producers. With consumption low but rising steadily, and having no indigenous industry to protect, Britain is a prime market for the rest of Europe. Accession to the EEC has boosted the wine trade, but even before 1973 Britain had established close links with particular regions, notably Bordeaux and Oporto. The comparative lack of regulation is another factor. Merchants, keen to exploit little-known regions, can set up business without much fuss or investment, and such merchants have stimulated interest in Rioja, Piedmont, and the Rhône, with the larger companies following their lead.

Other countries see Britain as an arbiter of taste. 'It is very difficult to get into the international market,' says Robert Mondavi, who has done more than anyone to establish the Napa Valley's reputation, 'but important that we be there. In that market, England in particular is important, because they have a reputation for being impartial.' As the centre of the international auction market, London is the clearing house for fine and rare wines, many of which are not available from any other source. Most of the customers are in the trade, but private buyers are welcome. Because most of the buyers are professionals the auctions provide an early warning of price increases, and are worth following just for that.

Auctions are, however, unlikely to be the collector's primary source of fine wines, and there are five other methods of buying wine in Britain. These are: traditional wine merchants, specialists, supermarkets, high-street chains, and wine clubs.

Thirty years ago the fine wine business in Britain was neatly organized. A group of traditional merchants, with lists built around the Crus Classés of the Médoc, sold to a small, upper-middle-class clientele. As well as private clients this included restaurants, universities, city institutions, and private clubs. Port, négociant-bottled Burgundy, and hock made up the rest of the list. There was little from the Rhône or Alsace, and none of the table wines of Spain and Italy. California meant Hollywood, and Australia cricket. It was all very cosy and consumption was static.

This began to change in the late 1950s, as the country moved from the austerity of the post-war years toward relative affluence. The large brewers, attracted to the traditional wine trade by its need for capital and general lack of it, and the distillers, wanting to diversify and sensing a shift in drinking habits, moved into wine. They started with basic table wine, but moved up-market, aided by two changes in the law. The first was the abolition in 1964 of fixed margins (resale price maintenance), and the second was the adoption of a more liberal licensing policy. Soon the high-street wine shop became commonplace. It was convenient, carried no class connotations, and while the staff frequently had little wine knowledge, prices were keen.

The Crown in Southwold, where Suffolk wine merchants Adnams moved in 1985. Their restaurant has an extensive list of reasonably priced fine wines.

Supermarkets

The most significant change in wine retailing, both for fine and everyday wines, has been the emergence of the supermarkets over the last two decades. Starting from scratch, they have become the country's largest wine merchants, accounting for about half of total sales. Their sales are dominated by own-brand wines at the lower price levels, but the best of them have moved increasingly into fine wine. Sainsbury's, the market leader, have a 'Vintage Selection' available in larger stores. Included are a Meursault, well-selected clarets from petits châteaux to Crus Classés, fine Sauternes, and vintage Champagnes.

Allan Cheeseman, the chief wine buyer for Sainsbury's, believes that as people grow more knowledgeable and confident about wine, supermarkets will take an even bigger share of the fine wine market. 'We have taken customers from the high-street shops in the past', he says, 'because of the convenience of doing all their shopping in one place. But as we improve our range, particularly with the "Vintage Selection", we will get more customers from the traditional merchants.' This should be making the others nervous, because Sainsbury's, though unwilling to reveal sales figures, are believed by trade sources to account for about 15 per cent of the total UK wine market.

Wine Merchants

Britain's best traditional merchants have responded well to the changes of the past couple of decades—they have had to in order to survive. In an era of rising prices and high interest rates, most can no longer afford to hold large stocks of mature claret and vintage port.

There is the occasional fortunate one like Berry Bros. & Rudd who are backed by Cutty Sark whisky, but even they have begun selling claret *en primeur*, that is in the year following the vintage, several years before the wine will be ready to drink. Increasingly the traditionalists have had to look to other regions, finding quality wines at reasonable prices, and convincing their customers to give them a try. In doing so they rely on their greatest strength, their expertise. People go to them for advice, something that is not available from supermarkets or most wine chains.

The trade card of a nineteenth-century London wine merchant. London, Victoria and Albert Museum.

The first chance to assess a fine wine merchant is through his list. The best of them, such as Lay & Wheeler and Corney & Barrow, have catalogues as informative as many books. There are notes on vintages, regions, and individual wines, giving the style, approximate date of maturity, and, occasionally, serving suggestions. Look first at the classics. A fine wine merchant should stock a good range of Bordeaux, with the top Crus Classés and well-selected Crus Bourgeois and petits châteaux. Stocks may well extend back through the classic vintages of the 1960s.

Burgundy is the region that tells most about a merchant. A good list will have a selection of domaine-bottled wines as well as the pick of the top négociants. If the list is simply line after line of négociant Burgundy from one or two houses, it means the merchant is not making an effort. In Burgundy you have to go looking for the good wines; they do not come to you.

Gone are the days when merchants bottled their own port. Vintage port is all bottled in Oporto now, so look for a good choice of vintages from the top shippers, and some of the good value 'single quinta' wines. There should also be some exquisite ten and twenty-year-old tawnies.

Apart from the classics, the merchant should be making an effort to sell the produce from one or more of the newer fine wine regions. Adnam's, for example, had a perfunctory Italian list until 1984. They have since visited the Italian vineyards, and have come up with a short selection of that difficult country's best estates.

It is the extras, though, that give the traditional merchant the edge in selling fine wine. Apart from advice, he should offer storage, credit, and delivery. And he should be willing to locate rare and unusual wines not on his list.

Specialists

The specialist is similar to the traditional wine merchant, but will sell a narrower range. Expertise is crucial here, for the wines will not be as familiar as Bordeaux and Burgundy. The specialist knows this. If a customer is disappointed with a bottle of claret, he will probably shrug it off. If the same thing happens with a Barolo, that is usually the end of the Italian experiment.

The specialist is sometimes the only source for certain wines. The Wine Studio for California, Windrush for the Pacific Northwest, and Yapp Brothers for the Rhône and Loire Valleys, are such merchants. Another plus for the specialist is his (or her) enthusiasm. He is probably concentrating on the wines of a particular region, less because he has identified a gap in the market, than because he genuinely likes the wines and wants to share his passion.

High-Street Chains

The large high-street chains are in danger of being squeezed at both ends. On the one hand there are the traditional fine wine merchants and the specialists, with increasing sophistication in marketing, and on the other, the supermarkets, which can rival the chains for both price and convenience. However, as long as the UK fine wine market continues to expand, there will be an incentive for the innovative merchant.

Wine Clubs

The Wine Society is the pioneer wine club, but many more have moved into this area. They are usually exclusively mail order and charge a membership fee. In the case of the Wine Society it is £10 ($15) for lifetime membership. Most have regular mailings of special offers, and organize tastings to get to know their members. The best of them are like traditional wine merchants with the enthusiasm of the specialists.

The USA

The United States may be an enterprise culture, and this the era of deregulation, but nobody seems to have told the wine trade. It is bound up by regulations and restrictions that are the legacy of Prohibition. From 1919 to 1933 the Volstead Act prohibited the production, importation, transportation and sale of alcoholic beverages in the United States. To secure repeal, Prohibition's opponents agreed to an important concession: regulation of alcoholic beverages would be left to the individual states. This allowed states with a strong temperance movement to remain 'dry' or to devolve power within the state. This 'local option' meant that one county or city might permit the sale of liquor while its neighbour

The Wine Society was the pioneer fine wine club. They maintain extensive cellars for their stocks and for those of their customers.

The story of Sherry-Lehmann on New York's Madison Avenue is the story of New York and of American fine wine retailing. Started by Sam Aaron in 1934, Sherry-Lehmann stock an unrivalled range of fine Bordeaux.

prohibited it. State licensing control gave the states a new and potentially vast source of revenue in the form of excise taxes.

For a foreign wine producer, state regulation means that the United States has effectively 50 separate authorities plus the Federal government. One respected producer in Alsace showed us a collection of labels and stack of forms needed to sell his wines in the different states and asked plaintively, 'It is one country, isn't it?'

Three of America's largest states illustrate the variety of regulations. California, the most populous state, has relatively few restrictions. This is to be expected from the country's most important producer. Here, wineries themselves are retailers, as are supermarkets, drug stores and specialist wine merchants. There are even wine supermarkets.

New York, the second largest state, is more tightly regulated, with the trade divided into importers, wholesalers, and retailers. It is an affluent market and competition is fierce. New York has as wide a range of wines as Great Britain, but wine shops cannot sell accessories, food, or wine books.

Pennsylvania, the fourth largest, has a state monopoly, with distribution and sale done entirely by the Pennsylvania Board of Control.

Wineries in California have stimulated interest in fine wines, especially in the home state, which is now one of America's most knowledgeable. For example, Kermit Lynch is an importer and retailer in Berkeley, and his shop, stacked with boxes and crates looks like a small warehouse. But what a warehouse! Burgundies from Bernard Maume and Robert Chevillon; Hermitage from Gérard Chave, and Côte-Rôtie from Robert Jasmin; Barolo from Aldo Conterno: selections from Europe's top growers with an emphasis on Burgundy and Rhône. They are all wines he imports himself, and though only an hour from the Napa Valley, he sells no California wines.

Such an operation is common enough in Great Britain, but highly unusual in America. Kermit Lynch could not have such a shop in New

In October 1985 Morrell's, one of New York's best fine wine merchants, moved to new premises on Madison Avenue.

York; it would be against the law, but California is one of the few states that allows importers to be retailers. Just down the street from Kermit Lynch is an entirely different sort of retailer, the Liquor Barn. Part of a chain, it is a supermarket selling only liquor, wines, and beer. There is an enormous selection of good, bad, and indifferent wines, very little advice, and very keen prices.

A New Yorker must plan his purchases more carefully, as wine sales are restricted to licensed liquor stores. Supermarkets do not stock wine, nor do drug stores. And there are restrictions at point of sale. Credit sales are illegal, and if the customer wants to taste before buying, he is out of luck. It is illegal to open wine for tasting in a retail shop. Chain stores are also illegal. These restrictions are annoying, but New York's wine merchants cope as any retailer in New York copes. They work out what they can do and then go at it harder than anyone else. So New York has an astonishing range of fine wines. It is America's most important market for Cru Classé Bordeaux and two shops in particular, Sherry-Lehmann and Morrell, stock unrivalled ranges.

Though New York is more regulated than California, the wine drinker is well enough served. Not so in Pennsylvania. There wine is sold only through state stores. The choice is representative rather than comprehensive, and not very inspired. And if a Pennsylvanian wants a wine not on the state list, he must go to the store and fill out a form which the manager passes on to the distributor. Some time later the wine arrives—sometimes. If it is a wine produced in small quantities, the chances are that the US allocation will have been taken up by retailers in more flexible jurisdictions. Pity the poor Pennsylvanian.

Not surprisingly, the restrictions show through in sales. In California, with relatively little regulation, the yearly average is 23 bottles per person; in New York, it is 15 bottles; and in Pennsylvania, with the state monopoly, the figure is only 7 bottles per person (*Wines & Vines*, 1985).

3   Auctions and Investment

Auctions

Auction houses are an important part of the fine wine trade, functioning as the wholesale market for mature classics which have disappeared from merchants' lists, and as the principal means by which private clients dispose of excess stock—particularly wines which have achieved a price higher than they wish to drink at. The shrewd consumer can use the salerooms as a way into the wholesale wine trade, but *caveat emptor*: the auction houses will reveal all they know about a wine's provenance, but they may not know the complete history of older bottles, and there is no merchant to go to for redress. Auctioneers act as agents for the vendor, not the buyer.

The international trade is based in London and is dominated by Christie's and Sotheby's with the former the more important. Christie's hold two fine wine sales a month at their King Street salerooms during a season lasting from September to July, and monthly sales of lesser wines at South Kensington. The King Street sales are divided between Bordeaux and Fine Wines, the latter including Burgundy, port, Germany, and other fine wines as well as older claret and Sauternes. A new company with British and American backing, International Wine Auctions, held its first sale in June 1985. They plan quarterly sales in London.

Because of its restrictive laws, America is not an important auction centre. Illinois is an exception, and Christie's hold frequent sales there, as does the American-owned Chicago Fine Wine Company. Christie's also organize regular sales in Amsterdam and Geneva.

Admission to auctions is by catalogue, and these are available by subscription, or individually from the auctioneer, or by post. A subscription is a good idea, because it saves money on the price of the catalogue and ensures that you will have sufficient time to read it and make decisions. Furthermore, both Christie's and Sotheby's send a list of prices realized to their subscribers after the sale. This is handy for keeping up with trends in the market. In addition, Christie's allow subscribers admission to pre-sale tastings—an excellent opportunity to learn about fine wines.

Michael Broadbent, Head of Christie's Wine Department, London, conducting a sale in Chicago.

Catalogue Symbols and Terms

Read the catalogue carefully, and be sure you understand the rules. Calculate any extras, such as duty, VAT (Value Added Tax at 15 per cent), delivery, and buyer's premium when deciding your bid. Sotheby's introduced a 10 per cent buyer's premium (i.e. 10 per cent of the selling price) in 1984, and Christie's have done the same beginning in September 1986. Set a firm figure for each lot and stick to it. It is easy to get carried away in the bidding and spend more than your budget will allow. You can also bid by post by filling in the form at the back of the catalogue. Be sure to state the maximum price for each lot and, if bidding for several lots, the order of preference, and maximum total expenditure. The auctioneer will not automatically buy it at your maximum, but will always try to secure it for you at a lower price.

Wines are sold either FOB, ex cellars, In Bond, Duty Paid, Duty Paid but Available in Bond, or Duty and VAT Paid. Most wines fall into the last two categories.

FOB (Freight on Board): seldom seen, it means that the buyer pays all the charges for carriage, duty, and VAT (Value Added Tax at 15 per cent) from the shipment point in country of origin. Auctioneers will usually arrange shipment of such wines for private clients.

Ex cellars: wine lying at the château with all shipment, duty, and VAT to be paid by the buyer. Usually only large lots are sold in this way.

In Bond: wines stored in bonded warehouses free of duty. Duty currently stands at the equivalent of £8.82 per dozen bottles for table wine, £14.56 for Champagne, and £17.54 per dozen bottles for vintage port. Overseas buyers need not pay the duty if the wine is to be shipped out of Britain. As there are quite a few overseas buyers, a private buyer living in the United Kingdom is at a disadvantage bidding for wines in bond.

Duty Paid and Subject to VAT (indicated with a † in the catalogue): these wines have had the excise duty paid but are still liable for VAT at 15 per cent of the selling price.

Duty Paid but Available in Bond (indicated with a ‡ in the catalogue): bidding takes place at duty-paid prices, but overseas buyers can subtract excise duty from the final cost. British clients must still pay VAT.

Duty and VAT Paid: wines marked without daggers or other qualifications are not liable for duty or VAT. These wines, from private cellars, represent the best buy for private clients.

Another feature to watch out for in the catalogue is an indication of options. Offered at the auctioneer's discretion, options give the successful bidder for the first of several lots of the same wine the right to buy as many of the remaining lots as he wants at the same price. The catalogue will say if options are to be offered. They generally are.

Bidding at auction is usually per dozen bottles or equivalent (e.g. six magnums, twenty-four half-bottles). A lot is usually at least a dozen bottles; if it is more, the bid is multiplied by the lot size. For example, the

Title pages from two of Christie's early wine sales. Their first wine auction was held in 1766.

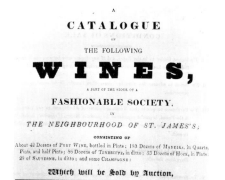

A selection from a 'Finest and Rarest Wine' sale at Christie's, London.

price of a lot of three dozen bottles would be the successful bid times three. Smaller lots or ones made up of several different wines are sometimes sold 'per lot'.

A bidding guide is provided in the form of estimates printed to the right of each lot. The estimate gives a minimum and maximum price based on recent history of the wine. When it is a wine which seldom appears, or when it is a mixed lot, the estimate sometimes appears as a single number with a plus sign, suggesting a minimum but leaving it open ended.

What to Buy at Auction

Red Bordeaux is the mainstay of the auction houses. It is the longest-lived of red wines, and the one in greatest supply. The market changes very rapidly, and predictions made in late 1985 may not apply in a year's time. Prices for mature wines from classic vintages have increased rapidly over the past three years, partly because of the strong dollar, and partly because of the greater world-wide interest in fine wines. The best buy for medium-term drinking is 1979. These wines are currently selling for about two-thirds the price of the more highly regarded 1978 vintage.

Compare the following prices from 1984 auctions: Pichon-Lalande 1978, £250 ($325); Pichon-Lalande 1979, £125 ($162); Palmer 1978, £400 ($520); Palmer 1979, £260 ($338); Léoville-Las-Cases 1978, £210 ($273); Léoville-Las-Cases 1979, £145 ($188). The 1979s closed the gap somewhat in 1985, but they still look to be a good buy. For the longer term, consider 1981. The first of three very good vintages in Bordeaux, 1981 looks the most likely to be left behind by fashion. They also sold at significantly lower

A wine auction in the Napa Valley, California.

opening prices than either 1982 or 1983, so an equivalent percentage increase for them would still make them attractive buys.

Vintage port prices are rising rapidly, due mainly to American demand. Philip Tenenbaum of the Chicago Fine Wine Company says that his clients concentrate on the greatest vintages. They are buying 1963s for the short to medium term, and moving on to 1977s for the long term. This leaves private buyers in the UK with the very good 1966s and the even better 1970s. Prices for the 1966s are already pretty high, reflecting their maturity. Restaurants and wine merchants are buying this wine for current consumption. Although prices for the best 1970s have risen sharply in the past two years, they were very low, and even now look attractive. In May 1985 both Taylor and Graham 1970 were selling for £180–£190 ($225–38) a dozen, less than the 1977s were making. The 1975 vintage is another attractive buy for current consumption.

The 1983 vintage ports were released in July 1985 at prices 20 per cent up on the 1982s, on average £120 ($150) per dozen duty paid, and were oversold by two or three times. Whether this was due to port shippers seeing the strength of demand and withdrawing stock into reserve, or genuine overselling is not yet clear, but speculation in the 1983s is now high and is having a knock-on effect on older vintages.

Burgundy makes up a small proportion of auction sales, and only a few domaines regularly achieve high prices. The two most prominent are the Domaine de la Romanée-Conti and Domaine Comtes de Vogüé. White wines do better than reds, and such is the scarcity of Grands and Premiers Crus from the Côte de Beaune that these are usually snatched up at high prices. It is still possible, however, to find good red Burgundy at reasonable prices, since its uneven quality inhibits potential buyers.

The vintage to buy is 1980, especially from the Côte de Nuits. Underrated from the start, the wines have turned out rather well, and are currently quite reasonable. Another vintage to consider is 1976, a year of big, tough wines. Originally well regarded, the year has turned up too many duds, and prices reflect this disappointment. The best vintage currently available is 1978, though prices are high. The 1983 vintage is prestigious, tannic and for long-term keeping, but with some risk due to rot, particularly in the Côte de Nuits. 1985 is more plummy and regular, and good to excellent throughout Burgundy. Prices, however, are astronomical. Particular care is needed when buying red Burgundy at auction, but with the current price differential between it and claret, it is worth taking a chance.

There is no doubt that the real bargains at auction are mature German wines, especially wines of Auslese and higher quality of the 1971 and 1976 vintages. Most still sell for less than £100 ($150) a dozen, and even Wehlener Sonnenuhr Auslese 1971 from Prüm Erben, a really outstanding wine, sold for only £115 ($144) a dozen in May 1985. This is less than the price of a good 1983 Sauternes. Consider these fine German wines as an alternative to the sweet wines of France.

Wine Investments

The 1982 Bordeaux vintage brought many first-time buyers into the *en primeur* market, and increased interest in wine as an investment. Top wines from that year have doubled or trebled in price, and some have disappeared from the market altogether. The following vintage has shown healthy increases too, as buyers who missed out on the 1982s have purchased the very good 1983s. Certainly anyone who bought wines from leading properties at opening prices has made a handsome profit.

1984 had no investment potential, as the prices asked bore no relation to quality, whatever relation they might have had with supply and demand. Following the excellent and much-touted quality of the 1985s, the 1984s may even fall in price from the opening offers of summer 1985.

Investing in wine is not a popular subject with some wine merchants. Peter J. Morrell, a leading New York merchant said, 'I certainly don't advise customers to invest. It takes wine away from the consumer and drives up prices. I've never been in favour of commodity speculators.' But Michael Broadbent takes the opposite view. 'The investor or speculator is a very useful chap,' he claimed. 'All right, if you pull out the speculative element, prices could fall by 40 per cent, but it would also mean the end of the supply of old vintages.'

We take a broad view of investment. For a wine lover, en primeur purchases are a good investment if the value of the wine at maturity has outpaced the return available from traditional sources. It has recently done much better than that, and by adding a few extra cases as investments in good years, the collector can finance future requirements by selling the excess. In addition, anyone planning a cellar should take note of the investment market. He can use the information to time purchases, find bargains, and plan sales of his stock.

Boom or Bust?

The recent past has seen a boom in fine wine prices (similar booms also occurred in the 1860s and 1920s). In 1971, Bordeaux of the great 1961 vintage was widely available and reasonably priced. Henry Townsend's list had Ducru-Beaucaillou and Léoville-Las-Cases for £2.50 ($6.12) per bottle; Palmer for £4.50 ($11.00); La Mission-Haut-Brion at £5.00 ($12.25); Latour at £8.75 ($21.43); and Mouton-Rothschild for the princely sum of £10.00 ($24.50). The cost of living has increased roughly fourfold since then, while these wines have rocketed out of sight. Ducru-Beacaillou and Léoville-Las-Cases sell for about £80.00 ($120); La Mission-Haut-Brion is pushing £200 ($300) a bottle; the others have passed that mark and are still climbing. As the graph below shows, the really spectacular rise begins in 1981.

Wine prices began to rise sharply a decade earlier with the release of the fine 1970s. Opening prices were reasonable, and allocations quickly taken up. Prices rose throughout the year. The following spring, the good but variable 1971s were offered at prices much higher than the previous vintage. Mouton-Rothschild's price went from FF 36,000 per tonneau in 1970 to FF 120,000 in 1971, while Lafite rose from FF 59,000 to FF 110,000.

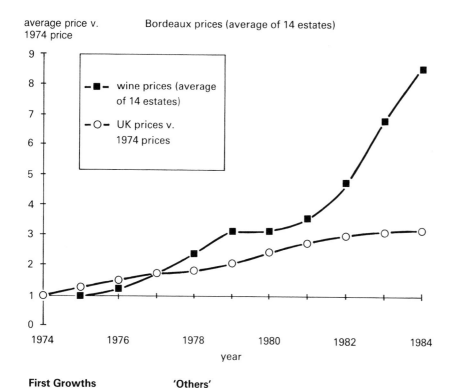

First Growths	**'Others'**	
Ch. Lafite-Rothschild	Ch. Cheval-Blanc	Ch. Léoville-Las-Cases
Ch. Latour	Ch. Pétrus	Ch. La Mission-Haut-Brion
Ch. Margaux	Ch. Beychevelle	Ch. Ducru-Beaucaillou
Ch. Mouton-Rothschild	Ch. Palmer	Ch. Gruaud-Larose
Ch. Haut-Brion	Ch. Pichon-Lalande	

There were similar increases throughout the Crus Classés. Ducru-Beaucaillou went from FF 8,000 to FF 28,000 and Léoville-Las-Cases from FF 8,000 to FF 20,000. (Figures courtesy John Armit Wine Investments.) Still there were buyers.

When the poor 1972s were offered in the spring of 1973 at similar prices, the danger signs were there. Many buyers, anxious to retain a position in what had suddenly begun to look like a seller's market, took up their allocations. Some of the biggest buyers were the brewing and distilling giants who had entered the trade in the previous decade.

The crash soon came. With the winter of 1973–4 came the energy crisis and lengthy recession. Bordeaux produced two more mediocre, plentiful vintages in 1973 and 1974. What had looked a seller's market in 1972 had turned completely around. Companies holding vast, overpriced stocks, dumped them, and the market did not fully recover until the 1978 vintage.

There are similarities with the current situation. Prices for the great 1982s have risen sharply in the three years since their release. The 1983 vintage opened at higher prices than the 1982s and sold quickly. Prices have risen steadily in the past two years. The 1984 vintage is inferior to the previous two, though better than 1972, and châteaux have set prices at or above the levels for 1983. This time, though, the trade has not rushed to buy, particularly in Great Britain.

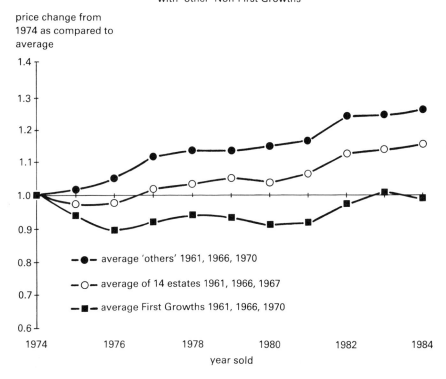

Comparison of Classified First Growths
with 'other' Non-First Growths

price change from
1974 as compared to
average

—●— average 'others' 1961, 1966, 1970

—○— average of 14 estates 1961, 1966, 1967

—■— average First Growths 1961, 1966, 1970

year sold

(First Growths and 'other' Non-First Growths listed opposite)

Michael Broadbent believes that the biggest difference between now and 1973 is the greater spread of ownership—what he refers to as 'a more "pure" demand: one not based on an inflationary flight out of money into a commodity'. There are more private buyers in the market, and fewer large speculators. There is also greater world-wide interest in fine wine.

Guidelines for Investment

The cornerstone of any investment portfolio is Bordeaux and specifically wines from the top Crus Classés in the best vintages. It is best to buy en primeur, when prices are keenest, and to hold stocks as long as possible; five or six years is the minimum. The reasons for claret's pre-eminence are simple. It is the most highly regarded red wine in the world; it requires many years ageing to reach its peak; and the best properties have a reputation for consistency and quality based on decades of experience. Above all it is 'négociable', that is, it has an international currency.

Second choice is vintage port, another wine requiring substantial bottle age. This means that much of the wine will have been consumed before maturity, and remaining bottles will be at a premium. Port from the top shippers also has a reputation for consistency. What it does not share with claret is a world-wide following. Until very recently one country, Great Britain, took over 90 per cent of the total output. This has changed over the last decade with American drinkers developing a taste for port, and its investment profile is likely to change.

Red Burgundy, apart from a couple of famous domaines, has never been a good investment, because of the number of small producers, and the wide variation in quality within the region, and even within individual vineyards. White Burgundy from the top Crus and producers has potential for investment.

German wines are not a good investment, mainly because demand and supply are more evenly matched and they are less easy to understand than Bordeaux or port. Italian wines have yet to make an international reputation; the same is true for California. When auctions become a more regular feature of US wine sales, the picture for California may be different. Right now there is only a small secondary market for mature bottles in the country which consumes virtually all the best wines.

One region with real potential is the northern Rhône. Not generally regarded as investment wines, the two great reds, Côte-Rôtie and Hermitage, have developed a strong following since the very fine 1978 vintage. They are long-lasting wines of high quality, produced in small quantities, and there are at least three producers whose wines merit consideration as investments (see p. 36).

Bordeaux: What to Buy

The Premiers Grands Crus might seem the obvious choice, and they do perform well as investments. But our research shows that they are not the

This bottle of 1787 Lafite with the initials of Thomas Jefferson, third president of the United States, sold for £105,000 ($150,000) at Christie's, London, in December 1985. This was, by a considerable margin, the highest price ever paid for a single bottle of wine.

very best. We looked at the performance at auction of fourteen estates over the period 1974 to 1984. We concentrated on three excellent vintages, 1961, 1966, and 1970. Three wines finished bunched together well ahead of the field. They were, in order, La Mission-Haut-Brion, Palmer, and Pétrus. These appreciated at a rate more than 50 per cent better than the average of the fourteen estates. Next came Ducru-Beaucaillou, Beychevelle, and Léoville-Las-Cases. Of the classified first growths only Lafite and Haut-Brion showed increases higher than the average for the fourteen properties, though none did badly.

One wine that would certainly be in the top group, if it appeared often enough at auction to get a reliable sample, is Ch. Trotanoy.

Moving to two more recent vintages, 1975 and 1978, the above information still holds, with a few qualifications. First, Pichon-Lalande is doing better since the 1978 vintage, as is Ch. Margaux. And the one wine of the acknowledged top eight excluded from our ten-year survey, Ch. Ausone, has now become one of the most sought-after wines of Bordeaux. It was excluded for the same reason as Ch. Trotanoy.

The 1975 first growths sold for between £80 and £100 ex cellars, and the top seconds for around £35 to £40. This was the first good vintage after the crash and prices were reasonable, in real terms lower than for 1971s.

Comparing specific wines from Henry Townsend's list and adding duty, carriage, and VAT we find that Léoville-Las-Cases sold for £49.70 ($89.50), Palmer for £67.00 ($121), and Mouton-Rothschild for £109.60 ($197). By the middle of 1985 the wines were selling at auction for the following prices: Léoville-Las-Cases, £280 ($350) per dozen; Palmer, £460 ($575) per dozen; and Mouton-Rothschild, £520 ($650) per dozen. Palmer is clearly maintaining its position as a high flyer, increasing in value by 687 per cent. Las-Cases went up by 563 per cent, and Mouton-Rothschild by 475 per cent. During this same period the UK Retail Price Index rose by 250 per cent.*

If we compare the same three châteaux from the 1978 vintage the prices are Léoville-Las-Cases, £88.13 ($180); Palmer, £101.30 ($208); Mouton-Rothschild, £181.42 ($372). The auction prices in the spring of 1985 were: Léoville-Las-Cases, £240 ($300); Palmer, £400 ($500); and Mouton-Rothschild, £600 ($750). The percentage increases are: Léoville-Las-Cases, 272 per cent; Palmer, 395 per cent; and Mouton-Rothschild, 330 per cent. There are a few points to make in comparison. First, as previously stated, 1975 was the first good vintage after the collapse, and prices were relatively low. By the time the 1978s arrived on the market in 1979 confidence had returned, and prices were moving back to the levels of the early seventies. In 1979 the French franc was strong against the dollar and the pound. The dollar was particularly weak at FF 4.30 to US $1.00. This compares to the mid-1985 exchange rate of approximately FF 8.5 to US $1.00.

It is too early to judge the impact of the trio of good vintages at the

*These increases are based on the auction price in sterling. Percentage increases in dollars will be lower because the dollar strengthened considerably between the fall of 1982 and the spring of 1985.

beginning of this decade. The 1981s have appeared on the market and more recently the 1982s, which are in great demand. If the 1982s continue to command high prices this will push up prices for older vintages like 1978 and 1975.

Here is a list of wines that are suitable for investment. Those marked with an asterisk are particularly good choices:

*Premiers Grands Crus
and Equivalents*
Ch. Lafite-Rothschild
Ch. Latour
Ch. Margaux
Ch. Mouton-Rothschild
Ch. Haut-Brion
Ch. Ausone*
Ch. Cheval-Blanc
Ch. Pétrus*

Other Médocs
Ch. Palmer*
Ch. Ducru-Beaucaillou*
Ch. Léoville-Las-Cases*
Ch. Gruaud-Larose
Ch. Pichon-Lalande*
Ch. Grand-Puy-Lacoste
Ch. Cos d'Estournel
Ch. La Lagune*

Graves
Ch. La Mission-Haut-Brion*
Domaine de Chevalier

St-Emilion
Ch. Canon
Ch. Figeac
Ch. Magdelaine

Pomerol
Ch. Certan de May*
Ch. La Conseillante
Ch. L'Evangile
Ch. La Fleur Pétrus*
Ch. Lafleur*
Ch. Latour à Pomerol*
Ch. Trotanoy*

Note the number of starred properties in Pomerol. This reflects both the current fashion for these wines, and the tiny production at most estates. The total production of all the Pomerols listed above, including Ch. Pétrus, is about the same as the annual output of Mouton-Rothschild. This scarcity is bound to make them expensive. John Armit, who as Managing Director of Corney & Barrow was largely responsible for introducing fine Pomerols to the English public, and who includes them in his investment portfolios, has been pleasantly surprised by their success but is reluctant to predict how high the prices might climb. 'I've often thought in the past they had reached a plateau,' he said, 'and I've always been proved wrong. Really they are just being discovered.' There is no question that the biggest change in the price hierarchy of Bordeaux has been the rise of several Pomerols to the level of and above the top second growths. And this has happened in the last six or seven years.

Before going on to consider other investments, here is a summary of advice to keep in mind when buying claret as an investment. Most of the rules apply equally to other wines.

1   Buy at the opening price. (In the United States this is called buying futures.)

2   Buy only the best properties with a proven record of appreciation, and only in the best vintages.
3   Store the wines in bond and save the duty and VAT. For an overseas buyer this facilitates resale on the London or Bordeaux markets.
4   Be prepared to hold on to the wines for at least five or six years.
5   Be prepared to hold the wines even longer if the market is in a trough. You should not commit to wine money that you may need to realize in a hurry.

Vintage Port

Conventional investment wisdom concerning vintage port is that it is a poor buy *en primeur,* and only begins to appreciate as it approaches maturity. Certainly our research into eleven years of price changes at auction appears to bear this out. But increasing demand for vintage port in the United States and from BES schemes will change this, and the 1983 vintage has been an important indicator.

As the accompanying graph shows, port prices barely kept pace with inflation from 1974 to 1982, but since then have been climbing steeply. The price of Taylor 1963 rose by 120 per cent in three years, Graham 1963

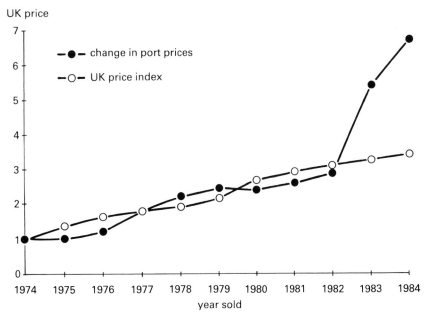

Port price changes from 1974

Port Suppliers

Cockburn	Fonseca	Sandeman
Croft	Graham	Taylor, Fladgate & Yeatman
Dow	Quinta do Noval	Warre

by 103 per cent, and Fonseca 1963 by 140 per cent. Figures for the 1966 vintage were: Taylor 95 per cent; Graham 130 per cent; Fonseca 120 per cent. The 1970 vintage was: Taylor 58 per cent; Graham 56 per cent; Fonseca 56 per cent. Prices continued to rise sharply in 1985, and the greatest increases have been for the outstanding 1977 vintage. In late 1982 Taylor's 1977 sold at auction for £82 ($135) a dozen. By May 1985 the price had increased to £230 ($288) and had overtaken the very good 1970s. This is an increase of 280 per cent in two and a half years. The same is true of Graham's 1977, which sold in late 1982 for £68 ($112) a dozen, and by May 1985 for £185 ($231) a dozen, an increase of 272 per cent. (See footnote p. 33.)

The leap in prices for the 1977s contradicts past patterns and may mean that young port from good vintages will become an attractive investment. The reason we have chosen the 1983 vintage over 1982, which was also declared, is that the three shippers whose wines perform best at auction—Fonseca, Graham, and Taylor—all preferred 1983 to 1982.

Other Wines for Investment

If you would like to commit part of your money to wines not usually considered for investment, try northern Rhône and white Burgundy. The former has been attracting wine drinkers because of its inherent quality and because it has been underpriced. There are three producers in particular worthy of attention.

First choice should be Paul Jaboulet's Hermitage 'La Chapelle'. The 1978 La Chapelle sold in 1980 for £92 ($200) per case, and made £420 ($525) at auction in May 1985. In March of the same year a case of 1961 La Chapelle sold for £1,700 ($1,955). The appreciation of 456 per cent (though only 262 per cent in dollars) for the 1978 La Chapelle outdoes even the best Bordeaux of that vintage, and marks this wine as one to watch. Another Hermitage worth considering is Gérard Chave's. He and Jaboulet are generally reckoned to be the best producers in this vineyard, and Chave's production is tiny. There is no auction record to go by, but it is still a good bet. The third producer of note is Etienne Guigal. His speciality is Côte-Rôtie, and the wines worth investing in are his single vineyard Côte-Rôties, 'La Mouline' and 'La Landonne'. The rules that apply for claret hold here too. Buy these wines only in the best years, and buy them as soon as they appear on the market.

White Burgundy should be approached with care, but the great wines of the Côte de Beaune are in such short supply that there is a flourishing secondary market. Le Montrachet itself is so expensive that it is better to turn to the Grands Crus immediately surrounding it and, as always in Burgundy, to the best producers. Top of the list is the Domaine Leflaive. In 1981, his 1978 Chevalier-Montrachet sold for £165 ($330) per dozen retail. In May 1985 it sold for £740 ($925) at auction. Even Leflaive's less good 1979s have shown substantial increases at auction. The Grands Crus of Louis Latour, particularly his Corton-Charlemagne and Chevalier-Montrachet, 'Les Demoiselles', also show well at auction.

To this list can be added another name: Louis Jadot. He, like Louis Latour, makes Corton-Charlemagne and Chevalier-Montrachet that command world-wide attention. White Burgundy has a shorter lifespan than the red wines under discussion, and it quickly disappears from the market. If you are interested in adding some white Burgundy, stick to the Grands Crus of the Côte de Beaune.

Selling the Wine

So far in this discussion we have assumed that wines purchased for investment would be placed for sale through the auction houses. This is the usual way of disposing of small, privately owned lots. Auctioneers charge a commission for effecting the sale. At both Christie's and Sotheby's it is now 10 per cent, though substantial private holdings and bona fide trade stocks attract a lower commission rate at Christie's.) It must be remembered, however, that Sotheby's charge a 10 per cent buyer's premium, making a total commission of 20 per cent on the sale. Wine merchants from whom stock was purchased will sometimes buy back mature wines from their clients, or even exchange them for a selection of younger wines.

Overseas residents can also participate in this market. The wine merchants recommended in this book usually offer storage for wines purchased from them, frequently with the option of keeping them in bond. The wines can be sold through the salerooms at the appropriate time, with the wine merchant making the arrangements. For Americans this is especially useful, because restrictive laws in many states prohibit such activity at home.

Cellars at Lay and Wheeler of Colchester in the 1920s and today. Like most good wine merchants, Lay and Wheeler provide storage for their customers' purchases.

Investment Companies

There is no reason why a collector cannot oversee his own wine investments by following the suggestions outlined above. There are, however, a number of specialist wine investment companies. Two well-established firms with good records are John Armit Wine Investments and Collins Wines. Both act for overseas as well as British clients.

Wine investment companies have mushroomed in the last year as a result of the British Government's Business Expansion Scheme. Set up to encourage investment in high-risk industries, the BES offers generous tax relief providing the money remains invested for five years. For investors who preferred less risky ventures, land and property were early targets, but when the Chancellor of the Exchequer made these ineligible, attention turned to wine. There are at least ten such companies with more than five million pounds to spend, and almost certainly more to follow.

The question is what effect this new money will have on the market. First of all, the companies were set up too late to take advantage of the opening prices for 1982 and 1983 Bordeaux. The first vintage available to them en primeur is 1984, a much less attractive investment though there may be substantial buying of the better 1985s. Money will probably go into older vintages of Bordeaux and vintage port pushing up prices. Of more concern is what will happen in five years' time when, presumably, most of the companies will be liquidated. If a substantial amount of wine appears on the market in 1989–90, it could depress prices. The Chancellor of the Exchequer has changed this somewhat in the 1986 Budget by limiting BES tax concessions to companies trading over half their stocks each year. This should ensure a more regular flow of wines into the market. Still, the private investor should be prepared to sell earlier or hold on to his stocks during this period.

It is essential that wines be properly stored. Trapps cellars near London Bridge provide cellarage for wine merchants and private clients.

4 France

BORDEAUX

The Market

Though the 1984 vintage was of no better than average quality, Bordeaux
has been enjoying an unusual run of successful vintages. Since 1975 there
have been only three years in which the quality has been less than good—
not surprising in Napa, but atypical of Bordeaux—and 1981, 1982, and
1983 represent the best three consecutive vintages since 1947, 1948, and
1949.

Hailed as 'the vintage of the century', 1982 is probably the best since
1961, and the publicity surrounding it brought large numbers of first-time
buyers into the en primeur market. The French franc was weak and the
dollar strong, and American buyers in particular rushed to buy this
vintage. The great growths opened at record prices, and promptly sold
out. Within a year many of the top wines were unavailable, and where
négociants still held stock, the prices had trebled or quadrupled from the
opening price.

Then the 1983s came on to the market. The producers looked not at the
1982 opening price, but rather at the current one, and set the 1983 price
accordingly; another record. Now 1983 is a very good, classically styled
vintage, and after a few perfunctory complaints, the world rushed to buy
again. For those who missed out on 1982 and found the prices too high by
mid-1984, the 1983s represented an opportunity to get into the market,
and enthusiasm for Bordeaux generated by the previous vintage, carried
over for the 1983s. Those who purchased the 1982s en primeur have done
very well. The wines have appeared on the market at three times the
opening price, or in the case of some smaller properties, have not re-
appeared at all. The 1983s increased in value by about 50 per cent within a
year, a spectacular rise measured against any vintage except the previous
one.

The question was whether the Bordelais could sustain this momentum
with the 1984 wines, which were not nearly as good as 1982 or 1983. Most
prices were between 10 and 20 per cent higher than the previous year's
levels. This disappointed wine merchants, and there was no rush to buy
from Britain. Demand in the United States was stronger, but there was no
reason to buy the 1984s en primeur with very good wines from 1981 and
1979 available at reasonable prices and with another good vintage (1985)
on the way. The 1979s are an especially good buy at auction as they lack
the 'classic' status of 1978 and 1975. They are beginning to drink well too
and will keep into the 1990s. But look to the 1981s for the longer term.

Rare treasures in the cellars at Château
Lafite.

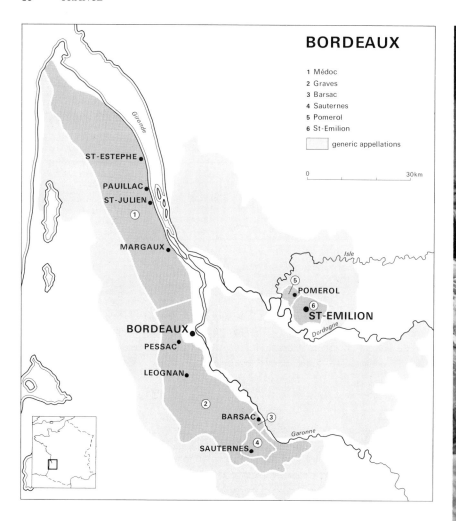

BORDEAUX

1 Médoc
2 Graves
3 Barsac
4 Sauternes
5 Pomerol
6 St-Emilion

generic appellations

0   30km

Repairing casks in the cooperage at
Château Loudenne.

The ageing cellars at Château Lafite. Each vintage is stored in new 225 litre oak barrels for 18 to 24 months before bottling.

The Trade

Bordeaux has historically been the most outward looking of France's fine wine regions, depending mainly on markets in northern Europe for its prosperity. In the nineteenth century, for example, it was the British aristocracy that made the reputations of the great Crus Classés.

The trade was dominated by a group of merchants known as 'négociants', who acted as bankers to the châteaux. The last two decades have seen their power decline, as the individual estates have assumed a greater role in the marketing of their wines. Two factors are chiefly responsible for this shift in power: the first is the change to château bottling; the second is the slump in the mid-seventies which found many négociants with excess stock at a time of high inflation.

The Background

Bordeaux prospered in the mid-nineteenth century. Its wine was fashionable and prices rose steadily. But a combination of phylloxera and economic slump in Europe and America precipitated a steady decline during the last two decades of the century. The proprietors turned to the négociants for finance, signing fixed-term contracts which gave the merchants exclusive rights to the wine for five or ten year periods. Many contracts gave négociants not just the wine, but also substantial authority over the running of the property. Firms such as Calvet, Cruse, and Barton & Guestier had enormous influence.

These firms were 'négociant-éleveurs' who not only sold wines but were responsible for the 'élevage' ('raising' or 'bringing up'), as their counterparts in Burgundy still are. Each spring they took delivery of a substantial proportion of the young wine and assumed responsibility for it in their own cellars. They shipped some abroad in cask to be bottled by their agents or by individual wine merchants, and the rest they bottled themselves. It was the négociants, not the châteaux who set prices and decided which markets to exploit. Even in the 1960s Calvet was still buying as much as 50 per cent of Ch. Cheval Blanc in cask.

The move toward château bottling gathered momentum after the Second World War with the Premiers Grands Crus leading the way. This coincided with the changes in the British retail trade outlined in Chapter 2. Wine broker and writer David Peppercorn has watched the changes during his career. 'When I first travelled to Bordeaux in the fifties very few people in the trade visited the vineyards. The large French and German houses had agents who imported the wines and sold to the retail trade. They also held substantial stocks, and there was a greater trade in mature wines.'

With the wines being bottled at the château, it was no longer necessary for a négociant to have extensive cellars and the consequent expense this entailed. A computer to keep track of stock, a telex, and a good commercial sense were all that were required. And a new generation of British wine merchants, keen to find the best wines, began visting the châteaux to try the wines for themselves. They bought the lesser wines directly from the châteaux, and the others through négociants in Bordeaux.

Since the Second World War the United States has established itself as the most important market for the top Crus Classés. Unlike their opposite numbers in Britain, American wine merchants have never had close ties with the Bordeaux négociants. Fine wine consumption has only taken hold in the last twenty-five years, and promotion trades heavily on the glamour of such top estates as Lafite and Mouton-Rothschild. Château-bottled claret is a natural for the prestige brand-conscious American market.

Vintage Assessment: Red Bordeaux

1985: A large crop and much bigger than expected. In contrast to 1984, the Merlot produced well. The wines are deep coloured, fleshy and fruity, a cross between 1982 and 1983, thus a very fine vintage indeed. With this quality, there was much speculation as to the price of the 1985s, since the 1984s came out at up to 20 per cent more than the 1983s, for wines of much lesser quality. However, the first prices seen in January and February 1986 were the same as the 1984s, which shows that the Bordelais are more sensitive than was feared about the long-term health of their market.

1984: Not in the same class as the three previous vintages; more like 1980. Best in the Médoc, where Cabernet Sauvignon dominates. Merlot production virtually wiped out by cold, wet weather at flowering, resulting in tiny quantities of St-Emilion and Pomerol.

1983: Very good vintage, the third in a row, but eclipsed by its great predecessor. A hot, humid, showery summer gave way to a glorious warm autumn, and those who picked late made the best wine. A classic vintage, more tannic than 1982 but with plenty of fruit. Good everywhere, but best in Margaux, where Ch. Margaux made the wine of the vintage. Other properties in this commune, notably Palmer, made better wine than in 1982.

1982: Probably the best vintage since 1961, but unlike it in that it was abundant as well as good. Dark, rich, concentrated wines of an almost Californian opulence, but enough tannin and acidity to ensure a long life. Great in Pomerol, but outstanding everywhere, except perhaps Margaux. St-Julien was particularly successful in the Médoc. A good vintage for Crus Bourgeois.

1981: Another very good vintage, but not as consistent as 1982 or 1983. Better in the Médoc than on the right bank, though there are some very good Pomerols. Prices are still reasonable, making this a good one to buy for the 1990s.

1980: A light vintage of average quality; for drinking not cellaring.

1979: A large vintage of good quality, which has turned out better than many critics expected. Very good wines in St-Emilion, Pomerol, and the Graves. Delicious medium-weight claret for drinking over the next decade.

1978: A very good vintage saved by a glorious autumn. Classic, well-balanced wines in the Médoc, where Cabernet Sauvignon was very successful; more variable in St-Emilion and Pomerol. Lesser wines are drinking well now, though the classified growths are still immature. Good keeping qualities.

1977: The poorest vintage in the past decade. Drink up.

1976: Heavy rains at harvest diluted what might have been an excellent vintage. Still good, though, with a lot of flavoury wines which are drinking well now. Uneven, so choose with care.

1975: Tough, full-bodied and tannic wines. Many are still years from maturity, and critics fear that some will dry out before shedding their tannin. No doubt, though, that there are some very fine wines, if only for the very patient. Even the 1978s are further evolved.

1974, 1973, 1972: Not much to recommend from these years, though 1973 had some admirers early on. A risky buy. Drink up.

1971: A very good year in St-Emilion and Pomerol, less consistent in the Médoc. Ripe, flavourful wines, now fully mature.

1970: An outstanding vintage, especially in the Médoc, where the best wines since 1961 were produced. Some are still a bit awkward, but should be delicious when mature. Just about ready, and should keep well.

1966: A very good vintage which has taken a long time to develop. Now quite expensive.

1961: Small vintage of very high quality. The 'vintage of the century' until 1970 and 1982 came along. Rare and very expensive.

All Crus Classés wines of Bordeaux are now château bottled. Note also the communal appellation, more specific than a regional one.

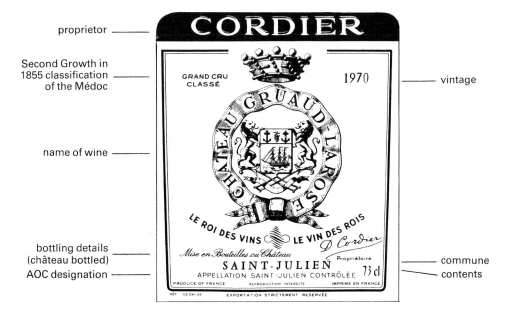

proprietor

Second Growth in 1855 classification of the Médoc

name of wine

bottling details (château bottled)

AOC designation

vintage

commune

contents

Recommended Producers: Médoc

The Grands Crus Classés (1855 Classification)

	Commune
Premiers Crus (First Growths)	
Ch. Lafite-Rothschild	Pauillac
Ch. Latour	Pauillac
Ch. Margaux	Margaux
Ch. Mouton-Rothschild*	Pauillac
Ch. Haut-Brion	Pessac
Deuxièmes Crus (Second Growths)	
Ch. Rausan-Ségla	Margaux
Ch. Rauzan-Gassies	Margaux
Ch. Léoville-Las-Cases	St-Julien
Ch. Léoville-Poyferré	St-Julien
Ch. Léoville-Barton	St-Julien
Ch. Durfort-Vivens	Margaux
Ch. Gruaud-Larose	St-Julien
Ch. Lascombes	Margaux
Ch. Brane-Cantenac	Cantenac
Ch. Pichon-Longueville-Baron	Pauillac
Ch. Pichon-Longueville-Lalande	Pauillac
Ch. Ducru-Beaucaillou	St-Julien
Ch. Cos-d'Estournel	St-Estèphe
Ch. Montrose	St-Estèphe
Troisièmes Crus (Third Growths)	
Ch. Kirwan	Cantenac
Ch. d'Issan	Cantenac
Ch. Lagrange	St-Julien
Ch. Langoa-Barton	St-Julien
Ch. Giscours	Labarde
Ch. Malescot-Saint-Exupéry	Margaux
Ch. Boyd-Cantenac	Cantenac
Ch. Palmer	Cantenac
Ch. La Lagune	Ludon
Ch. Desmirail	Margaux
Ch. Cantenac-Brown	Cantenac
Ch. Calon-Ségur	St-Estèphe
Ch. Ferrière	Margaux
Ch. Marquis-d'Alesme-Becker	Margaux

	Commune
Quatrièmes Crus (Fourth Growths)	
Ch. St-Pierre	St-Julien
Ch. Talbot	St-Julien
Ch. Branaire-Ducru	St-Julien
Ch. Duhart-Milon-Rothschild	Pauillac
Ch. Pouget	Cantenac
Ch. La Tour-Carnet	St-Laurent
Ch. Lafon-Rochet	St-Estèphe
Ch. Beychevelle	St-Julien
Ch. Prieuré-Lichine	Cantenac
Ch. Marquis-de-Terme	Margaux
Cinquièmes Crus (Fifth Growths)	
Ch. Pontet-Canet	Pauillac
Ch. Batailley	Pauillac
Ch. Haut-Batailley	Pauillac
Ch. Grand-Puy-Lacoste	Pauillac
Ch. Grand-Puy-Ducasse	Pauillac
Ch. Lynch-Bages	Pauillac
Ch. Lynch-Moussas	Pauillac
Ch. Dauzac	Labarde
Ch. Mouton-Baronne-Philippe	Pauillac
Ch. du Tertre	Arsac
Ch. Haut-Bages-Libéral	Pauillac
Ch. Pédesclaux	Pauillac
Ch. Belgrave	St-Laurent
Ch. Camensac	St-Laurent
Ch. Cos-Labory	St-Estèphe
Ch. Clerc-Milon-Rothschild	Pauillac
Ch. Croizet-Bages	Pauillac
Ch. Cantemerle	Macau

*declared a First Growth in 1973

MARGAUX

The best news to come out of the Médoc in the last decade has been the renaissance of Ch. Margaux. Plagued by inconsistency in the sixties and seventies, this famous property made a spectacular return to form in 1978 under new ownership. Since then it has regularly produced one of the three or four best wines on the left bank, and may be making the best wine in the Médoc at the moment.

With Ch. Margaux in eclipse the best wine in the commune used frequently to be the third growth, Ch. Palmer. Palmer suffered with the rest of the commune in 1982, but returned to its best in 1983. Ch. Giscours is another third growth making good wine in a robust style, while Ch. d'Issan makes consistently good and well-priced wine. Ch. Prieuré-Lichine, a fourth growth, is also reliable and very reasonably priced.

There are five second growths in Margaux, though they do not all perform up to that standard. Ch. Brane-Cantenac, after a disappointing period, is again making very good wine and Ch. Durfort-Vivens produced very good wine in both 1982 and 1983.

Cru Bourgeois wines of note in Margaux include Ch. d'Angludet, Ch. Bel-Air-Marquis d'Aligre, Ch. Labégorce-Zédé, and Ch. Siran.

ST-JULIEN

No commune in the Médoc could be said to provide more wine-drinking pleasure than St-Julien, where the standards are consistently and exceptionally high. There are no Premiers Crus here, but two second growths are performing at or near that level. Ch. Léoville-Las-Cases, the firmest and most backward wine in a commune known more for softness and elegance, turns out impeccable wines year after year. Its only rival is Ch. Ducru-Beaucaillou, where the resident proprietor, Jean-Eugène Borie, makes a wine of great concentration and harmony. Both these estates are worth following.

A short step behind comes another second growth, Ch. Gruaud-Larose, the pride of Cordier, the négociants, who also own the very good Ch. Talbot. Ch. Léoville-Barton is another very good second growth, making classic, cedary claret that ages particularly well, while the third Léoville, Ch. Léoville-Poyferré made an outstanding 1982 and one of the best 1983s. Ch. Langoa-Barton, sister property to Léoville-Barton, is also good, and

Château Gruaud-Larose is one of two St-Julien Crus Classés owned by the négociants Cordier. It is now one of the most consistently fine of all Bordeauxs.

Ch. Branaire-Ducru, a fourth growth, makes consistently fine and reasonably priced wine. Ch. Beychevelle, a favourite in Great Britain, rounds out the group of top-class wines from this commune.

St-Julien is the smallest commune in the Médoc and most of its area is occupied by Crus Classés. One Cru Bourgeois of note, though, is Ch. Gloria, owned by the octogenarian Henri Martin, who in 1984 purchased Ch. St-Pierre.

PAUILLAC

Pauillac is the most famous of the Médoc communes, and claims three of the world's greatest wines. Ch. Lafite-Rothschild is more than just a great wine; it is an international symbol of luxury. It is, thankfully, back to deserving such eminence after inconsistent performances in the sixties and early seventies. Old vines, rigorous selection, and a brilliant wine-maker have achieved this for the most richly perfumed and delicate of the great Pauillacs.

At the southern end of the commune, adjoining St-Julien, is Ch. Latour, which produces great wine of an entirely different style. Opaque when young and concentrated, Latour is the biggest wine of the Médoc, though recent vintages have displayed a lighter style (for Latour, that is). The most consistently fine of the first growths, Latour is also the most modern in technique.

Next door to Lafite in the north of the commune is Ch. Mouton-Rothschild, which was classified at the top of the second growths in 1855. In 1973 the authorities officially recognized what the market had long made plain, and Mouton was promoted to Premier Grand Cru status. In style more akin to Latour than to Lafite, Mouton is dense and concentrated but more immediately showy than Latour. If Lafite is brilliant, and Latour statuesque, then Mouton is spectacular.

Close behind this trio in quality, but a long way behind in price, is Ch. Pichon-Lalande. Bordering Latour near St-Julien, Pichon-Lalande displays some of the characteristics of that commune. It is softer than most Pauillacs and attractive when young. The high proportion of Merlot in the blend contributes to this, but despite its immediate charm, good vintages last very well.

Two fifth growths come next in the order of merit in Pauillac. Ch. Grand-Puy-Lacoste, owned since 1978 by the Bories of Ducru-Beaucaillou fame, is producing wine of second growth standard. Rich, full-bodied Cabernet is produced at Ch. Lynch-Bages, a long-time favourite in Britain.

Ch. Pichon-Longueville-Baron, a second growth, has been eclipsed of late by Pichon-Lalande, and, though less consistent, made excellent wines in 1982 and 1983. Ch. Haut-Batailley, another Borie property, is producing stylish wine at a reasonable price and bears watching. Another improving property is Ch. Pontet-Canet. The unclassified Les Forts de Latour, second wine of Ch. Latour, is reckoned to be of second growth quality, and priced accordingly.

As with St-Julien, Pauillac is not the best place to look for Crus Bourgeois. Among the best are Ch. Fonbadet (not technically Cru Bourgeois), Ch. La Couronne, and Ch. Haut-Bages-Monpelou.

ST-ESTEPHE

The most northerly and largest of the fine wine appellations of the Médoc, St-Estèphe produces wines of power and concentration rather than charm. Ch. Cos d'Estournel is the top wine here, a second growth to rival Pichon-Lalande, Ducru-Beaucaillou, and Léoville-Las-Cases. A high percentage of Merlot makes Cos more elegant than its neighbours, but it retains the solid structure of a great St-Estèphe.

Ch. Montrose, the other second growth of this commune, is one of Bordeaux's great long-distance runners. Unyielding in youth (and sometimes in middle age) Montrose can mature into a meaty, vigorous wine, almost as concentrated as Latour. Both the 1961 and 1970 are still a long way from maturity.

Ch. Calon-Ségur is a difficult estate to assess. This third growth is capable of producing truly great wine, as in 1982, but it is also notably inconsistent.

This large commune with only five classed growths is especially rich in Crus Bourgeois. Best known is Ch. de Pez, a wine of classed growth standard. Ch. Haut-Marbuzet and the Cordier-owned Ch. Meyney are very good. The latter has improved considerably in the last few years, while the former is the commune's most elegant Bourgeois. Other notable wines are Ch. Les-Ormes-de-Pez; Ch. Marbuzet, the second wine of Cos d'Estournel; Ch. Phélan-Ségur; and Ch. Tronquoy-Lalande.

MOULIS AND LISTRAC

These two communes north-west of Margaux contain no Crus Classés, but several very good wines that usually sell at reasonable prices. The best of these is Ch. Chasse-Spleen in Moulis, a dark, stylish wine that would certainly be included in any reclassification of the Médoc. Other properties worth considering are Ch. Poujeaux (or Poujeaux-Theil), a good wine usually needing time to come around; Ch. Gressier-Grand-Poujeaux; Ch. Dutruch-Grand-Poujeaux; and Ch. Brillette.

Listrac has no estate as good as Chasse-Spleen, but Ch. Clarke, a Rothschild property, is getting better and better and should soon be among the leading Crus Bourgeois. Two of the best-known wines of this commune are Ch. Fourcas Dupré and Ch. Fourcas-Hosten.

HAUT-MEDOC

Something of a catch-all appellation including fifteen communes not considered good enough for separate recognition, the Haut-Médoc contains two Crus Classés currently making very fine wine. Third growth Ch. La Lagune is not far behind the top second growths, and until 1983 represented the best value for money in the whole Médoc. Their 1982 price, announced early, was a great bargain, and it was no surprise that they upped the price for the 1983. It is still good value.

Ch. Cantemerle, a respected fifth growth, lost its way in the seventies, but is back on form under Cordier management. Cantemerle made a very good 1982 and an even better 1983. This is a property to follow.

There is a host of Crus Bourgeois in the Haut-Médoc with Ch. Cissac, Ch. Lanessan, and Ch. Sociando-Mallet leading the way. Cissac, a great favourite in Britain, is a full-bodied Médoc that ages well. Ch. Lanessan is one of the region's most reliable wines, and Sociando-Mallet, of robust Cabernet Sauvignon style, is challenging the Crus Classés of the region. Other good wines are Ch. Citran, Ch. Coufran made predominantly of Merlot, and Ch. Villegeorge.

MEDOC

Formerly called the Bas-Médoc (describing geography not wine) but now simply Médoc, this region has no Crus Classés, but several Crus Bourgeois worthy of note. Among them are Ch. La Cardonne, a part of the Rothschild empire; Ch. Loudenne, owned by Gilbey's and much respected in Britain; Ch. La Tour de By; and Ch. Potensac, under the same ownership as Léoville-Las-Cases, and it shows.

Recommended Producers: Graves

Grands Crus Classés (1959 Classification)

Red	Commune	White	Commune
Ch. Haut-Brion	Pessac	Ch. Bouscaut	Cadaujac
Ch. Bouscaut	Cadaujac	Ch. Carbonnieux	Léognan
Ch. Carbonnieux	Léognan	Domaine de Chevalier	Léognan
Domaine de Chevalier	Léognan	Ch. Couhins	Villenave-d'Ornon
Ch. de Fieuzal	Léognan	Ch. La Tour-Martillac	
Ch. Haut-Bailly	Léognan	(Kressmann La	
Ch. La Mission-Haut-Brion	Pessac	Tour)	Martillac
		Ch. Laville-Haut-Brion	Talence
Ch. La Tour-Haut-Brion	Talence	Ch. Malartic-Lagravière	Léognan
		Ch. Olivier	Léognan
Ch. La Tour-Martillac (Kressmann La Tour)	Martillac	Ch. Haut-Brion*	Pessac
Ch. Malartic-Lagravière	Léognan	*added in 1960	
Ch. Olivier	Léognan		
Ch. Pape-Clément	Pessac		
Ch. Smith-Haut-Lafitte	Martillac		

Cabernet Sauvignon-based red and the best dry white wine of the region are produced in Graves. The red wine is similar to the Médoc, but is a bit drier, perhaps, and matures earlier. The white is austere in youth, but full and vigorous in maturity. Different in style from the rich, buttery Chardonnays of Burgundy, the best Graves is equal in quality. Alas, it is also now equal in price.

Ch. Haut-Brion is the great name of this region, a first growth in the 1855 classification and the only non-Médoc to be included. Haut-Brion matures more quickly than its peers but maintains this level for years, a trick of suspending time that no other claret can match. There is a tiny quantity of Haut-Brion Blanc produced each year and sold at a very high price.

Cabernet Sauvignon: the most adaptable of the great red varietals producing dark, tannic wines with the aroma of cassis, cedar, and, in California occasionally, mint. The principal grape of the Médoc, where, blended with Merlot, it produces classic claret. It is grown very successfully in California and Australia.

Chardonnay: the white grape of Burgundy and Champagne and a notable success in America and Australia. The Chardonnay produces full-bodied, richly flavoured wines: the finest dry whites in the world.

Riesling: the classic grape of Germany and along with the Chardonnay one of the two most important white varietals. Even sweet examples retain a crisp acidity and clean finish and all Rieslings have a fine, flowery aroma. It is responsible for Alsace's greatest wines and is also successful in California (Johannisberg Riesling) and Australia (Rhine Riesling).

Pinot Noir: the grape of red Burgundy, producing richly perfumed wines with less tannin and generally less colour than the Cabernet Sauvignon. Important in Champagne, where it is blended with Chardonnay and Pinot Meunier. Pinot Noir has proved less successful outside of France.

The Hôtel Dieu, or Hospices de Beaune, is a hospital supported by wine. Each November wines produced from vineyards belonging to the hospital are sold at auction and the prices watched as a guide by the rest of Burgundy.

The harvest at Heitz Cellars under a cloudless California sky. The grapes are tipped into the *fouloir-égrappoir* (stemmer-crusher), where they are de-stemmed and the skins lightly broken before going into the fermentation vats.

The harvest underway at Château Margaux, a Premier Grand Cru Classé of the Médoc. The wine of Margaux is characterized by an intense perfumed fragrance.

Spraying against parasites in Bordeaux. Advances in disease and rot control have meant fewer poor vintages, but such treatments are expensive and not all proprietors can afford them.

Barcos Rabelos were traditionally used to transport casks of young port from the vineyards down the river to the lodges in Vila Nova de Gaia. These beautiful ships now appear only on ceremonial occasions.

The Stag's Leap vineyard in Napa Valley, California.

Château Latour, a Premier Grand Cru Classé, is one of Bordeaux's longest-lived wines. The robust style and record of consistency have made it a great favourite in Britain and in the United States.

The château and cellars at Château Lafite, perhaps the world's most famous wine. After a period of inconsistency in the sixties and early seventies, Lafite is again making magnificent wine.

Stainless steel fermentation tanks at
Joseph Phelps in the Napa Valley,
California. Phelps are one of the most
technologically advanced of California
wineries.

The Confrérie des Chevaliers du Tastevin, founded in 1934, promotes the wines of Burgundy. Their dinners are held at the Château du Clos de Vougeot.

Opposite The Bordeaux cellars of the négociants Calvet et Cie.

The wine cellar at the 'Tour d'Argent', world-famous three-star Parisian restaurant.

Just next door, and formerly Haut-Brion's great rival, is Ch. La Mission-Haut-Brion. Formerly, because Haut-Brion bought the property in 1983. The winemaking is still separate and the La Mission style—dark, concentrated, and tannic—will remain. La Mission would be at the top of most people's list as a candidate for promotion to first growth. Ch. Laville-Haut-Brion is the white wine of La Mission-Haut-Brion, and considered by many to be the finest of the commune. Fermented in small oak barrels, the wine is unforthcoming in youth, though in maturity it is dry but very rich and concentrated.

Domaine de Chevalier deserves recognition because it produces an outstanding red and a great white wine year after year. And while it is not cheap it is very good value. Of the other reds, Ch. Haut-Bailly is probably the best, though it is less consistent than Domaine de Chevalier. Inconsistency is also the problem at Ch. Pape-Clément, which at its best produces one of the softest, most stylish wines of the commune. Ch. La Tour-Haut-Brion is the second wine of La Mission, but it is of such quality that it deserves separate mention, and Ch. de Fieuzal is currently making very good red wine and a fine, non-classified white.

Ch. Bouscaut is producing good-quality red and white wine, while Ch. Malartic-Lagravière makes reliable rather than exciting wine, both red and white. Ch. Carbonnieux makes better white than red.

Among the unclassified properties, Ch. Rahoul is making excellent red and white wine, and Ch. La Louvière's produce, both red and white, is as good as several classified estates.

Recommended Producers: St-Emilion

Premiers Grands Crus Classés (1954 Classification)

A		B	
Ch. Ausone		Ch. Beauséjour-Bécot*	
Ch. Cheval-Blanc		Ch. Beauséjour-Duffau-Lagarrosse	
		Ch. Belair	
		Ch. Canon	
		Ch. Figeac	
		Clos Fourtet	
		Ch. La Gaffelière	
		Ch. Magdelaine	
		Ch. Pavie	
		Ch. Trottevieille	

*demoted to Grand Cru Classé in 1984, but not yet ratified

St-Emilion is the largest of Bordeaux's fine wine appellations, and the quality ranges from the very finest to the very ordinary. If Margaux's return to glory is the good news in the Médoc, the revival of Ch. Ausone is its counterpart on the right bank. One of Bordeaux's oldest and smallest estates, Ausone was an underachiever for many years. Then in 1975 the owners brought in a new winemaker, Pascal Delbeck, *et voilà!* Ausone is

Château Ausone is now producing one of Bordeaux's finest wines: Madame Dubois Challon (left), proprietor of Château Ausone, and winemaker Pascal Delbeck (right) with Simon Loftus of Adnams wine merchants at a tasting of the Château's wines in London.

back on top. The 1979 challenges Margaux as the best of that vintage; the 1982 is one of the greatest of that great year; and the 1983 has been described by one British wine merchant as the finest young red wine he has ever tasted.

When Ausone was in eclipse, the undisputed leader in St-Emilion was Ch. Cheval-Blanc. Situated near the border with Pomerol, Cheval-Blanc is a bigger wine than Ausone. Rich and plummy, it is sometimes compared to Burgundy. Cheval-Blanc also produced a great wine in 1982.

The classification system in St-Emilion confuses as much as it clarifies. In 1954 two wines were chosen as Premiers Grands Crus Classés A and ten wines as Premiers Grands Crus Classés B. In addition seventy-two properties were classified as Grands Crus Classés. About 150 wines were designated Grands Crus, but had to submit tasting samples each year to maintain their rating. The rest were plain St-Emilion. In 1984 the system was revised, reducing the categories from four to two. Of the twelve Premiers Grands Crus Ch. Beauséjour-Bécot was demoted and added to the seventy-two Grands Crus Classés. These wines, plus six other estates, are now classified St-Emilion Grand Cru. Everything else in simply St-Emilion. We have included the original twelve Premiers Grands Crus from the 1954 classification, because there is such an enormous difference in quality within the new grouping of ninety estates. The market will still look at the old classification.

Of the former Premiers Grands Crus Classés B, the best are Ch. Figeac, neighbour of Cheval-Blanc but with a high proportion of Cabernet Sauvignon and a more Médoc style; Ch. Canon, whose quality matches the best second growths of the Médoc; Ch. Belair, under the same ownership and management as Ausone and enjoying a similar revival; and Ch. Magdelaine, owned by the J.-P. Moueix family and made with the same care and brilliance as their Pomerols. Ch. Pavie, the largest of the Premiers

Grands Crus, is again making fine wine after some so-so vintages in the early seventies; Clos Fourtet, following its purchase by André Lurton, is back in fine form; and Ch. La Gaffelière has shown recent improvement.

Within the large group of Grands Crus that were formerly Grands Crus Classés there are several properties making wine as fine as their more highly regarded neighbours. The best of these from the St-Emilion Côtes are Ch. L'Angélus; Ch. L'Arrosée, unusual for its high proportion of Cabernet Sauvignon; Ch. Balestard-la-Tonnelle, big, rich wine; Ch. Cadet-Piola, elegant wines and a notable 1982; Ch. Canon-la-Gaffelière, stylish but expensive; Ch. La Clotte, delicious Pomerol-like wine; Ch. Couvent-des-Jacobins, big, full-bodied, consistently fine; Clos des Jacobins, Cordier-owned, and now doing well; Ch. Curé-Bon-La-Madeleine, well-sited vineyard making consistently good wines; Ch. Fonplégade, large property, consistent record; Ch. Fonroque, another J.-P. Moueix property making very full-bodied St-Emilion; Ch. Franc Mayne, soft, fruity wines: Ch. Haut-Sarpe, a big concentrated wine, usually reliable; Ch. Larmande, deep-coloured, complex wine from an estate to watch; Ch. Moulin-du-Cadet, well-made stylish wine; Ch. Pavie-Decesse, under the same ownership as Pavie, making good, age-worthy wine; Ch. Soutard, very well-made, long-lived wines from this large property; Ch. Troplong-Mondot, a large estate, producing one of the best St-Emilions year after year.

In the St-Emilion 'Graves' the best properties include Ch. Corbin-Michotte, where Jean-Noël Boidron is responsible for wine of consistently high quality; Ch. Croque-Michotte, a well-sited vineyard making full-bodied wine; Ch. La Dominique, admirably situated next to Cheval-Blanc, and a producer of rich fine wine; Ch. Grand-Corbin-Despagne, big, sturdy wine of good quality; Ch. La Tour Figeac, best of the three La Tour Figeac properties.

Recommended Producers:

Pomerol

Next door to St-Emilion is the smallest of the fine wine appellations of Bordeaux, and, until the 1960s, the most neglected. Pomerol is making up for that now with a vengeance. It is Ch. Pétrus that has made the name of Pomerol famous, and prompted people to try these distinctive wines.

The dominant grape here is Merlot. With less tannin than the Cabernet Sauvignon, it produces softer wines that are immediately attractive, but age well. The J.-P. Moueix family own Ch. Pétrus and strive for perfection in every aspect, from vineyard through to finished product. They also own what many consider to be Pomerol's second best wine, Ch. Trotanoy.

Ten years ago Pétrus was priced with the first growths of the Médoc, and Trotanoy with the seconds. Now Trotanoy is climbing toward first growth price and Pétrus operates in a market of one. Christian Moueix believes that both these properties made their finest ever wines in 1982.

One of the reasons that Pomerols are so expensive is the tiny production at most properties. There is no better illustration of this than Ch. Lafleur, where production is around 1,000 cases. This is deeply coloured, long-lasting wine of the highest order.

Ch. La Fleur Pétrus, another Moueix property, is also in the top flight of Pomerols. A very firm wine, it is less concentrated than either Pétrus or Trotanoy. Ch. La Conseillante is leaner and more restrained than most Pomerols, but in good vintages, such as 1970 and 1982, it is a most fragrant and elegant wine. Ch. L'Evangile is a big wine, needing a decade or more to soften, while Vieux Château Certan, once this commune's most famous property, makes a drier wine, more Médoc in style.

Ch. Certan de May has recently begun to make exceptionally good wine. Latour-à-Pomerol is another property making very good wine in a full, fruity style. Ch. Le Gay, a small property under the same ownership as Ch. Lafleur, makes rich, concentrated wine, but only in tiny quantities.

There is no classification in Pomerol, but several other properties are recognized as making wine which is good but not of the same quality as the wines listed above. These include Ch. de Sales, the largest property in Pomerol and a very reliable one; La Grave-Trigant-de-Boisset, a Moueix estate making flavoury, early-maturing wine; Ch. Petit-Village, under the same ownership as Cos d'Estournel, and producer of a very fine 1982; Ch. Nenin, a big property, producing reliable rather than exciting wine; and Ch. L'Enclos, a fine, deep wine that ages well.

Sauternes and Barsac

The great sweet white wines of Bordeaux, like dry Graves, are a product of the Sauvignon and Sémillon. In the best years the grapes are attacked by botrytis cinerea. The fungus reduces the water content of the grapes leaving a higher proportion of sugar, which produces a rich, more concentrated wine, higher in alcohol, with a varying amount of residual sugar. The wines are commonly known by the most famous commune, Sauternes, and they are regaining favour in international markets after several years in the doldrums. A great vintage in 1983 will no doubt assist this.

Vintage Assessment: White Bordeaux

1985: A very good vintage for dry white wines, whose quality has been improving steadily in the 1980s. The hot weather during vintage time only caused problems to those châteaux without cooling equipment. The dry wines will be full of flavour and very attractive. In Sauternes and Barsac, the dry autumn prevented the appearance of botrytis, and an untypical wine was made, fully sweet due to the grapes being roasted rather than affected by noble rot, and high in alcohol. Not a classic vintage. Even so, some Crus Classés in Sauternes are offering their wine en primeur, perhaps to benefit from the fine reputation of the 1985 reds.

Pouring the grapes into the crusher at Château d'Yquem.

1984: A better-than-average year for both dry and sweet white varieties, though it is still early days for both. Early maturing wines.

1983: A potentially great vintage for Sauternes and a very good one for Graves. The sweet wines are a good bet for long-term ageing.

1982: Better for Graves than Sauternes. The dry wines may be a bit too ripe, but are very flavoury. Sweet wines are deficient in acid and are probably best drunk over the next 5 years.

1981: Very good in Graves, no better than average in Sauternes. The dry wines are ripe and full of flavour now, though the best should keep well. Sweet wines are better balanced than 1982 but lack the depth of a really good vintage.

1980: A much more successful vintage for white Bordeaux, both dry and sweet, than for red. Graves are particularly good, full-bodied and well-balanced and the best need a few more years. Sauternes are good, medium-bodied wines that are mostly ready to drink now.

1979: A good vintage, better for Sauternes than for Graves. Dry wines lack fruit and flesh and should be drunk now. Sauternes have sufficient fruit and depth and should still improve.

1978: A good vintage for Graves, rather less so for Sauternes. Dry wines are good now, and perhaps should be consumed before the fruit fades. Sauternes missed botrytis and thus lack richness and depth.

1977: A poor vintage for both dry and sweet varieties.

1976: A good vintage for Graves and a very good one for Sauternes. The best dry wines are delicious now, but should keep well, while the finest Sauternes are still developing.

1975: A great year for both dry and sweet Bordeaux. Very good, balanced wines in Graves, a bit less ripe than 1976, but with more style. It is the same story in Sauternes, and the 1975s are probably the better vintage for long-term keeping.

1974: A dull vintage. Avoid.

1973: A big vintage of average quality that is now past its best. Some Sauternes should still be all right, but none will improve.

1972: A below-average vintage now past its prime.

1971: A very good year for both dry and sweet varieties. All wines are ready now, and the better Graves are delicious. Sauternes also in its prime but should keep well.

1970: A great vintage for Graves, though the wines are now difficult to find. Very good for Sauternes, though perhaps not as good as 1971. The sweet wines are well balanced and should last.

Earlier vintages: Very few older Graves would still be in good condition, but fine Sauternes last an amazingly long time. Some older vintages to look for are 1967, 1961, 1959, 1955, 1953, 1949, 1947 and 1945.

Left The coat of arms of the illustrious Château d'Yquem.

The Grands Crus Classés (1855 Classification)

Premier Grand Cru (First Great Growth)

Ch. d'Yquem	Sauternes

Premiers Crus (First Growths)

Ch. Guiraud	Sauternes
Ch. La Tour-Blanche	Sauternes
Ch. Lafaurie-Peyraguey	Sauternes
Ch. de Rayne-Vigneau	Sauternes
Ch. Sigalas-Rabaud	Sauternes
Ch. Rabaud-Promis	Sauternes
Clos Haut-Peyraguey	Sauternes
Ch. Coutet	Barsac
Ch. Climens	Barsac
Ch. Suduiraut	Sauternes
Ch. Rieussec	Sauternes

Deuxièmes Crus (Second Growths)

Ch. d'Arche	Sauternes
Ch. Filhot	Sauternes
Ch. Lamothe	Sauternes
Ch. Doisy-Védrines	Barsac
Ch. Doisy-Daëne	Barsac
Ch. Suau	Barsac
Ch. Broustet	Barsac
Ch. Caillou	Barsac
Ch. Nairac	Barsac
Ch. de Malle	Sauternes
Ch. Romer	Sauternes

Recommended Producers:

Sauternes

The greatest of the sweet white wines is Ch. d'Yquem, one of the world's finest wines. Everything about the property is conducted in the most meticulous manner, from vineyard cultivation to vinification, ageing and bottling, and the result is a golden, honeyed wine, very sweet but in a delicate balance that lasts almost indefinitely.

For those unable to afford the exquisite pleasures of Ch. d'Yquem, there are, fortunately, a number of very good Sauternes at reasonable prices. Ch. Suduiraut is the second-best property, and after some uneven examples in the early seventies, is back on form. Ch. Guiraud, bought by Canadian interests in 1981, made a very good 1983, after several indifferent years. This is a heartening sign, because Guiraud should be one of Sauternes' great estates. Ch. Rieussec, now majority-owned by Domaines Rothschild, also made a very good 1983, as did Ch. Lafaurie-Peyraguey. The second growth Ch. Filhot makes a good wine in a lighter style.

Among the Crus Bourgeois, look out for Ch. de Fargues, controlled by the Lur Saluces family of Ch. d'Yquem; Ch. Raymond-Lafon, owned by the winemaker at Ch. d'Yquem, and producer of a fine 1983; and Ch. Gilette, which produces several wines of varying richness, all of high quality.

Barsac

Barsac is the other major sweet wine commune, and the style is similar to Sauternes but a shade drier. Its two Premiers Crus are regularly among the best wines of the region. Ch. Climens is a luscious wine, sweeter than other Barsacs, and consistently good. Ch. Coutet, the other great Barsac, is less sweet, with a tangy acidity on the finish that makes it refreshing.

The second growth, Doisy-Védrines, is a traditional property making rich wines that age well, while Doisy-Daëne makes more modern, lighter wines and succeeded especially in 1983. Among the Crus Bourgeois, notable wines are made at Ch. Roumieu, and Ch. Padouën, while Ch. Liot makes consistently good wines at reasonable prices.

BURGUNDY

Buying fine red Burgundy is like playing dungeons and dragons. The hazards are numerous and well disguised, but the rewards are immense, for the Côte d'Or represents perfection in the Pinot Noir grape. Unlike Cabernet Sauvignon which produces fine wines in California, Australia, and Italy, the Pinot is a reluctant traveller. Making good wine from this grape has been difficult and frustrating for generations in Burgundy; it has been almost impossible elsewhere.

Fine Burgundy has an intense, perfumed fragrance when young, and none of the mouth-puckering tannins that make a young Bordeaux so off-putting. It combines this fragrance with an aroma less easy to define, for there is a hint of freshly composted soil balancing the perfume in great Burgundy: a 'Bal à Versailles' of the barnyard.

The 1983 vintage highlights some of the problems facing winemakers in Burgundy, and, farther down the chain, those consumers trying to buy it. Much heralded in the press, 1983 has certainly produced some of the greatest wines of the past twenty years, but it lacks the consistency of the 1982 and 1983 vintages in Bordeaux. A hot, humid summer encouraged rot; there were hailstorms that did particular damage in Chambolle-Musigny and Vosne-Romanée. Hot weather at harvest made temperature control during fermentation difficult, and some wines are overly tannic and out of balance.

Irregular vintages are the norm in Burgundy, and there is seldom a vintage of consistently high quality. The climate and the fickleness of the grape are partly responsible, but it is also due to the number of growers producing wine in the same vineyard. Unlike Bordeaux, where specific properties are classified, in Burgundy it is the vineyards that are ranked. Anyone owning a plot within the vineyard is entitled to the appellation. Some are conscientious and dedicated, while others are content to sell their produce on the vineyard's reputation. So, while Chambertin is potentially one of Burgundy's greatest wines, not all Chambertin lives up to the potential. The name of the producer is of paramount importance in Burgundy.

The small size of plots in many of the great vineyards also makes it difficult for some growers to assemble enough wine to make bottling economically feasible. Even in a good year the yield from one *climat* might only be a few dozen cases. In the past this production was sold to négociants, who would blend it with other wines from the same vineyards. But growers are increasingly opting to bottle wines themselves, as domaine wines have begun attracting premium prices.

The position for white Burgundy is less complicated. Put simply, it is

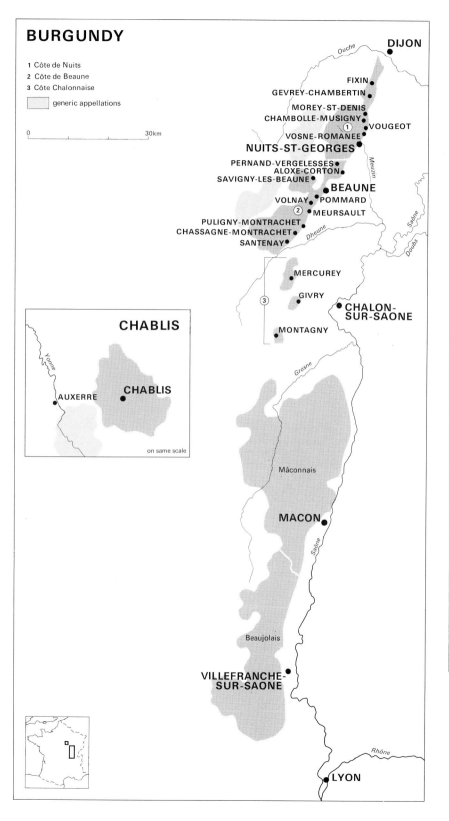

BURGUNDY

1 Côte de Nuits
2 Côte de Beaune
3 Côte Chalonnaise

generic appellations

0   30km

DIJON

Ouche

FIXIN
GEVREY-CHAMBERTIN
MOREY-ST-DENIS
CHAMBOLLE-MUSIGNY
① VOUGEOT
VOSNE-ROMANÉE
NUITS-ST-GEORGES
Meuzin

PERNAND-VERGELESSES
ALOXE-CORTON
SAVIGNY-LES-BEAUNE
BEAUNE
VOLNAY POMMARD
② MEURSAULT
PULIGNY-MONTRACHET
CHASSAGNE-MONTRACHET
SANTENAY
Dheune

Saône
Doubs

MERCUREY
GIVRY
CHALON-
SUR-SAONE
③
MONTAGNY

Grosne

CHABLIS

Yonne

AUXERRE

CHABLIS

on same scale

Mâconnais

MACON

Saône

Beaujolais

VILLEFRANCHE-
SUR-SAONE

Rhône

LYON

the finest expression of what is currently the most fashionable white varietal, and is produced in such small quantities that demand always exceeds supply. The Chardonnay is an easier grape than the Pinot Noir, as its success in America, Australia and New Zealand proves. The classic whites of the Côte de Beaune have set the standard for these other regions.

The finest wines are generally barrel-fermented at a low temperature, and kept in wood until bottling. The time of bottling depends on the style the winemaker seeks. If he wants to emphasize fresh, ripe fruit, he will bottle early; if seeking a bigger wine with a distinct oaky flavour, he will leave the wine in barrels, a proportion of them of new wood. At the top level, most winemakers opt for the latter style. The result is a wine that is full of fruit but a bit harsh when young, with the oak dominating the fruit. It matures—and for great white Burgundies this might take five to eight years—into a buttery, rich wine, luscious but distinctly dry, with a vanillin taste as a reminder of the oak.

The Chardonnay produces another white wine that is included within the broad appellation of Burgundy, but is better known by its regional name, Chablis. Farther north than the Côte d'Or, Chablis produces a steelier Chardonnay, drier and more austere. There is greater variation in Chablis with fewer warm summers to ripen the grapes. But in good years like 1983, Grands and Premiers Crus from Chablis produce ageworthy wines with an emphasis on the fruit rather than on the weight of the varietal.

The Trade

The trade in Burgundy is divided between négociant-éleveurs, and proprietors who vinify, age and bottle the wine from their own vineyards. The most important négociants own substantial domaines, but they also purchase young wine from other growers to age and bottle under their own labels. An important difference between Burgundy and Bordeaux is the size of the holdings. Château Mouton-Rothschild, for example, is about 70 hectares (170 acres), and produces roughly 22,500 cases of Premier Grand Cru wine, while the Domaine Dujac in Morey-Saint-Denis is 11 hectares (27 acres) and produces as many as nine different wines. Each wine must be vinified, aged and bottled separately, and in some years the production from one vineyard may be no more than a few dozen cases.

The position of the négociant is very strong. Most growers do not own enough land to make domaine bottling economically feasible; they must sell the young wine to a négociant. Because of their size the négociants have certain commercial advantages. They have (at least the good ones do) an established reputation for quality, and they produce wines in sufficient quantities to guarantee continuity of supply. They also have a strong enough marketing organization to promote their wines around the world.

Those proprietors who bottle their own wines can be divided into three groups. There are the pioneers of domaine bottling such as Armand Rousseau, Marquis d'Angerville, and Henri Gouges. They are joined by

Le Montrachet vineyard. The greatest and most sought-after dry white wine in the world comes from this 7½ hectare (18.5 acre) vineyard in the communes of Puligny and Chassagne-Montrachet in Burgundy's Côte de Beaune. The total production averages about 2,500 cases.

relative newcomers such as Jacques Seysses who have come prepared to invest substantial sums in developing both vineyards and cellars. Finally there are the small producers who have been persuaded to bottle their wine by exporters who then take on the task of selling them.

Of late there has been much discussion of the relative merits of domaine versus négociant bottled Burgundy with some consumers believing the former to be the Holy Grail. There is so much poor, overpriced Burgundy about that it would be reassuring to think there was some easy method of avoiding it. In truth there is not. There are some excellent domaines and some négociants who maintain consistently high standards. But there are both négociants and domaines turning out dull characterless wine year after year.

'I believe there is too much made of this,' said John Avery of the Bristol wine merchant that is one of Britain's best for Burgundy. 'The fact is that "élevage" and bottling are different and distinct skills from running a vineyard. Some proprietors have these skills, but many do not. Nor do they have the resources of a négociant. Say a man produces two barrels of Corton-Charlemagne. If he keeps it himself, he won't even have enough wine to keep the barrels topped up, at least not with Corton-Charlemagne.'

Rebecca Wasserman is an American whose company in Beaune represents many of the finest small domaines. 'There is always going to be a place for the négociant in Burgundy,' she said, 'because many growers cannot afford to bottle their own wine. What the good small domaines have done though is force many négociants to raise their standards. That's because they have shown people what true Burgundy tastes like.'

Some négociants, such as Joseph Drouhin, have responded by signing contracts for grapes rather than young wine. This gives them control over the vinification, as well as the ageing and bottling.

Burgundy seems to be on the rise. This might seem a peculiar description of one of the world's two most prestigious wine regions. But in the past few years there has been a noticeable improvement in quality. Négociants such as Joseph Drouhin, Louis Jadot, and Faiveley are making better wines than ever, and a new generation of enthusiastic university trained winemakers is appearing in domaines throughout the region. We have certainly been living in a golden age for Bordeaux. Are we about to see the same in Burgundy?

Classification

Burgundy is classified by vineyard in its fine wine regions, and planting is restricted to two grape varieties: Pinot Noir for red and Chardonnay for white. At the top of the hierarchy are the Grands Crus, 23 for red and 6 for white. These are identified by vineyard alone, e.g., Chambertin, Musigny, Montrachet, and do not require the commune name on the label.

In the next rank are the Premiers Crus, whose names appear on the label preceded by the name of the commune, e.g., Gevrey-Chambertin (Commune)—Clos St-Jacques (Vineyard), or Meursault (Commune)—

vineyard
(Grand Cru)

producer

VIN NON FILTRE
DÉCANTATION
RECOMMANDÉE

MIS EN BOUTEILLE
AU
DOMAINE

CLOS LA ROCHE
APPELLATION CLOS LA ROCHE CONTROLÉE

1980

DOMAINE DUJAC

75 cl

S.C.E. DU DOMAINE DUJAC PROPRIÉTAIRE A MOREY-ST-DENIS (CÔTE-D'OR)
PRODUCE OF FRANCE
FILIBER A NUITS

bottling details
(domaine
bottled)

AOC
designation

vintage

contents

Clos La Roche is a Grand Cru, so the name appears alone on the label, with its own Appellation Contrôlée status. Premiers Crus vineyards must be preceded by the name of the commune and bear the communal AOC.

Charmes (Vineyard). There are over 200 Premiers Crus, but many are not sold under their own names. They are blended together and sold as Beaune Premier Cru or Pommard Premier Cru. This is perfectly legitimate. The best of the Crus are known by name, and some approach or surpass Grand Cru quality. Charles Rousseau, for example, prefers his Clos St-Jacques to several of his Grands Crus from the vineyards adjoining Chambertin.

The next level encompasses all wines with commune or village names, e.g. Gevrey-Chambertin, Nuits-St-Georges, Aloxe-Corton. These wines can vary widely in quality, though the same rule as for the greatest growths applies here. Look first for the name of the producer; a good domaine or négociant is the best guarantee. Here, though, a word of caution is in order. The Burgundian habit of annexing the name of the most famous vineyard can lead to confusion. Take for example the famous white wines of the Côte de Beaune, where both Chassagne and Puligny have annexed Le Montrachet. Bâtard-Montrachet is a Grand Cru, only slightly less exalted than Le Montrachet itself. A wine labelled simply Puligny-Montrachet or Chassagne-Montrachet is a village wine. It may be good, indeed should be, but it is certainly not a Grand Cru.

Chablis's classification includes the commune name even with the Grands Crus. So, the Grand Cru Les Clos is Chablis Les Clos. There is an enormous difference between Chablis and a Chablis Grand Cru.

Vintage Assessment: Red

Vintages matter a great deal in Burgundy, which is on the northern fringe of red wine cultivation. Ideal conditions occur two or three times a decade, so winemakers have had to learn to cope. The vintage is second in importance to the producer, whose name is always the first thing to look for.

1985 (red and white): The total harvest will be slightly above 1984 in quantity and equal to 1983 (but quite different) in quality. Chablis harvested 60 per cent more than was expected, but this was unable to hold down prices. In the Côte d'Or the lack of rain from August to the end of October had not been seen for decades. The red wines have a beautiful colour, a rich, plummy fruit and perfect balance; they are less tannic, and less serious than the 1983s, and will mature faster. Prices at the Hospices de Beaune showed a startling rise of 86 per cent over 1984, and the average rise from the growers seems to be in the 50 per cent range. The white wines will be magnificent, with less alcohol than the flamboyant 1983s and more flavour than the elegant 1984s. This is a year for the collector, and although prices at the Hospices de Beaune went up by 'only' 20 per cent for the white wines, prices at the property have risen further.

1984: A difficult summer in Burgundy as elsewhere in France. Cold early on and wet in August. No better than average.

1983: The sort of year that makes a vintage chart meaningless. Some growers made the best wines since 1949. Others, who could not cope with the problems of rot and hot weather during fermentation, failed. Burgundians, eager for a '1982 Bordeaux' have been beating the drum for the 1983, so they will be expensive. Choose with care.

1982: A huge crop leading generally to light, pleasant wines for early drinking, but more concentrated wines from experienced growers.

1981: The least attractive vintage since 1977. Some wines have a green, undernourished character. Drink now.

1980: The best vintage for quality and price for wines from the Côte de Nuits. Initially condemned, the wines have surpassed expectations, though many from the Côte de Beaune live down to the early evaluation. Buy now for drinking over the next few years.

1979: The opposite of 1980. A vintage that initially looked promising but has faded rather quickly. Better in the Côte de Beaune but for drinking, not keeping.

1978: A small vintage of elegant, well-balanced wines. The best still have a lot of life, and some of the sturdier Côte de Nuits have yet to mature. Scarce and expensive.

1977: Mean, stringy wines that never did show well. Drink up.

1976: A difficult and atypical Burgundy vintage. The product of a hot summer, many have unusually high tannin levels for Pinot Noir, and appear unlikely ever to come around. The best, though, have masses of fruit and an heroic structure. Choose very carefully.

1975: A complete washout. Avoid.

1974: Hard wines that never had much charm, and are now past their best.

1973: This vintage was all right in its time: light, everyday wines but not a stayer.

1972: The fourth of four consecutive good to very good vintages, followed by three mediocre years to redress the balance. The 1972s suffered because it was not a good year for Bordeaux and they were caught in the mid-seventies slump. Some very good wines still; firm and fully mature.

1971: A very good vintage and most wines are now at their best. Scarce and expensive.

1970: A good vintage, though not as fine as 1969 or 1971 due to over-production. The wines appeared soft when young, but many have lasted well.

1969: A very good vintage of big, old-fashioned wines. Good examples from the Côte de Nuits still have a future. Scarce and very expensive.

Earlier vintages: The sixties were a good decade for Burgundy, and besides 1969, good wines were made in 1966, 1964, 1962, and 1961. These wines occasionally appear at auction.

Vintage Assessment: White

The Chardonnay produces more consistent results than the Pinot Noir, and there have been few recent vintages that have not been at least good for white Burgundy. This is fortunate for the consumer, because the already high prices would otherwise be astronomical.

1985: (see above)

1984: More successful for white than red with well-balanced wines for relatively early drinking.

1983: The hot summer produced some wonderfully rich, exotic wines, and a lot of unbalanced, over-alcoholic ones. The prices are very high, and it will be necessary to choose carefully. Outstanding for Chablis.

1982: A good year for whites though overproduction caused some to be too dilute. In the main these are ripe, well made, and for early drinking. Chablis was less successful, though the wines are good.

1981: A very good year for white Burgundy with lean, well-balanced wines that need some bottle age. The best will begin to show well in two or three years. An excellent year for Chablis.

1980: The poorest year since 1977. Most wines are a bit tart and lack fruit. If they were inexpensive they might be worth considering, but as they are not it is best to avoid them.

1979: A large vintage of, on the whole, very good quality. Most are drinking well now, and a few will improve. Huge crop in Chablis, and these wines are fully mature.

1978: An outstanding vintage. Fruity with plenty of weight and enough acid to ensure their future. The best wines have disappeared from the retail market, and occasionally surface at auction. Very expensive. A great year in Chablis.

1977: Never was much good. Avoid.

1976: Same problem as with the reds, though a number of whites have turned out rather well. Big, buttery Chardonnays lacking acidity. All but the best are on the decline.

Earlier vintages: The best white Burgundies can last a decade or more, but most do not. There are still some good wines from 1973, which was an excellent vintage, and from 1971, which received more publicity and achieved higher prices. Buying white Burgundy older than 1971 is a risky business.

Côte de Nuits

FIXIN
Grands Crus: none

Important Premiers Crus: Clos du Chapitre, Cheusots, Perrière

Just north of Gevrey-Chambertin, Fixin's wines are big and sturdy, but often lacking in elegance. Because it is less well known than its neighbours the wines are frequently good value.

Recommended Producers

Philippe Joliet
Pierre Gelin
Guy Berthaut

GEVREY-CHAMBERTIN
Grands Crus: Chambertin, Chambertin Clos de Bèze, Chapelle-Chambertin, Charmes- (and Mazoyères) Chambertin, Griotte-Chambertin, Latricières-Chambertin, Mazis-Chambertin, Ruchottes-Chambertin

Important Premiers Crus: Cazetiers, La Combe-aux-Moines, Combottes, Estournelles, Lavaux, Clos Prieur, La Romanée, Clos St-Jacques, Les Varoilles

It is in Gevrey, which annexed the name of its great vineyard, that the most famous names of red Burgundy begin. The commune's fame is founded on the reputation of its two great vineyards, Chambertin and Chambertin Clos de Bèze. At their best they are powerful, full-bodied wines, which require more ageing than any of the great reds. The other Grands Crus are said to be like the two great growths but to lack that extra measure of elegance, body or concentration. There is an enormous range of styles, and, alas, of quality, even among the greatest wines of the commune. The name Chambertin is a guarantee, but it is one way. It guarantees a sale for the winemaker, but not always quality for the consumer. Gevrey-Chambertin illustrates perfectly the first rule for choosing Burgundy: look first for the supplier's name, then for the vineyard or commune. In this section we shall concentrate on the leading domaines. Négociant wines will be treated in a separate section.

Proprietor Jacques Seysses sampling the wine from a cask at Domaine Dujac in Morey-St-Denis. Note the shallow silver *tastevin*, traditional in Burgundy.

Recommended Producers

Domaine Camus	Domaine Pernot-Fourrier
Domaine Clair-Daü	Domaine Henri Rebourseau
Domaine Drouhin-Laroze	Domaine Joseph Roty
Domaine Dujac	Domaine Armand Rousseau
Domaine Faiveley	Domaine Tortochot
Philippe Leclerc	Domaine Louis Trapet
René Leclerc	Domaine des Varoilles

MOREY-ST-DENIS

Grands Crus: Bonnes Mares (a part), Clos des Lambrays, Clos de la Roche, Clos St-Denis, Clos de Tart
Important Premiers Crus: Clos de la Bussière, Les Monts Luisants (white), Clos des Ormes, Sorbés, Le Clos Sorbés

Less well known than its neighbours along the Côte de Nuits, Morey-St-Denis is currently producing some of its best wines. The style is firmer than Chambolle-Musigny in the south, and fuller bodied; perhaps less elegant than Gevrey-Chambertin in the north. Although recognition has now come to Morey-St-Denis, it has never been a popular appellation and its success is well deserved.

Recommended Producers

Domaine Clair-Daü	Domaine Hubert Lignier
Domaine Dujac	Domaine Ponsot
Clos de Tart (Monopole)	Domaine Georges Roumier
Clos des Lambrays (Monopole)	Domaine Bernard Serveau
Domaine Georges Lignier	

CHAMBOLLE-MUSIGNY

Grands Crus: Bonnes Mares (the greater part), Musigny
Important Premiers Crus: Amoureuses, Charmes

Chambolle-Musigny is known for the silky, elegant style of its wines, and it is another commune bursting with new ideas and talented winemakers. One of Burgundy's greatest estates, Domaine Comte de Vogüé is here, making highly prized Musigny, as well as Bonnes Mares.

Recommended Producers

Domaine Clair-Daü	Domaine Daniel Moine
Domaine Clerget	Domaine Georges Roumier
Domaine Jean Grivot	Domaine Comte de Vogüé

VOUGEOT
Grand Cru: Clos de Vougeot
Important Premiers Crus: Cras, Clos de la Perrière, Petits Vougeots

One of Burgundy's most famous names because of its 125-acre Grand Cru Clos de Vougeot, this commune's reputation has suffered of late. The great vineyard now has around 75 owners, and all the range of quality one would expect from such a fragmented property. It is especially important with Clos de Vougeot to seek out the best growers.

Clos de Vougeot: the largest of the Grands Crus of the Côte de Nuits and the most parcelated, with some seventy-five different owners. The Château du Clos Vougeot is the headquarters of the Confrérie des Chevaliers du Tastevin. Founded in 1934, this organization promotes Burgundy wines. Each year they select outstanding examples which bear the Tastevin label.

Recommended Producers

Domaine Bertagna	Domaine Machard de Gramont
Domaine Clair-Daü	Domaine Mongeard-Mugneret
Domaine J.-J. Confuron	Domaine Georges Mugneret
Domaine René Engel	Domaine Henri Rebourseau
Domaine Jean Grivot	Domaine Georges Roumier
Domaine Hudelot-Noëllat	

FLAGEY-ECHEZEAUX AND VOSNE-ROMANEE
Grands Crus: Echézeaux, Grands Echézeaux, Richebourg, La Romanée, Romanée-Conti, Romanée-St-Vivant, La Tâche
Important Premiers Crus: Beaux-Monts, Brûlées, Grande-Rue, Malconsorts, Clos des Réas, Suchots

There are two distinct villages but one appellation, Vosne-Romanée, producing, along with Gevrey-Chambertin, the most famous wines of the Côte de Nuits. This is the home of the Domaine de la Romanée-Conti, producer of sometimes fabulous but always fabulously expensive Burgundies. Their Monopoles of Romanée-Conti and La Tâche head a list which includes Richebourg, Romanée-St-Vivant, Grands Echézeaux, Echézeaux, and a small holding in Le Montrachet. Romanée-Conti is Burgundy's most celebrated name and in good years their wines do have an added dimension, a depth of flavour that singles them out. After a decade or more of producing wines below their possible level of quality, the growers of Vosne-Romanée are showing much improvement.

Recommended Producers

Domaine Robert Arnoux	Domaine Machard de Gramont
Domaine René Engel	Domaine Mongeard-Mugneret
Domaine Jean Gros	Domaine Georges Mugneret
Domaine Hudelot-Noëllat	Domaine Gérard Mugneret
Domaine Henri Jayer	Domaine Pernin-Rossin
Domaine Jacqueline Jayer	Domaine de la Romanée-Conti
Domaine Henri Lamarche	

NUITS-ST-GEORGES
Grands Crus: none
Important Premiers Crus: Les Argillats, Clos de l'Arlot, Boudots, Cailles, Chaignots, Clos des Corvées, Cras, Clos des Forêts, Les Hauts Pruliers, Clos de la Maréchale, Aux Perdrix, Perrière, Les Porets, Les Pruliers, Les St-Georges, Les Vaucrains

The principal town of the Côte de Nuits, Nuits-St-Georges has no Grands Crus, but several of its Premiers Crus approach that standard. These are among the sturdiest of all red Burgundies, and generally need more bottle age than their neighbours.

Recommended Producers

Domaine L. Audidier
Robert Chevillon
Domaine Henri Gouges
Domaine Machard de Gramont
Domaine Jean Grivot

Domaine Alain Michelot
Domaine Georges Mugneret
Domaine Gérard Mugneret
Daniel Rion

Côte de Beaune

LADOIX-SERRIGNY
Grands Crus: see Aloxe-Corton
Important Premiers Crus: Les Maréchaudes, La Toppe au Vert (appellation Aloxe-Corton)

ALOXE-CORTON
Grands Crus: Corton (to which a vineyard name may be appended, such as Bressandes, Languettes, Pougets, Renardes, Clos du Roi, etc.), Corton Charlemagne
Important Premiers Crus: Les Fourniers, Les Maréchaudes, Les Paulands

These two communes and Pernand-Vergelesses form the points of a triangle with the great vineyard of Corton in the middle. Most of the vineyard is in Aloxe-Corton, but a substantial part of Corton-Charlemagne is in Pernand. It is much the largest Grand Cru in Burgundy, and it is confusingly sub-divided. Besides Le Corton itself there are the well-known Grands Crus, such as Bressandes, Renardes, and Clos du Roi. Any wine labelled simply Corton, or Corton followed by a vineyard desig-nation, is a Grand Cru. If it is labelled Aloxe-Corton followed by a vineyard name, it is a Premier Cru. Corton is the only Grand Cru red of the Côte de Beaune, and in style it resembles the biggest wines of the Côte de Nuits. It is a wine that needs substantial bottle age.
   The other Grand Cru, Corton-Charlemagne, is the first of the great white wines of the Côte de Beaune, which begins at Ladoix-Serrigny. A powerful, concentrated Chardonnay, Corton-Charlemagne is generally reckoned to be second only to Le Montrachet in the hierarchy.

Recommended Producers

Domaine Bonneau du Martray
Domaine Chandon de Briailles
Domaine Chevalier
Domaine Dubreuil-Fontaine
Le Prince de Mérode
Domaine Rapet Père et Fils

Domaine Daniel Senard
Domaine Tollot-Beaut
Domaine Tollot-Voarick
Charles Viénot
Domaine Michel Voarick

PERNAND-VERGELESSES
Grands Crus: see Aloxe-Corton
Important Premiers Crus: Fichots, Ile des Vergelesses

Pernand produces both red and white wines which are frequently good value, and some of the reds are particularly good. Look especially for the Premier Cru Ile des Vergelesses.

Recommended Producers

Domaine Bonneau du Martray
Domaine Chandon de Briailles
Domaine Dubreuil-Fontaine

Domaine Rapet Père et Fils
Domaine Tollot-Voarick

SAVIGNY-LES-BEAUNE
Grands Crus: none
Important Premiers Crus: Aux Vergelesses, Clous, Dominodes, Guettes, Lavières, Marconnets, Serpentières

Mainly red wine here, and, at its best, on a par with its more famous neighbour, Beaune, but usually considerably less expensive.

Recommended Producers

Domaine Pierre Bitouzet
Simon Bize et Fils
Domaine Chandon de Briailles

Domaine Bernard Clair
Domaine Louis Ecard-Guyot
Domaine Tollot-Beaut

BEAUNE
Grands Crus: none
Important Premiers Crus: Avaux, Boucherottes, Bressandes, Cent Vignes, Champimonts, Cras, Epenottes, Fèves, Grèves, Marconnets, Clos des Mouches, Clos de la Mousse, Clos du Roi, Teurons, Vignes Franches

Burgundy's commercial heart and its most beguiling town, Beaune is the largest wine-producing commune in the Côte de Beaune. Almost all the wine is red and, as Beaune is the headquarters of several famous négociants, it is no surprise that they are major landowners.

Recommended Producers

Robert Ampeau et Fils	Domaine Michel Gaunoux
Domaine Besancenot-Mathouillet	Domaine Michel Lafarge
Coron Père et Fils	Domaine Tollot-Beaut

The Hospices de Beaune

One of Beaune's landmarks, the Hospices de Beaune is a fifteenth-century hospital whose charitable works are supported by vineyard and farmland endowments. The vineyards now total 138 acres: all, except for a plot in Mazis-Chambertin, in the Côte de Beaune. They are the legacies of merchants and growers and produce a total of 34 wines, 25 red and 9 white. Many Hospices wines are not made with the produce of a single vineyard, but are blended from excellent plots within the same commune. The famous Dr Peste, for example, is assembled from five Corton vineyards, including Bressandes and Clos du Roi.

The wines are auctioned for charity on the third Sunday in November, and the prices are watched closely by other producers as an indication of the market. Prices for Hospices wines are generally higher than their quality warrants because of the charitable aspect, and many critics reckon the sale has an inflationary effect. This was seen in the result of the 1985 auction, which showed an overall increase of 80 per cent over 1984, albeit the quality was much higher, with red wines fetching 86 per cent more and white wines 'only' 20 per cent more.

The annual wine sale at the Hospices de Beaune. Each November the wines of the Hospices de Beaune are auctioned to support the organization's charitable works. Prices are generally very high and are watched by other domaines and négociants as a guide.

The following, listed by appellation and cuvée name, make up the 34 wines of the Hospices de Beaune:

Red

Mazis-Chambertin: Cuvée Madeleine Collingnon
Corton: Cuvée Charlotte Dumay; Cuvée Docteur Peste
Pernand-Vergelesses: Cuvée Rameau-Lamarosse
Savigny-lès-Beaune: Cuvée Forneret; Cuvée Fouquerand; Cuvée Arthur Girard
Beaune: Cuvée Nicholas Rolin; Cuvée Guigone de Salins; Cuvée Clos des Avaux; Cuvée Brunet; Cuvée Maurice Drouhin; Cuvée Hugues et Louis Bétault; Cuvée Rousseau-Deslandes; Cuvée Dames Hospitalières; Cuvée Cyrot Chaudron
Pommard: Cuvée Cyrot Chaudron; Cuvée Dames de la Charité; Cuvée Billardet
Volnay: Cuvée Blondeau; Cuvée Général Muteau; Cuvée Jehan de Massol; Cuvée Gauvain
Monthélie: Cuvée Lebelin
Auxey-Duresses: Cuvée Boillot

White

Corton-Charlemagne: Cuvée Françoise de Salins
Corton-Vergennes: Cuvée Paul Chanson
Meursault: Cuvée Jehan Humblot; Cuvée Loppin; Cuvée Goureau
Meursault-Genevrières: Cuvée Baudot; Cuvée Philippe le Bon
Meursault-Charmes: Cuvée de Bahèzre de Lanlay; Cuvée Albert Grivault

POMMARD
Grands Crus: none
Important Premiers Crus: Arvelets, Clos Blanc, Epenots, Jarollières, Pézerolles, Rugiens Bas, Rugiens Haut, Clos du Verger

Pommard, one of the most popular communes in the American market, produces solid, flavoury wines, lacking the elegance of Volnay, and usually needing more bottle age.

Recommended Producers

Domaine du Comte Armand
Domaine Michel Gaunoux
Domaine Machard de Gramont
Domaine de Montille

Domaine Jacques Parent
Ch. de Pommard
Domaine Pothier-Rieusset

VOLNAY
Grands Crus: none
Important Premiers Crus: Caillerets, Cailleret Dessus, Champans, Clos des
Chênes, Clos des Ducs, Fremiets, Pousse d'Or, Santenots, Taille Pieds

Elegance and balance are the hallmarks of Volnay, the most attractive red
wines of the Côte de Beaune. Another reason to follow closely the fortunes
of this commune is the extraordinary number of fine winemakers.

Recommended Producers

Domaine Robert Ampeau
Domaine Marquis d'Angerville
Domaine Louis Glantenay
Domaine Michel Lafarge

Domaine Lafon
Domaine de Montille
Domaine de la Pousse d'Or
Domaine Jacques Prieur

MEURSAULT
Grands Crus: none
Important Premiers Crus: Charmes Dessous, Charmes Dessus, Genevrières
Dessous and Genevrières Dessus, Goutte d'Or, Perrières Dessous and
Perrières Dessus, Poruzots, Santenots Blanc

The largest of the great white wine communes, Meursault has no Grands
Crus, but three Premiers Crus of world renown: Genevrières, Perrières,
and Charmes. Fine Meursault is rich and buttery with great length, and it
should age well.

Uphill from the Premier Cru Perrières is the commune of Blagny, whose
finest vineyards run into both Meursault and Puligny-Montrachet. The
commune wine is sold as Meursault-Blagny.

Recommended Producers

Robert Ampeau et Fils
Bitouzet-Prieur
Pierre Boillot
Jean François Coche-Dury
Albert Grivault
François Jobard
Domaine des Comtes Lafon

Domaine Pierre Matrot
Domaine Michelot-Buisson
Domaine René Monnier
Pierre Morey
Domaine Jacques Prieur
Domaine Ropiteau-Mignon
Guy Roulot et Fils

PULIGNY-MONTRACHET
Grands Crus: Montrachet, Bâtard-Montrachet, Bienvenue-Bâtard-Mont-
rachet, Chevalier-Montrachet
Important Premiers Crus: Champ Canet, Clavoillons, Combettes, Folatières, Garenne, Hameau de Blagny, Pucelles, Referts

The commune of Puligny, in best Burgundian tradition, added on the name of its greatest vineyard, Le Montrachet. Not to be outdone, its neighbour to the south, Chassagne, which shares the vineyard, did the same. Montrachet is the greatest white wine of Burgundy and the finest dry white wine in the world. Concentrated fruit and intense floral aroma are the hallmarks of this wine, which ages gracefully and well.

The other Grands Crus clustered around Le Montrachet show similarities in style with Chevalier-Montrachet perhaps the closest. The production of these great wines is small and prices have spiralled in the last few years. Montrachet is ludicrously expensive, and it seems inevitable that the others will follow. The Premiers Crus are still affordable, and there are some very fine producers.

Recommended Producers

Robert Ampeau et Fils
Domaine Chartron et Trébuchet
Henri Clerc
Domaine Leflaive

Domaine René Monnier
Domaine Jacques Prieur
Domaine Etienne Sauzet
Domaine Baron Thénard

CHASSAGNE-MONTRACHET
Grands Crus: Bâtard-Montrachet, Criots-Bâtard-Montrachet, Montrachet
Important Premiers Crus: (red and white except for En Cailleret, red only; and Caillerets, white only) Abbaye de Morgeot, Boudriotte, Caillerets, En Cailleret, Grands Ruchottes, Morgeot, Clos St-Jean

Chassagne shares both Montrachet and Bâtard-Montrachet with Puligny, and has one tiny Grand Cru, Criots-Bâtard-Montrachet. A major difference is that Chassagne is an important producer of red wine, though in the United States and Britain it is best regarded for its white.

Chassagne differs from Puligny in that it is less floral and more robust, while neither possesses the obvious, rich fruit of Meursault.

Recommended Producers

Domaine Bachelet-Ramonet
Domaine Blain-Gagnard
Jean-Noël Gagnard
Domaine Gagnard-Delagrange
Domaine du Duc de Magenta

Domaine Albert Morey et Fils
Domaine Marc Morey
Domaine Michel Niellon
Domaine Jacques Prieur
Domaine Ramonet-Prudhon

SANTENAY
Grands Crus: none
Important Premiers Crus: Gravières, Clos des Tavannes

Tucked away at the end of the Côte de Beaune, Santenay is an anti-climax after the great white wine communes. But there are some good buys here: honest rather than exciting Pinot Noir that sells on its merits instead of the commune name.

Recommended Producers

Domaine Belland
Domaine René Fleurot
Domaine Fleurot-Larose
Domaine des Hautes Cornières

Domaine Lequin-Roussot
Mestre Père et Fils
Domaine de la Pousse d'Or

Good Value from Lesser Communes

Several communes in the Côte de Beaune with less favourably sited vineyards produce good red and white wine at reasonable prices. Auxey-Duresses, north-west of Meursault, produces white wine in the style of its illustrious neighbour but with less depth.

Chorey-Lès-Beaune is primarily red wine from vineyards on flat land south of Aloxe-Corton. Monthélie produces wines of a higher class from sites which border Volnay. St-Aubin in the hills behind Puligny and Chassagne-Montrachet has red and white wine, and both should be consumed young to capture the fruit. St-Romain also produces red and white wine and is best known for the latter. The red wine from most of these communes can be sold under the appellation Côte de Beaune—Villages.

Côte Chalonnaise

The bulk of the wine from the Burgundy appellation is produced south of the Côte d'Or. In the region immediately south of Santenay there are a number of producers who have worked hard to improve standards. The communes here are Mercurey and Givry, mostly red wine; Rully, divided between red and white; and Montagny, white wine only.

Recommended Producers

Domaine de la Folie, Rully
Domaine Jacquesson, Rully
Domaine Michel Juillot, Mercurey
Bernard Michel, Montagny

Domaine de la Renarde, Rully
Hugues de Suremain, Mercurey
Domaine Thénard, Givry
A. and P. de Villaine, Bouzeron

Recommended Négociants

The prosperity of the top négociants is founded upon significant domaines, and generally these are their finest wines. The increase in domaine bottling means that there is less fine wine sold in bulk to the négociants, but they still play a most important part. The négociants' role—blending, ageing and bottling—is crucial, because many growers' holdings are too small or fragmented to make domaine bottling feasible. The best of the négociants apply the same skill and care to their bought-in wines as to the produce of their own vineyards.

Bouchard Père et Fils

With excellent holdings in Beaune and Corton, Bouchard Père is the largest domaine in the Côte de Beaune. Their best red wine is Le Corton, but they are probably best known for their range of Beaune Premiers Crus and the Grands Crus whites. Their commercialized bottlings are not always up to the same standard.

Red	*White*
Le Corton	Le Montrachet
Beaune Grèves Vigne de l'Enfant Jésus	Corton-Charlemagne
Beaune Clos de la Mousse	Chevalier-Montrachet
Volnay Caillerets Ancienne Cuvée Carnot	

Joseph Drouhin

A large domaine in Chablis and the Côte d'Or forms the backbone of this family-owned firm, which is making wines as fine as anyone at the moment. A fire in 1972 hampered Drouhin for a while, but they have fully recovered. Drouhin's wines are balanced; elegant rather than massive, and age well.

Red	*White*
Chambertin	Le Montrachet (Marquis de Laguiche)
Bonnes Mares	Corton-Charlemagne
Musigny	Bâtard-Montrachet
Chambolle-Musigny	Beaune Clos des Mouches
Clos de Vougeot	Chablis Les Clos
Beaune Clos des Mouches	

Négociants Bouchard Père & Fils own the largest domaine in the Côte de Beaune. One of the best *monopoles* of their more than 80 hectares (200 acres) of vineyard is the Beaune Grèves Vigne de l'Enfant Jésus. The wines are stored in cask and in bottle in vast cellars under their fifteenth-century headquarters, the Château de Beaune.

Faiveley

Like Bouchard and Drouhin, Faiveley are a family firm, and their speciality is big red wines from the Côte de Nuits. The house style tends toward rich, full-bodied, age-worthy wines, and they have the ideal sites to realize this. Faiveley's wines were very successful in 1983.

Red

Chambertin Clos de Bèze
Latricières-Chambertin
Mazis-Chambertin
Clos de Vougeot
Echézeaux
Nuits-St-Georges Clos de la Maréchale
Mercurey, Clos des Myglands

Louis Jadot

Jadot are best known for producing some of Burgundy's most elegant white wines, and have recently been achieving the same high standard with their reds.

Red

Beaune Boucherottes
Beaune Clos des Ursules

White

Corton-Charlemagne
Chevalier-Montrachet Les
    Demoiselles
Puligny-Montrachet Les Folatières

Louis Latour

One of the most famous négociants in Burgundy, Louis Latour's domaine is based on the great Corton vineyard. Latour's condemnation of the 1980 vintage (unfair, as it turns out) and Anthony Hanson's revelation that the Latour red wines are pasteurized have hurt his standing somewhat, but the wines, especially the whites, are still very good.

Red

Chambertin
Romanée St-Vivant
Corton Clos de la Vigne au Saint
Corton-Grancey

White

Corton-Charlemagne
Chevalier-Montrachet Les
    Demoiselles

Other reliable négociants are Chanson, with a large range of Beaune Premiers Crus; Jaffelin, controlled by Drouhin but a separate enterprise with a good range, especially of whites; Leroy run by Mme Lalou Bize-Leroy, co-owner of the Domaine de la Romanée-Conti, big, rich wines, and expensive; Prosper Maufoux, reliable wines across the range, also under the Marcel Amance label; Moillard, fruity, early-maturing wines; Remoissenet, very good white wines and traditional supplier to Avery's of Bristol; Ropiteau Frères, owners of the Ropiteau-Mignon domaine, very good whites.

Chablis

Grands Crus: Blanchot, Bourgos, Les Clos, Grenouilles, Les Preuses, Valmur, Vaudésir. La Moutonne is within Vaudésir and Les Preuses
Important Premiers Crus: Fôrets, Fourchaume, Les Lys, Montée-de-Tonnerre, Montmains, Monts de Milieu, Vaillons

Gathering the harvest in Chablis. In this very northerly vineyard it is a struggle every year to get grapes of sufficient ripeness.

Located about ninety miles north-west of Beaune, Chablis is nevertheless included in the Burgundy classification. In this northerly setting the Chardonnay struggles to ripen and produces wines of greener colour and less richness than the Côte de Beaune, but with firm fruit and good balance. That is in good years. In poor ones the wine is tart and skinny with little charm. Fortunately, improvements in frost control and vinification techniques have lessened the risk of a really bad vintage.

There are four categories of Chablis: Grand Cru, of which there are seven, all grouped around the village of Chablis; Premier Cru; Chablis; and Petit Chablis, which seems to be an attempt to expand the vineyards into less suitable land. Grands Crus and Premiers Crus are very much better than ordinary Chablis and almost always worth the extra money. Of the Grands Crus, Vaudésir, Grenouilles, and Les Clos have the finest reputations, but, as elsewhere in Burgundy, the best growers make the best wines, and it is their names that you should look for first.

Recommended Producers

René Dauvissat
Domaine Defaix
Jean Durup
William Fèvre (Domaine de la Maladière)
Henri Laroche (Domaine Laroche and Domaine La Jouchère)
Long-Depaquit
Louis Michel
J. Moreau et Fils
François Raveneau

RHONE

No French region has received as much favourable attention over the past few years as the Rhône Valley. It is really two distinct regions. The northern Rhône stretches from Vienne to Valence; all the fine red wine of this area is the product of the Syrah grape. The southern Rhône, between Pont-St-Esprit and Avignon, is one of the largest vineyards in France, producing fine Côtes du Rhône as well as ordinary table wine. A number of grape varieties are grown, the Grenache and Mourvèdre being the most important. The principal fine wine of the southern region is Châteauneuf-du-Pape.

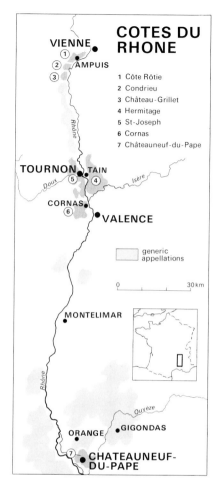

COTES DU RHONE

1 Côte Rôtie
2 Condrieu
3 Château-Grillet
4 Hermitage
5 St-Joseph
6 Cornas
7 Châteauneuf-du-Pape

Northern Rhône

The discovery, or more properly rediscovery, of the northern Rhône, was long overdue. Fashionable in the nineteenth century, the great wines of Hermitage and Côte-Rôtie were struggling for recognition, and a fair price, in more recent times. But when price increases for Bordeaux and Burgundy were leading merchants and consumers to seek alternatives, a great vintage in 1978 was the extra push the region needed. There followed successful vintages in 1979 and 1980; a mediocre one in 1981; a fine one in 1982; and, in 1983, wine to rival 1978 and 1961.

The growing conditions in the northern Rhône are difficult. The Syrah is grown on steep terraces, overlooking the river. The coarse, rocky soil produces wines of great concentration and depth. Tannic, alcoholic, and overpowering when young, they mature into the nearest thing to a great Médoc. It can, however, take ten, fifteen, or even twenty years for the wines to mature; many who have tried a young Hermitage must be wondering what all the fuss is about.

Rhône wines are classified by commune with no further distinction such as Grand or Premier Cru. 'La Chapelle' is the name given by Jaboulet to their finest Hermitage.

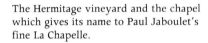

The Hermitage vineyard and the chapel which gives its name to Paul Jaboulet's fine La Chapelle.

Northern Rhône: Vintage Assessment

1985: A very healthy vintage for both red and white, close to 1976 in quality, with a deep colour and high natural alcohol. Hermitage will be particularly good, especially the red. These wines are becoming increasingly fashionable, and there is no stock in the growers' nor the négociants' cellars. Prices will probably show a rise of 20 per cent over 1984, which is justified by the quality, but a disturbing trend in any event.

1984: Not a great year. In common with the rest of France, the Rhône had a cool summer with more rain than usual. Better weather in early autumn improved things, but this is still a vintage to wait and see about before buying. With so many other good vintages available, there is no need to rush to buy.

1983: A great vintage, the best since 1978. Even the lesser appellations, such as Crozes-Hermitage and St-Joseph, need four or five years of bottle age. Hermitage and Côte-Rôtie both need at least a decade and should be at their peak early in the next century.

1982: A very good year, which will probably suffer from comparison with the 1983s, though this vintage may be better for Côte-Rôtie. Very concentrated wines built for long ageing. If prices for 1983s begin to spiral, this vintage will be a very good buy.

1981: There are good wines to be found but they are in the minority. With so many good vintages surrounding it, 1981 is a year to avoid unless the price is very attractive.

1980: A good vintage, especially for Côte-Rôtie, though the wines lack the depth of an outstanding vintage. All but the most concentrated Hermitages should be drinking well over the next few years. Guigal's Côte-Rôties are exceptions and need several years' more ageing.

1979: A good year for Hermitage; less so for Côte-Rôtie. Another year which lacks the depth of a great vintage. This is a very attractive vintage for current consumption, and would provide a good introduction to these wines.

1978: To the northern Rhône what 1982 was to Bordeaux. Great wines throughout the region, worth making an effort to find. The best still need five or six years and should last well into the twenty-first century.

1977: Even this far south the weather can play tricks. A year to avoid.

1976: A big, tough vintage, not unlike Burgundy, but more successful here. Lacking the overall balance of the 1978s, but still very good. The best wines still need a couple more years and should last well.

1975, 1974, 1973: An unusually depressing trio of vintages for this region. These wines need drinking now.

1972: A good vintage, especially in Hermitage, which like Burgundy suffered from lack of immediate acclaim because this was a poor year in Bordeaux. These wines are at their best now.

1971: A good vintage, but some of the wines are showing their age. Drink up.

1970: A very good vintage. Hermitage and Côte-Rôtie are delicious now and will keep.

1969: A great vintage, now scarce. Both Côte-Rôtie and Hermitage were successful. Wines to drink to realize the full potential of the region.

1961: Though there were other good vintages in the 1960s, this vintage stands out. As good for Hermitage and Côte-Rôtie as it was for Bordeaux, the 1961s have disappeared from the market. Jaboulet's La Chapelle is going for £150 ($210) a bottle at auction.

CÔTE-RÔTIE

The northern Rhône begins with one of its greatest wines, Côte-Rôtie, a powerful, long-lived wine that rivals Hermitage itself. This is strictly a red wine appellation, but the rules allow the addition of up to 20 per cent white Viognier to the Syrah to produce a more elegant wine. In practice all the growers use considerably less. This wine has developed a cult following in Great Britain and the United States, largely due to some outstanding winemakers.

Recommended Producers

Emile Champet	Paul Jaboulet Aîné
Max Chapoutier	Robert Jasmin
Marius Gentaz-Dervieux	J. Vidal-Fleury
Etienne Guigal	

CONDRIEU AND CHATEAU GRILLET

Just south of Ampuis is the commune of Condrieu, home of a northern Rhône speciality. Nestled amongst the terraces of Syrah is one of France's rarest white wines. Made from the Viognier grape, Condrieu is pale golden, with a sweet, peachy aroma: a full-bodied dry wine which is

Côte-Rôtie ('Roasted Slope'). The Syrah grape produces powerful, long-lived red wines from these steeply terraced slopes overlooking the Rhône.

flowery and fruity the moment it is made. It is one fine wine that does not improve with age as the intense fruity taste fades after about three or four years.

Château Grillet is a small appellation within the Condrieu area which covers one property; Viognier is used to make a similar wine there. It has the same forceful aroma and, while it lasts a bit longer, is still best drunk within three or four years of the vintage. It is very rare and consequently extremely expensive. Condrieu, by comparison, is only moderately expensive, and there are several good producers.

Recommended Producers

Château Grillet   Paul Multier (Ch. du Rozay)
Etienne Guigal   Georges Vernay

HERMITAGE

Hermitage is the greatest of all Rhône reds, and at its best can rank with the finest wines of Bordeaux and Burgundy. The vineyard looms above the town of Tain at a bend in the Rhône, so that the slope faces directly south. Steeply terraced plots similar to Côte-Rôtie mean that cultivation by machine is impossible, and tending such vineyards and harvesting the crop is back-breaking work. Gérard Jaboulet told us that one man could work nine or ten hectares in Châteauneuf-du-Pape but in Hermitage he could only work two.

Hermitage is an inky purple–black when young, as tannic as the most backward Bordeaux, with the bouquet closed up. Over the years it lightens to a brilliant purplish hue, which in maturity has an amber tinge. The nose is raspberries, blackcurrants and spice, and the taste firm, even in maturity. The nearest equivalent would be a Paulliac from a great vintage, say a Château Latour.

Recommended Producers

Chapoutier et Cie   Domaine Grippat
Gérard Chave   Paul Jaboulet Aîné
Delas Frères   Domaine Sorrel
Albert Desmeure

ST-JOSEPH AND CORNAS

On the opposite (or west) side of the Rhône are two appellations producing good, modestly priced wine from the Syrah. St-Joseph is a fruity, lighter-style wine, at its best with three or four years of bottle age. The second, Cornas, is a brawny, unrefined cousin of Hermitage. Here the Syrah produces wine with the same power and forceful tannins, but without the same balance and elegance in maturity. Cornas is entirely red, but St-Joseph has a fine reputation for its floral white wines.

The St-Joseph appellation covers a wide area on the west bank of the Rhône. Here the Syrah produces a lighter, fruitier style of wine than in either Côte-Rôtie or Hermitage.

Recommended Producers

St-Joseph   *Cornas*

Chapoutier et Cie   Guy de Barjac
Delas Frères   Auguste Clape
Bernard Gripa   Delas Frères
Jean-Louis Grippat   Paul Jaboulet Aîné
Raymond Trollat   Robert Michel

CROZES-HERMITAGE

This appellation, surrounding Hermitage and to the south, is particularly good value. The wines do not have the body or structure of an Hermitage (with the possible exception of Paul Jaboulet's Domaine de Thalabert), but possess a lovely plummy fruit and soft spicy flavour that allows them to be drunk two to three years after the vintage.

Recommended Producers

Chapoutier et Cie   Paul Jaboulet Aîné
Delas Frères   Tardy and Ange
Albert Desmeure

Southern Rhône

South of Valence there is a break of some seventy miles before vineyards begin in earnest. The great bulk of wine produced here is ordinary Côtes du Rhône, but its leading wine, Châteauneuf-du-Pape, was the first to adopt a system of regulation which later became known as Appellation Contrôlée.

There are thirteen approved grape varieties in Châteauneuf-du-Pape, but the Grenache dominates. Other important varieties are Syrah, Mourvèdre, Cinsaut, and the white Clairette. Because of this it is difficult to describe a typical Châteauneuf-du-Pape, though the dominance of Grenache means that the wines do not require as much cellaring as the Syrah to the north. The best examples need six to eight years and should be good up to the age of twelve to fifteen.

Châteauneuf-du-Pape has improved greatly over the past few years and its top estates are now making very fine wine. There is also white Châteauneuf-du-Pape, which has benefited enormously from modern cold-fermentation techniques. It represents only a fraction of the total production, is designed to be consumed young, and commands a similar price to the red.

Châteauneuf-du-Pape is not the only fine wine from the southern Côtes du Rhône, although it is the best known. Almost as powerful in body is Gigondas, a big, sturdy wine with a plummy, spicy bouquet and a rich tannic taste. Gigondas has the same high (minimum 12.5 degrees) alcoholic content as Châteauneuf, and the same low-yielding vines (maximum 35 hectolitres per hectare—roughly 1,900 bottles per acre—one of the very lowest in France). It is an impressive, long-lasting wine, but rarely has the finesse of Châteauneuf-du-Pape and, as such, sells for a half to two-thirds of the price. Next door to Gigondas is Vacqueyras, about mid-way in style between Gigondas and a good Côtes du Rhône-Villages.

Currently very fashionable are the rich, sweet Vins Doux Naturels of Beaumes de Venise. These are made with the Muscat grape and achieved recognition as an alternative to Sauternes and kept it through sheer quality. They are very sweet and best drunk young, either as an aperitif or at the end of the meal.

Southern Rhône: Vintage Assessment

Vintages here are not as consistent as in the northern Rhône, which is perhaps surprising considering that Châteauneuf-du-Pape is farther south. The last great vintage was 1978, though both 1981 and 1983 were very good.

1985: The success of the Grenache this year produced a crop of 2 million hectolitres, compared to an average of 1.8 million and 1984's 1.68 million. A very healthy vintage, with some problems of fermentation due to the very hot weather, and rather low acidity. The best wines are from Châteauneuf-du-Pape. A vintage for medium-term drinking, much better than 1984, but less fine than 1983. Because of the large volume of wine,

Châteauneuf-du-Pape produces the finest wine in the southern Rhône. This commune pioneered the Appellation Contrôlée system.

prices for Côtes du Rhône Villages are stable, but those for the better appellations—Châteauneuf-du-Pape, Gigondas—will move up 10 per cent, a normal increase in view of quality and less than the increase seen in the northern Rhônes.

1984: Still early, but this vintage looks more successful here than in the north. Solid, well-balanced wines should result.

1983: Not as exceptional here as in the north, which has been the rule for most of the past decade, but still very good. An uneven vintage, though the best are better than 1981 and should last well.

1982: A very hot, dry summer led to some over-alcoholic wines, quick maturing which are nowhere near as good as these from the north. Choose carefully.

1981: What looked like an unpromising summer produced some very good wines. Generally, the good colour, balanced fruit and tannin augur well. The wines are becoming expensive.

1980: Workmanlike wines from this vintage, which is slightly inferior both to 1981 and to 1979.

1979: As in the north, this is an ideal vintage for current drinking. Most are completely ready; the others are drinking well and will improve.

1978: A great vintage for Châteauneuf-du-Pape, and a good bet for long-term cellaring even now. The best wines have the structure of Hermitage and should be left until the 1990s.

1977: An unexciting vintage. Drink up.

1976: A good vintage, but less successful than in the north. A good choice for current drinking.

Earlier vintages: Not many Châteauneufs live beyond twelve years unless it is a very good vintage. Some 1970s, 1971s and 1974s might still be drinking well, but unless the wines have been properly cellared it is unwise to take a chance.

Recommended Producers

Châteauneuf-du-Pape	*Gigondas*
Château de Beaucastel	Domaine François Ay
Domaine de Beaurenard	Domaine Roger Combe
Les Cailloux	Domaine Les Pallières
Chante Cigale	Domaine St-Gayan
Château Fortia	
Clos du Mont-Olivet	*Muscat de Beaumes de Venise*
Domaine de Mont-Redon	
Château La Nerte	Domaine de Coyeux
Clos des Papes	Domaine Durban
Château Rayas	Paul Jaboulet Aîné
Domaine du Vieux Télégraphe	J. Vidal-Fleury

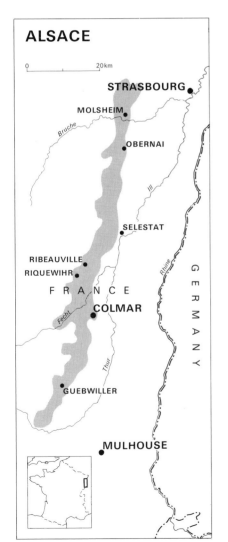

ALSACE

Alsace, with the simplest and clearest vineyard classification in France, is, paradoxically, the least appreciated. Perhaps the predominance of German grape varieties has led to misunderstanding. Indeed, the greatest wine of Alsace is Riesling, but unlike their German counterparts, the wines of Alsace are vinified completely dry. This makes them an ideal accompaniment for food. Alsace has one appellation, namely Alsace, and each wine is identified by grape variety, California-style. The use of such phrases as 'cuvée tradition' and 'réserve personnelle' have no legal force, but indicate the grower's feelings about the quality of the wine.

The Alsatians have recently recognized twenty-five sites as Grands Crus, though this does not have the same force as it does in Burgundy. The vineyards were chosen for their track-record; they have been producing fine wine over a period of years. The Alsatians have given legal status to two of their special wines: Vendange Tardive, that is, late-picked grapes that are vinified off-dry to medium sweet, and Sélection de Grains Nobles. These latter rarities combine the sweetness of a German Beerenauslese with the alcohol levels of Sauternes. Vendange Tardive and SGN wines can be produced from only the four finest grape varieties—Riesling, Muscat, Gewürztraminer and Tokay—and only in the ripest vintages. Some outstanding examples were produced in 1976, 1983, and again in 1985. These recent vintages have helped Alsace gain the recognition it deserves, for they are years of astonishing quality, comparable to 1982 Bordeaux or 1978 in the northern Rhône. With the spiralling cost of white Burgundy, consumers would be wise to give the wines of Alsace a try.

One of the specialities of Alsace is the Gewürztraminer, and the finest examples of this big, spicy, full-flavoured white wine are found here. But the king of Alsace is the Riesling. If you love this flowery, aromatic grape, but are uncomfortable with the sweeter versions from across the Rhine, Alsace is for you. The other two principal varieties are the Pinot Gris, known as Tokay d'Alsace, and the Muscat. Tokay d'Alsace comes in a

Vineyards between Turkheim and Niedermorschwihr in the Alsace. The wooden baskets, called 'hottes', are still widely used for the harvest.

variety of styles from light and fruity to sweet and full-bodied, while the Muscat is generally used to make a lighter, grapier wine, lacking the character and complexity of the other three.

Vintage Assessment

1985: Quantity is higher than was expected from one of the driest years in history. Quality is extremely high, almost on a par with 1983, but more like 1976, another hot dry year. Unlike 1983, very little noble rot developed and the 'Sélection de Grains Nobles' wines were still being harvested in December. Prices have risen on average by 50 per cent since the launching of the 1983 vintage, and demand is still firm as these wines have been underpriced for too long. Alsace has recently had a justified success, and it is to be hoped that, with the excellent 1985 vintage now in bottle, prices will not rise further.

1984: A no-better-than-average vintage, with wines in a lighter style. No reason to buy these as long as the 1983s are still around.

1983: What a great year 1983 was throughout France, and Alsace is no exception. Easily the best vintage since 1976, with wines of weight and style from all the grape varieties. Many producers made Vendange Tardive and Sélection de Grains Nobles wines which should be delicious well into the next century.

1982: A good vintage of wines that are drinking well now. It was a big vintage, unlike the better 1983, so there should be some bargains among the 1982s.

1981: Better than 1982, these wines have been drinking well for the past

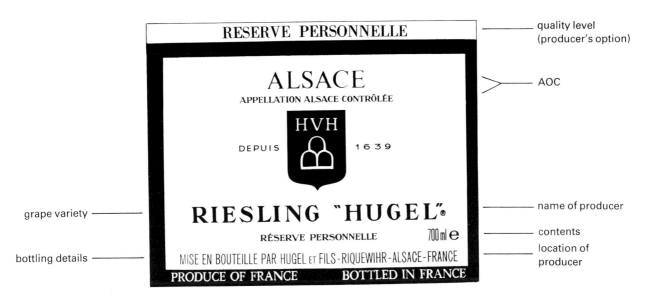

quality level (producer's option)

AOC

grape variety

name of producer

contents

location of producer

bottling details

Alsace wines are identified by grape variety, and a single appellation covers the entire region. In 1983, 25 sites were designated Grands Crus, but many producers, including Hugel, prefer the old style of labelling, according to quality level rather than site name. The vintage is given on the neck label.

two years and the better Rieslings and Gewürztraminers should last a while yet.

1980: An average vintage of wines which, on the whole, lack fruit. You can be fussy with Alsace, as it is one of the few regions where it is still a buyer's market. Be careful with this vintage.

1979: A good vintage, especially for Riesling; the 1979s are now at their best.

1978: A solid, if unexciting vintage. Drink up.

1977: A mediocre vintage of skinny, charmless wines.

1976: A great vintage, the product of a memorably hot summer, Rieslings at Réserve Personnelle level are still gloriously fresh, and Vendange Tardive and Sélection de Grains Nobles wines are mere adolescents.

Earlier vintages: There are some 1971s still around and they are worth a try, just to see how good a mature Alsace can be. Otherwise, it is best to be careful with older vintages from this region.

Recommended Producers

There is a very high standard among Alsace's leading winemakers who are divided into two groups: grower-négociants, who own vineyards but also buy in grapes; and proprietors, who only make wine from their own holdings.

Négociants
Leon Beyer
Dopff 'Au Moulin'
Hugel et Fils
Kuentz-Bas
Gustave Lorentz

Proprietors
Jos. Meyer
Rolly-Gassman
Domaine Weinbach (Mme Faller)
Zind-Humbrecht

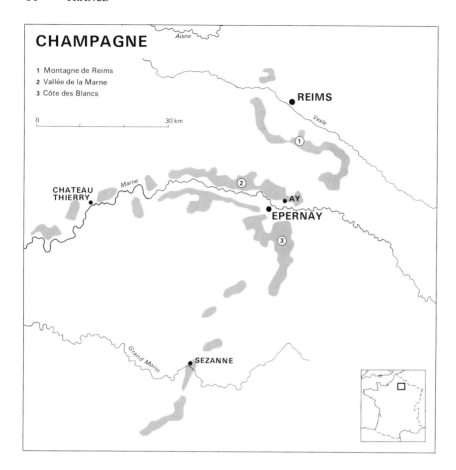

CHAMPAGNE

1 Montagne de Reims
2 Vallée de la Marne
3 Côte des Blancs

0 _____ 30 km

Aisne

REIMS

Vesle

①

CHATEAU
THIERRY   *Marne*

②

AY
EPERNAY

③

Grand Morin

SEZANNE

Above Producing Champagne is labour intensive and therefore expensive. The new wine is racked to remove the impurities of the first fermentation and then allowed to rest for a time in barrels or, more usually, tanks.

Opposite top left The various casks are blended and bottled with the addition of *liqueur de tirage* (sugar dissolved in Champagne) to induce a second fermentation. The tightly-corked bottles are then laid down for two or three years, occasionally for longer periods.

Opposite top right The second fermentation will have thrown a sediment which must be removed. The bottles are placed in *pupitres*, where they are rotated and gradually tilted downwards to make the sediment collect on the cork. This is known as 'le remuage'.

Opposite centre left The bottles finish standing upside down with the impurities lodged in the neck of the bottle.

Opposite centre right The *dégorgeur* then freezes the neck of the bottle so that the sediment can be removed in one piece. A small quantity of dissolved sugar, known as 'liqueur d'expédition' is then added, the amount depending on the sweetness desired. Even brut Champagnes have some additional sugar.

CHAMPAGNE

Champagne has a clear identity in the market. It is the wine of celebration, and this image has been of incalculable advantage to the producers. But it has its drawbacks: Champagne is seen as an expensive, single-purpose wine. Many prestige cuvées are indeed expensive and of questionable value at this price, but non-vintage Champagnes, which are the pride of the great houses, are fairly priced for wines so well made.

Champagne is a blended wine, and the winemaker's skill is of paramount importance. It is his job to smooth over nature's shortcomings, and conjure up consistent fine wine year after year. With prices for white Burgundy and California Chardonnay frequently higher than for non-vintage Champagne, it is time for a reappraisal of Champagne's role. Excellent as an aperitif, fine as an accompaniment to fish, soups and even lighter meats, it is one of the very finest white wines.

In the best years merchants set aside a part of the crop to declare as a vintage. Of late, more and more of them have further subdivided this vintage by adding so-called luxury cuvées. The majority of these, Veuve Cliquot's 'La Grande Dame', Mumm's 'René Lalou', Canard-Duchêne's 'Charles V', are sold in fancy bottles, most of which are very pleasing to

Right A new cork, such as the one on the far left, is driven into the bottle and secured by the familiar wire clamp. The wine is then ready to be shipped. Over the years the cork shrinks, but even the twenty-year-old one on the right still fits snugly enough.

look at, but of which only one—Gosset's 'Grande Millésime'—equals the beauty of the original luxury cuvée, Moët & Chandon's 'Dom Pérignon'. Some highly prestigious Champagne houses, Bollinger and Pol Roger, for example, prefer to keep to the classic Champagne bottle.

Classification

There is a classification system in Champagne, but because it is a blended wine such details seldom appear on the labels. The classification is of great importance to the merchants and growers because it determines the price paid for the fruit. There are twelve Grands Crus, villages rated at 100 per cent; a further forty-one Premiers Crus rated between 90 and 99 per cent; and the rest of the region which is rated between 80 and 90 per cent. Each year a price is agreed between the growers and merchants, and that price is paid for all grapes from villages rated 100 per cent. The rest of the villages receive a percentage of the price that corresponds to their rating.

Harvesting under way in the Champagne commune of Verzenay.

The Trade

The Champagne trade is dominated by the merchant houses known as the Grandes Marques, who are especially strong in export markets. Each has developed a house style, as represented by the non-vintage wine. Bollinger, for example, aim for a full-bodied wine, and use a greater proportion of Pinot Noir to achieve this. Taittinger favour a lighter, more elegant style, and for them the Chardonnay predominates.

On each label there are initials which identify the type of producer. NM (Négociant-Manipulant) is the most important category which includes all the Grandes Marques. These merchants buy all or part of the grapes they need, usually from Grand Cru villages or the best Premiers Crus. RM (Récoltant-Manipulant) is a grower who is only permitted to make wine from his own grapes. CM (Co-opérative Manipulant) is a co-operative which vinifies wine from its members' grapes, which are sold under a variety of labels. MA (Marque Auxiliaire or Marque Autorisée) is a merchant who buys wine from producers or négociants to sell under a different label. His wine is most commonly seen as Buyer's Own Brand.

Ageing Champagne

Most Champagnes, even non-vintages, improve with a bit of time in the bottle. Commercial pressures lead to the release of many Champagnes before they are at their peak. This is a subject on which opinions differ, and England is in a minority when it comes to favouring well-aged Champagnes. The French, particularly, prefer the wine young, fresh and grapey.

Our advice is to buy non-vintage Champagne and keep it for at least six months to a year. Two years is not too long for the more full-bodied examples like Bollinger and Roederer. With time in bottle the wines take on a new dimension, and the varietal character begins to show.

Vintage Champagnes are, in principal, only put on the market when the producers consider them at or near their best. The 1979 has been available since mid-1984, and it is better now (early 1986) than it was then. Most Grandes Marques will agree that a vintage Champagne is very fine at ten years old, a little younger for those cuvées either wholly or mainly composed of white grapes. Of the smaller quality houses, Bollinger produce a late-disgorged vintage of about this age, and Krug keep back a proportion of their vintage wine for late release.

Recommended Producers

Billecart-Salmon: Better known in France than in export markets, though attracting attention in Britain and the United States for fresh vintage and non-vintage wines. Keenly priced.

Bollinger: One of the great names in Champagne, famous for full-bodied, distinctive non-vintage, delicious vintage; also for their speciality, a vintage RD (or recently disgorged). Wine bearing this classification has been allowed to stay on the yeast for several years before being disgorged, recorked and sold.

Deutz and Gelderman: Based, like Bollinger, in Ay, they produce full-flavoured wines to a high standard, especially their 'Cuvée William Deutz'.

Charles Heidsieck: One of the largest houses and well known in export markets, Charles Heidsieck produce a sound, competitively priced non-vintage and a range of vintage and prestige cuvées.

Heidsieck Monopole: A fine producer of old-fashioned style Champagne both vintage and non-vintage. Diamant Bleu is their prestige cuvée.

Krug: The bench-mark for fine Champagne and the epitome of a fine wine producer. Their wines are fermented entirely in small oak casks, and their non-vintage is itself a luxury cuvée. Small amounts of vintage Champagne are made in great years, and, more recently, a Rosé, and Blanc de Blancs from the Clos de Mesnil.

Laurent-Perrier: A large house whose standards have risen noticeably in the last few years. Good and well-priced non-vintage and vintage wines, as well as a non-vintage luxury cuvée, Grand Siècle.

Moët & Chandon: A very large company, now merged with the Hennessey Cognac group, which also controls Ruinart and Mercier Champagnes. Their non-vintage is the market leader in both Great Britain and the United States, and is competitively priced. Dom Pérignon is their finest wine, and the one that started the rage for prestige bottlings.

Mumm: An important producer, now controlled by Seagram. Their non-vintage Cordon Rouge is on the light side and René Lalou is the prestige cuvée.

Joseph Perrier: Familiar in Britain, this is always a good, light Champagne at a reasonable price.

Perrier-Jouët: Another part of the Seagram's empire and very popular in the United States. A fine, robust non-vintage, and Belle Epoque vintage in flower-painted bottles.

Piper Heidsieck: A producer of correct, rather than exciting wines, though consistent in both vintage and non-vintage.

Pol Roger: A family firm making perhaps the finest Champagnes of all the Epernay-based Grandes Marques, from a very high proportion of Grand Cru grapes. Their range has recently been extended to cover a vintage Blanc de Blancs and a special cuvée named after Winston Churchill, their most famous client.

Louis Roederer: One of the very best Champagnes right across the range. The luxury cuvée Cristal Brut gets a lot of attention, but Roederer's non-vintage is a real delight.

Salon de Mesnil: Only Blanc de Blancs vintage from this house. Elegant Champagne par excellence.

Taittinger: A house that has moved to the top rank in the past twenty years. Elegance and finesse rather than body are the style, throughout the range: non-vintage, vintage, and Comtes de Champagne Blanc de Blancs vintage.

Veuve Clicquot: Another great house whose non-vintage is in the full-bodied style. They produce a good vintage and a luxury vintage, 'La Grande Dame'.

LOIRE

The Loire Valley is an important source of pleasant, summery wines, but a few examples rise above the level of the everyday. Sancerre and Pouilly-Fumé are France's best pure Sauvignon Blancs: tart, spicy wines with lively fruit. But the region's greatest wines are the product of the Chenin Blanc. These sweet wines, with a high level of acidity, seem to live for ever, accumulating extra layers of flavour as they age. The two important areas for these sweet wines are Touraine and Anjou–Saumur.

Central Loire

POUILLY-FUME OR BLANC FUME DE POUILLY
These crisp, aromatic wines should be drunk young, though some will improve for two or three years in bottle.

Recommended Producers

Jean-Claude Dagueneau   Château du Nozet (Ladoucette)
Paul Figeat   Château de Tracy
Jean-Claude Guyot

SANCERRE
Wines similar to Pouilly-Fumé are produced here, perhaps in a more traditional style. This is another wine for early consumption.

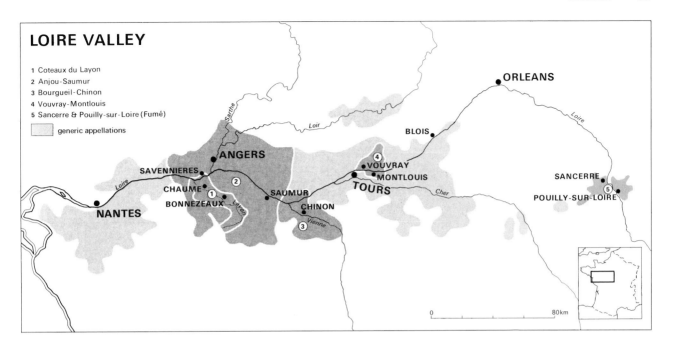

LOIRE VALLEY

1 Coteaux du Layon
2 Anjou-Saumur
3 Bourgueil-Chinon
4 Vouvray-Montlouis
5 Sancerre & Pouilly-sur-Loire (Fumé)

generic appellations

Recommended Producers

Philippe de Benoist	Gitton Père et Fils
Lucien Crochet	Lucien Picard
Vincent Delaporte	Jean Vacheron et Fils

Touraine

VOUVRAY AND MONTLOUIS

Touraine's greatest wine is Vouvray, where the Chenin Blanc produces an array of wines from dry to intensely sweet. The dry wines here can be very good, with more flesh and flavour than Sauvignons, and the sweet wines, at their best, can rival fine Sauternes. Across the river from Vouvray is the commune of Montlouis, where wines of similar style are made. The best red wines of the region are made in Chinon from the Cabernet Franc grape.

Recommended Producers

A. Foreau	Gaston Huet
André Freslier	Prince Poniatowski

Harvesting the Chenin Blanc crop in Vouvray. This grape, known locally as the 'Pineau de la Loire', is alone responsible for the great sweet wines of the Loire.

Anjou-Saumur

COTEAUX DU LAYON

This region is well known for its rosé, but its best wines come from the Côteaux du Layon Appellation, floral, honeyed white wine, particularly from two vineyards within the Appellation, Bonnezeaux and Quarts de Chaume, both of which have separate AOC status. The most notable dry Chenin Blanc comes from Savennières.

Recommended Producers

Jean Baumard   Jean-Pierre Chéné
Jacques Boivin   Pierre Yves Tijou

SAVENNIERES

This mostly dry white from the Chenin Blanc sets this commune apart from its neighbours. Good Savennières is difficult to taste when young, acidity predominating over closed-up fruit. Given a few years (at least five or six), the wine opens up and the honeyed flavour of the Chenin Blanc comes through.

Recommended Producers

Armand Bizard   Madame A. Joly
Domaine du Closel   Yves Soulez

5 Germany

Understanding the German Style

Riesling is the only one of the cépages nobles to find its classic expression outside France. Though only 20 per cent of German vineyards are planted with Riesling, this figure includes most of the greatest names. Some good wines are made with Müller-Thurgau, particularly in the Rheinhessen, but they never reach the same heights as the finest Rieslings.

There are three levels of German wine: Tafelwein or table wine, Qualitätswein or quality wine, and Qualitätswein mit Prädikat (QmP), quality wine with special attributes. Only this last concerns us. There are six categories of QmP, based on the sugar content—the 'must weight'—of the grapes at harvest. The basic category is Kabinett: wine made from ripe grapes harvested at the normal time. If the grapes are allowed to overripen they make a Spätlese wine. Auslese wine, the third category, is made from selected bunches picked late, and has a higher sugar content than either Kabinett or Spätlese. With this category begins the German grower's flirtation with real danger. Because of the northerly climate and short growing season, delaying the harvest can be risky. But to produce a fine Auslese wine usually requires that the grapes be left at least until late October, so a sudden frost or heavy rains can ruin the harvest.

Up to this category wines can be medium-dry to sweet, and the sugar is balanced by the natural acidity of the Riesling. The remaining three categories are intensely sweet, the German alternative to the great Sauternes. Beerenauslese and Trockenbeerenauslese (TBA) are made from individually selected ripe grapes left very late on the vine. In addition, TBA requires grapes affected by botrytis and shrivelled on the vine to raisin consistency. These wines, with very high degrees of sugar and relatively low alcohol content, are the peak of German winemaking and have no rival apart from the Alsatian Sélection de Grains Nobles. The sixth and last category, Eiswein, is made from grapes frozen on the vine, and the sugar content must reach that of a Beerenauslese.

There is no vineyard classification in Germany as there is in Burgundy and Bordeaux. Instead, each wine is treated on its merits. In theory any vineyard can produce wines in the top categories, provided that it meets the minimum must-weight regulations for its region. German labels give comprehensive information, but as there is no vineyard classification, and as the climate allows two or three good vintages a decade, it is essential to look for the name of the producer above all else. The State Domaine of the Nahe, for example, has vineyards scattered about the region, but the wines are of consistently high quality. Their name serves as a guarantee.

GERMANY

1 Mosel-Saar-Ruwer
2 Rheingau
3 Nahe
4 Rheinhessen
5 Rheinpfalz (Palatinate)

KOBLENZ

RAUENTHAL   WIESBADEN

ZELL

HATTENHEIM   ELTVILLE
RUDESHEIM   ERBACH
WINKEL

WEHLEN   GRAACH
PIESPORT   BERNKASTEL-   BAD
KUES   KREUZNACH   NIERSTEIN

TRIER   SCHLOSSBOCKELHEIM   OPPENHEIM
    DIENHEIM
LUXEMBOURG   NIEDERHAUSEN

G E R M A N Y

SAARBURG

MANNHEIM

WACHENHEIM
    FORST
DEIDESHEIM
RUPPERTSBERG

FRANCE

0   60 km

Gathering the Eiswein harvest in the famous Bernkasteler Doktor vineyard. German law requires that the grapes be frozen on the vine.

Principal Regions

There are eleven fine wine regions, of which five are the most important. These are the Mosel–Saar–Ruwer, and four areas in the Rhine Valley: Rheingau, Nahe, Rheinhessen, and Rheinpfalz. The Mosel river rises in northern France, flows along the Luxembourg–Germany border, and winds its way north-east to Koblenz, where it joins the Rhine. The Saar and Ruwer rivers flow into the Mosel near the triangle of Germany, Luxembourg, and France. Along with the Rheingau, this region produces Germany's most distinguished wines. Identifiable by the slender green bottle, Mosel wines epitomize the Riesling at its crisp, steely best. Leaner and more acidic than Rhine wines, they are, when the weather has favoured them, suffused with a flowery, aromatic bouquet. The taste is fresh, and a bit stern, and the finish clean, despite the sweetness.

Trier is the principal city of the Mosel–Saar–Ruwer, and home to some of its greatest estates. Bernkastel-Kues, downstream towards Koblenz, is another important centre, and home of the famous Bernkasteler Doktor vineyard. Other notable wine villages are Graach, Wehlen, and Zeltingen. They form the heart of the Middle Mosel. Saar wines are the crispest and freshest of the region, though in such a northern climate there are no wines that could be described as fat. Wiltingen is the principal town of the Saar, and the site of the famous Scharzhofberg vineyard. Other important villages are Ayl, Ockfen, and Kanzem. The Ruwer joins the Mosel east of Trier and is famous for one of Germany's greatest vineyards, Maximin Grünhaus at Mertesdorf. The region's other important village is Eitelsbach.

region (Anbaugebiet) ———

vintage ———

village (Gemeinde) ———

grape variety ———

quality category ———

contents ———

——— vineyard (Einzellage)

——— quality level

——— bottling details

——— producer

——— contents

MOSEL · SAAR · RUWER

19   81

Bernkasteler Doktor
Riesling Spätlese

Qualitätswein mit Prädikat · A. P. Nr. 157628102282

Erzeugerabfüllung · Estate bottled · Gutsverwaltung

Deinhard®

Bernkastel-Kues/Koblenz

750 ml
PRODUCE OF GERMANY

SHIPPED BY
Deinhard & Co
KOBLENZ · GERMANY

75 cl e
REGISTERED TRADE MARK

German labels contain comprehensive information, and the rules are the same for every region.

The Rheingau is one of Germany's smallest wine regions, but it contains the Rhine's greatest estates. Wiesbaden is the major city, and the great vineyards stretch south-west from here to where the Nahe joins the Rhine. Rauenthal, Kiedrich, Erbach, Hattenheim, Winkel, Geisenheim, and Rüdesheim are among the villages which produce wines with a world-wide reputation. The great Rheingaus have more weight and depth than Rieslings from the Mosel, but lack some of the cut. They are, however, well balanced with enough acidity to make them clean in the finish.

South-west of the Rheingau is the Nahe region. Larger than the Rheingau, but with fewer fine wine producers, much of the region is planted in Müller-Thurgau. The best vineyards though, as elsewhere in Germany, are predominantly Riesling. It is often said that Nahe wines combine the leanness and crispness of the Mosel with the weight and body of the Rheingau. This is true enough, but seems a backhanded compliment to a region whose best villages, such as Schloss Böckelheim and Nieder-hausen, produce individual wines of the highest quality.

Rheinhessen is the biggest of the German regions, but most of its production is of little interest to us. Only a few of the vineyards are planted in Riesling, and the area is best known as the home of Liebfraumilch and of a variety of branded wines in the lower price ranges. The finest wines come from the Rhine-front vineyards above Nierstein and Oppenheim.

Much the same is true of the Rheinpfalz even farther south, also known as the Palatinate. Many of the famous properties are mixed farms rather than being exclusively devoted to wine. The best vineyards here are in Wachenheim, Deidesheim and Forst. Because they come from a more southerly region, these wines are frequently more full-bodied and higher in alcohol than those from further north.

The Market

German wines have been overlooked during the boom of the last decade. There are three main reasons for this. The first is the difficulty in matching German wine with food—most consumers, especially in Great Britain and the United States, drink wine as a complement to food. The second, and according to Ian Jamieson of Deinhard's the most important reason, is the inconsistency of German vintages. Winemakers can count on two or perhaps three good vintages a decade. They must look with envy at Bordeaux where five of the six years from 1978 to 1983 produced good to outstanding wine. However, until 1983 the Germans had to look back to 1976 and 1971 to find years in which they produced consistently good vintages. But 1983 broke the run of bad luck. It was a year of ample sunshine, and a fine autumn, so the Riesling was able to ripen fully. This was especially true in the Mosel, and the region was very successful. There was not as much noble rot (or Edelfäule) as in 1976, but the wines have a natural concentration and sufficient acidity to ensure a long life.

Wines at Kabinett level are drinking well now, and should keep until the end of the decade. The same is true of Spätlese, but the Auslese wines are so full and balanced that they should easily see out the century. The final reason for the neglect of German wines is the tendency to drink them too young: perhaps the light style leads people to believe that they lack staying-power. This is simply not true. Good German wines not only keep well, but develop extra nuances of flavour in the bottle.

The picture, then, for German wines is pretty straightforward. If you have the chance to buy wines of Auslese or higher quality from the 1976 or 1971 vintages, by all means do so. If not, concentrate on 1983.

A fifteenth-century wine crane, and a more recent example in use until about a hundred years ago in the Rheingau commune of Oestrich. The cranes were used to load barrels on to barges for shipment to Cologne and to the industrial cities of the Ruhr.

Recommended Producers

Mosel–Saar–Ruwer

Bischöfliche Weingüter Trier: This large Mosel estate, the union of three church properties, still markets the wines under the individual names: Bischöfliches Priesterseminar, Hohe Domkirche, and Bischöfliches Konvikt. Priesterseminar wines include Erdener Treppchen and Dhroner Hofberger in the Mosel, and Kanzemer Altenberg, Wiltinger Kupp, and Ayler Kupp in the Saar. Hohe Domkirche produces wines in the Scharzhofberg vineyard. Bischöfliches Konvikt, the largest of the three, has holdings in Ayler Kupp and Ayler Herrenberger in the Saar; at Eitelsbacher Marienholz in the Ruwer; and Piesporter Goldtröpfchen in the Middle Mosel.

Deinhard: The jewel of Deinhard's Mosel estate is a holding in the famous Bernkasteler Doktor. But Deinhard's entire range of Mosels, emphasizing individual vineyard characteristics, is consistently well made.

Dr Fischer: A leading Saar estate featuring wines from Ockfener Bockstein and Wawerner Herrenberg.

Friedrich-Wilhelm-Gymnasium: Trier is to the Mosel as Beaune is

to the Côte d'Or, and this is one of its leading properties, with over 100 acres of prime vineyards. Look especially for Zeltingen-Sonnenuhr and Schlossberg; Bernkasteler-Graben and Bratenhöfchen.

Le Gallais: Supervised by Egon Müller, this estate produces very fine Wiltinger Braune Kupp.

von Hövel: Scharzhofberger and Oberemmeler Hütte come from this very good Saar estate.

Reichsgraf von Kesselstatt: One of the largest Mosel estates, von Kesselstatt make old-fashioned Rieslings, emphasizing individual vineyard characteristics. Ninety-eight per cent of the vineyards are planted in Riesling, and their special pride is Josephshöfer. Other estates controlled by von Kesselstatt include Joseph Koch, van Volxem, and Felix Müller.

Egon Müller-Scharzhof: A great estate making one of the finest Scharzhofbergers. Recognized in Germany and abroad for this and other model Saar wines.

J. J. Prüm: A famous Mosel estate whose Wehlener Sonnenuhr would surely be a first growth if German classification allowed such comparisons.

S. A. Prüm Erben: Formerly part of the much larger Prüm estate with holdings in Wehlener Sonnenuhr and Graacher Domprobst, as well as Bernkasteler Badstube.

C. von Schubert: This single-vineyard Ruwer estate produces one of Germany's greatest wines. The Maximin Grünhäus vineyard is divided into three parts: Bruderberg (the brothers), Herrenberg (the gentlemen), and Abtsberg (the Abbot). This last is generally regarded as the finest, but all produce Riesling at its aromatic, delicate best.

Bert Simon: Energetic, modern estate producing fine, steely Saar wines, especially from vineyards in Serrig-Herrenberg and Würtzberg.

Staatliche Weinbaudomänen: Based in Trier and more conveniently known as the State Cellars, vineyards include Ockfener Bockstein and Herrenberg, and Serriger Vogelsang.

Dr Thanisch: Most famous for its Bernkasteler Doktor, Dr Thanisch also has holdings in Brauneberger Juffer Sonnenuhr and Graacher Himmelreich.

Vereinigte Hospitien: Another great Trier institution with extensive vineyard holdings in the Saar and Middle Mosel. Their best wine is probably Scharzhofberger.

Rheingau

Deinhard: The Rheingau estate of the Koblenz merchant has important holdings in Oestrich-Lenchen and Doosberg; Rüdesheim-Berg Rottland, Berg Schlossberg, and Berg Roseneck; also Winkel-Hasensprung and Jesuitengarten. The Winkeler wines are particularly fine, but the standards throughout the range are high.

Staatsweingüter Eltville: The State Wine Cellars are Germany's largest and set standards for the entire region. A collection of seven estates is run

Maximin Grünhaus, the estate of the von Schubert family in the Ruwer, produces one of Germany's great wines.

from the headquarters in Eltville, and there are important holdings in Rüdesheim-Berg Schlossberg and Berg Roseneck; Erbach-Marcobrunn and Steinberger; Hochheim-Domdechaney and Kirchenstück. The wines are full-bodied, and in some cases heavy, lacking the drive of the very best smaller estates.

Schloss Groenesteyn: Based in Kiedrich, this is an old and very fine estate owning sites in the best vineyards of Rüdesheim-Berg Rottland, Berg Roseneck, Berg Schlossberg, and Bischofberg.

Schloss Johannisberg: A single-vineyard estate, the most famous in all of Germany, it has given its name to the Riesling grape in America. A variety of coloured capsules distinguish quality levels. The wines at their best are among the longest-lived of all German wines.

von Mumm: With important holdings at Johannisberg and Rüdesheim, this estate, linked with Schloss Johannisberg, is famous for traditional, wood-matured Rieslings.

Schloss Reinhartshausen: Formerly owned by the Prussian royal family, this estate's holdings include vineyards in Erbach—Marcobrunn and Schlossberg; and in Hattenheim—Nussbrunnen and Wisselbrunnen. These old-fashioned, powerful Rieslings are excellent for long-term ageing.

Schloss Schönborn: A large, well-known estate and sole owner of the fine Hattenheimer Pfaffenberg as well as other choice sites in Erbach, Winkel, Rüdesheim and Hattenheim. Big, full-flavoured wines.

Schloss Vollrads: This single-vineyard estate is one of Germany's greatest. In style, firmer and more austere than most of its neighbours, Vollrads might be at home in the Mosel. The wines age beautifully.

Nahe

August E. Anheuser: An old-established estate with sites in Kreuznach-Brückes and Kahlenberg; Niederhausen Hermannshöhle; and Schlossböckelheimer Königsfels. The wines are matured in wood and are true to the taste of each vineyard. Very fine, very stylish Rieslings.

Paul Anheuser: Anheuser is a famous name in the Nahe, and this estate was originally part of the previous one. Holdings in Kreuznach-Brückes, Kahlenberg, and Krötenpfuhl; Schlossböckelheim-Felsenberg and In Den Felsen.

Hans Crusius: A small, family-run estate producing wine of the highest standard. Especially good are Traiser Bastei and Schlossböckelheimer Felsenberg.

Staatliche Weinbaudomänen: The State Cellars set the standard for the region and their white label with a black eagle motif is well known in export markets. Founded in 1902, the Cellars have sites in Schlossböckelheim's two best vineyards, Kupfergrube and Felsenberg; also in Niederhausen at Hermannsberg, Hermannshöhle, and Steinberg; and throughout the valley. It is hard to think of a domaine in Germany making wines as consistently fine as these. Riesling at its very best.

The Hollenberg vineyard in Assmannshausen is a rarity in the Rheingau. It is planted primarily in Spätburgunder (Pinot Noir), and produces one of Germany's most sought-after red wines.

Rheinhessen

Bürgermeister Anton Balbach Erben: An old, well-respected Nierstein estate with sites in some of the town's finest vineyards, including Pettenthal, Hipping and Kranzberg.

Louis Guntrum: Merchants as well as estate owners, this family firm's holdings include, in Nierstein—Pettenthal and Orbel, and in Oppenheim—Sackträger and Kreuz. About 30 per cent of vineyards are planted in Riesling.

Freiherr Heyl zu Herrnsheim: Another important Nierstein estate, with holdings in Pettenthal and Hipping, and with sole ownership of Niersteiner Brudersberg.

Gustav Adolf Schmitt: Nierstein-based merchant and grower with a wide variety of wines. The best are Rieslings from Nierstein—Hipping, Kranzberg, Ölberg and Pettenthal.

Geschwister Schuch: A family business producing good wines from sites in Nierstein—Hipping and Ölberg and Oppenheimer Sackträger.

Heinrich Seip: An innovator with new grape varieties, and with good sites in Nierstein and Oppenheim.

J. & H. A. Strub: One of Nierstein's most respected estates, producing traditional wines from some of the town's best sites, including Hipping and Ölberg.

Rheinpfalz

Dr von Bassermann-Jordan: One of the finest Palatinate estates with vineyards planted almost entirely in Riesling. Sites in Deidesheimer Grainhübel, Forster Ungeheuer, and Ruppertsberger Reiterpfad.

Reichsrat von Buhl: Fine estate with a good reputation, in both Britain and the United States, for rich, aromatic Rieslings. Holdings include Kirchenstück and Jesuitengarten in Forst; Kieselberg and Leinhöhle in Deidesheim, as well as sites in Wachenheim and Ruppertsberg.

Dr Bürklin-Wolf: A famous estate, which like von Buhl owns parcels in the best Palatinate vineyards and enjoys a world-wide reputation. In Forst—Jesuitengarten, Kirchenstück, and Ungeheuer; in Deidesheim—Altenberg and Goldbächel; and in Ruppertsberg—Hoheburg and sole ownership of Geisbohl.

Dr Deinhard: Fine, middle-weight wines from vineyards planted mainly in Riesling. In 1973 the Koblenz merchants Deinhard acquired by purchase and long-term lease a part of this estate, and the wines are up to their usual high standards. Both properties have their headquarters at Dr Deinhard's in Deidesheim.

K. Fitz-Ritter: Well-known producer of sparkling wine, also of some fine, flavoury, still wines.

Eugen Spindler: Fine, traditional Rieslings come from this family property in Forst, where it also has some of its best vineyards; these include Jesuitengarten, Pechstein and Ungeheuer.

6 Italy

Italy has a long tradition of winemaking, and no region is without its local product. Many of the grape varieties are unique to this country, and the number of wines, as well as the volume, is astonishing. But although to the consumer the Italians are relative newcomers to the production of fine wine, there are three notable exceptions: Barolo and Barbaresco in Piedmont, and Brunello di Montalcino in Tuscany. More and more Italian growers, particularly in the north-east and Tuscany, are experimenting with cépages nobles to produce fine wines more acceptable to international tastes. There is an enormous amount of work to do.

The Market

Italian wines have a reputation, especially in the United Kingdom, as being rather ordinary table wines. There is still consumer resistance to paying a premium price for any Italian wine, regardless of quality. Producers have learned this to their cost: British consumers who willingly pay £10 ($15) for a middle-of-the-road Bordeaux baulk at the thought of spending the same amount on the finest Barolo.

ITALY

1 Trentino-Alto Adige   7 Chianti Classico
2 Amarone   8 Montalcino
3 Gattinara   9 Montepulciano
4 Barbaresco
5 Barolo
6 Chianti

Italian wines have achieved more success in the USA, but they have yet to accomplish what Bordeaux and Burgundy achieved years ago, namely to have their wines associated with quality in the public's mind. The lustre of the great names of Bordeaux rubs off on even the humblest petit château. The reverse is true in Italy. The reputation for cheap, ordinary wine tarnishes their finest examples.

The Italians are also hurt by disorderly marketing. There are so many small producers, and such a wide variety, that they have not established a clear identity in the market. They have proved less adept than the French at promoting wines by region with the emphasis on particular styles. Piedmont, which is the premier red wine region, does not have the high profile of Bordeaux, Burgundy, or even the northern Rhône. In part this is because it has not exported much of its finest wines, and it is difficult to establish a position in the market without a constant source of supply over several years. Now that producers are anxious to export, they have to educate the public about their wines. This is particularly true of big, tannic wines such as Barolo and Barbaresco, which require many years of bottle age. A bottle of 1978 Barolo opened now might be disappointing. At the same time, mature Barolo is almost impossible to find.

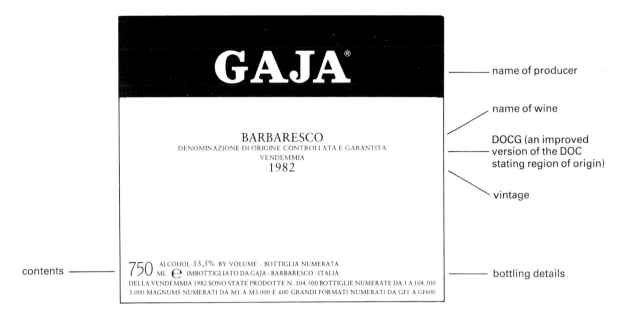

GAJA ———— name of producer

———— name of wine

BARBARESCO
DENOMINAZIONE DI ORIGINE CONTROLLATA E GARANTITA
VENDEMMIA
1982

———— DOCG (an improved version of the DOC stating region of origin)

———— vintage

contents ————

750 ML ℮ ALCOHOL 13,5% BY VOLUME - BOTTIGLIA NUMERATA
IMBOTTIGLIATO DA GAJA - BARBARESCO - ITALIA
DELLA VENDEMMIA 1982 SONO STATE PRODOTTE N. 104.500 BOTTIGLIE NUMERATE DA 1 A 104.500
3.000 MAGNUMS NUMERATI DA M1 A M3.000 E 600 GRANDI FORMATI NUMERATI DA GF1 A GF600

———— bottling details

Italian DOC and DOCG laws are comparable to the French AOC system. They guarantee that a wine comes from the specified region and is produced from the approved grape varieties. Barbaresco comes from a small area of Piedmont and is made entirely from the Nebbiolo grape.

Classification of Italian Wines

The Italian system of classification is also a problem. The DOC (Denominazione di Origine Controllata) is the equivalent of the French Appellation Contrôlée, but Italian regulations only permit established grape varieties. This means that winemakers experimenting, sometimes quite successfully, with Cabernet or Chardonnay, find that the wine does not qualify for a DOC label. The wines must be sold as 'vino da tavola', ordinary table wine, which is also the humblest of categories. This inevitably leads to confusion.

Piedmont: Vintage Assessment

1985: A harvest of reduced quantity, due to frost and hail damage, but of excellent to exceptional quality. The 1985s are a complete contrast to the 1984s, being higher in alcohol and lower in acidity, with an extraordinary depth of colour. The quality of the 1985s will confirm Italy as a producer of fine wines and will allow them to be sold at a good price.

1984: A cool, wet summer led to a disappointing vintage.

1983: These wines promise well in cask, and look to be very good, if not great.

1982: This is the vintage currently arriving and it is a great one, the best since 1978. Big, full-bodied wines in Barolo and Barbaresco that will need ten years at least. Recommended.

1981: This is an okay vintage, but the wines have more toughness than fruit. Might improve with age, but be careful.

1980: A light vintage of early maturing wines.

1979: A good vintage for Barolo and Barbaresco, overshadowed by its illustrious predecessor. The best-value vintage for drinking now.

1978: A great vintage of deep-coloured, concentrated wines, most still a long way from maturity. Very difficult to find.

1977: A poor vintage best forgotten.

1976: Better than 1977, but no great shakes. No reason to buy these.

1975: This never was a very good vintage and should be avoided.

1974: One of the three best vintages of the seventies, these wines are at their peak and absolutely delicious.

Earlier vintages: The best Barolos for drinking now are from the great 1971 vintage. They are, unfortunately, scarce and very expensive. There are good earlier vintages, such as 1970, 1967, and 1964, but as with any older wine, only buy these if you are confident that they have been stored properly.

Piedmont: Recommended Producers

Produttori di Barbaresco: A co-operative producing a variety of single-vineyard Barbarescos. Good quality and attractive prices.

Fratelli Cavallotto: Famous Barolo, particularly from Bricco Boschis. Available in the United States and Britain.

Casa Vinicola Ceretto: A model Piedmont property producing estate-bottled Barolo (Bricco Roche) and Barbaresco (Bricco Asili) from their own vineyards and very good wines from leased lands.

Pio Cesare: One of the best-known Barolo producers in export markets. Also very good Barbaresco.

Elvio Cogno: Outstanding Barolo La Serra and Brunate.

Aldo Conterno: One of two brothers producing outstanding wines, Aldo Conterno emphasizes fruit and fresh flavour. His Barolo has structure and more finesse than most.

Giacomo Conterno: Aldo's brother and owner of the family firm, which is over 200 years old. One of the most traditional, and longest lived of all Barolos.

Paolo Cordero di Montezemolo: A fine small producer of Barolo Monfaletto.

Fontanafredda: Much the largest estate in Piedmont and equipped with the most modern technology. Winemaker Livio Testa manages to make a range of fine, well-priced Barolos and good Barbaresco. A notable *méthode champenoise* named Contessa Rosa.

Angelo Gaja: A ceaseless innovator at his winery and a tireless promoter of Piedmont wines abroad, Angelo Gaja is the star of Italian winemaking. His estate-bottled Barbarescos, including three individual crus, 'Sori San Lorenzo', 'Sori San Tildin', and 'Costa Russi', set the standard for quality, but at a price.

Bruno Giacosa: Not a vineyard owner, but a skilled winemaker. Very good Barbaresco.

Castello di Nieve: A small, old estate producing outstanding Barbaresco.

Alfredo Prunotto: An outstanding producer, whose Barolo and Barbaresco enjoy a high standing in Italy and abroad.

Antinori's Tignanello benefits from the addition of Cabernet Sauvignon to the traditional Chianti grape, Sangiovese. Cabernet Sauvignon is grown on the right-hand slope.

Renato Ratti (Abbazia dell'Annunziata): Ratti is a prominent wine personality, as winemaker, writer, and judge of other wines. His own wines are, unsurprisingly, first rate.

Paolo Scavino: A fine, small Barolo producer whose wines are available in the United States.

Vietti: Produce small quantities of fine Barolo and Barbaresco.

Tuscany

Tuscany is famous as the home of Chianti. This light, agreeable product of the Sangiovese grape is most people's introduction to Italian wines. In the best region, Chianti Classico, it can produce a wine of real character. The great wine of this region, though, is Brunello di Montalcino. Produced in southern Tuscany from the Brunello, a Sangiovese strain, it is a very big, very dry red wine that reputedly lives indefinitely. The nearby Vino Nobile di Montepulciano has the makings of a first-rate wine, but Tuscany's future as a fine wine region may lie in other directions.

It is the firm of Antinori who have led the way in experiments with the Cabernet Sauvignon which, blended with the Sangiovese, makes a more elegant wine than Chianti. Their Tignanello is one of the best Tuscan reds. They also used to make and market the all-Cabernet Sauvignon Sassacaia, which is a rich, Bordeaux-like wine, and an indication of the promise this region holds for the great Médoc grape.

Tuscany: Recommended Producers

Marchesi L. & P. Antinori: Much the most famous and important of Tuscany's producers, Antinori start from a sound base with a good Chianti Classico. Their Tignanello and Sassacaia have already been mentioned, and their experiments include methods of vinification and ageing as well as viticulture.

Badia a Coltibuono: Traditional Chianti Classicos, especially Riservas.

Biondi-Santi: A Tuscan traditionalist who produces Italy's most famous—and most expensive—wine, Brunello di Montalcino Il Greppo.

Tenuta di Capezzana: Another firm with a sound base in Chianti producing new-style red wines. Their most famous, Carmignano, is the revival of a family tradition and is a blend of Sangiovese and Cabernet Sauvignon. They are also experimenting with Cabernet/Merlot blends.

Frescobaldi: Large-scale producer with very fine Chianti Montesodi.

Tenuta Il Poggione: A large estate in Montalcino making good Brunello di Montalcino and selling it at an attractive price.

Castello di Rampolla: Another innovator, but deserving of mention as the producer of one of the finest Chianti Classicos.

Castello Vicchiomaggio: Traditional Chianti and new-style barrique-aged reds.

Castello di Volpaia: Chianti Classico.

Other Regions

There are other fine wine pioneers in Italy, people prepared to wed traditional skills to the most up-to-date advances in vinification and ageing. It is not so much one region as individuals blazing the trail: in Torgiano, near Perugia, Giorgio Lungarotti has received international attention for his Sangiovese-based Rubesco di Torgiano. He is experimenting with Cabernet Sauvignon, Chardonnay and Gewürztraminer.

The Trentino–Alto Adige region in the north-east is an area of great experimentation. Twenty years from now this may be the most important fine wine region outside Piedmont. Growers have found that this relatively cool climate suits both Chardonnay and Pinot Noir ('Pinot Nero'), and the Merlot is also proving successful. Three producers to watch are Conti Martini, de Tarczal, and Zeni (especially for Chardonnay). The region is also home to Italy's finest producer of sparkling wines, Ferrari: they make vintage and non-vintage *méthode champenoise* wines that bear comparison with champagne.

In the Veneto, known for light-style reds and whites, is another notable innovator, Conte Loredan-Gasparini. The Venegazzú della Casa, a blend of Bordeaux grape varieties, is one of Italy's best red wines. Masi are traditionalists who make excellent Amarone, a powerful alcoholic speciality of Veneto. In Friuli, Mario Schiopetto makes a variety of wines with cépages nobles, including Cabernet Sauvignon, Merlot, and Riesling; and Angelo and Sylvio Jermann produce Tunina (an attractive white), and also a good Chardonnay.

Fine Italian wines have found greater acceptance in the United States than in any other market. Louis Iacucci's Goldstar Wines in Forest Hills, New York, specializes in the best of Italy.

7 Spain and Portugal

SPAIN

Spain, like Italy, is an historically important wine country, but, apart from sherry, relatively new to the production of fine wines. The Rioja region in the north dominates the country's quality table wine market with consistently good oak-aged reds. However, the practice of ageing wines in wood until they mature means that they do not acquire the nuances of flavour that bottle-ageing imparts to the fine wines of France.

Producers in Catalonia are experimenting with classic grape varieties and the results have been encouraging. Good Chardonnay and Cabernet Sauvignon are coming from this region around Barcelona, hitherto best known as the sparkling wine capital of Spain. Spain's greatest red wine, though, is Vega Sicilia. Produced by costly and painstaking methods at one estate near Valladolid from the native Garnacha and the classic Bordeaux varieties, Cabernet Sauvignon, Merlot, and Malbec, it is an expensive and highly prized rarity.

Rioja

There are four quality steps in the classification of red Rioja. These are 'sin crianza', without ageing in wood; 'con crianza', usually three years old, one of which must be spent in 225-litre Bordeaux-style barriques (barricas); 'Reservas', five-year-old wines which have spent at least two years in barricas; and 'Gran Reservas', seven-year-old wines which have spent three or four years in barricas. The final two categories contain most of the region's finest wines and, in the United States and Great Britain, some excellent bargains.

Recommended Producers

CVNE	Olarra
R. Lopez de Heredía	La Rioja Alta
Muga	

Catalonia

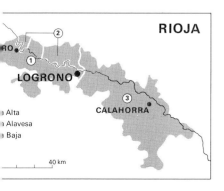

Catalonia's emergence as a fine wine region is chiefly the result of one company, Vinédos Torrés. A family company like Mondavi in California and Antinori in Tuscany, Torrés is helping to shape the country's fine wine industry. Their Gran Coronas Black Label, a mainly Cabernet Sauvignon blend, is one of Spain's finest wines.

Recommended Producers

Jean Léon
Torrés

Sherry

There are two principal styles of sherry—fino and oloroso, determined by the appearance or not of a surface layer of yeast on the young wine. Those which develop the layer of yeast, called flor, are destined to be finos; those that do not will be olorosos. Fermentation takes place in barrels or stainless steel tanks, but all the wine is matured in large oak casks, and it is here that sherry parts company from other fine wines. The casks called butts are filled only four-fifths full, encouraging that enemy of wine, oxidation.

The flor retards oxidation and wines in these casks are lightly fortified, and aged for a shorter period. They become delicate, fresh-flavoured wines, delightful when drunk lightly chilled. The wines which develop little or no flor are more heavily fortified and matured for a longer time in contact with air. Occasionally a wine will develop characteristics of both fino and oloroso. These wines, called Palo Cortado, combine the freshness and cut of a fino with the depth and body of an oloroso.

There are two subdivisions of fino sherries—Manzanilla and Amont-illado. The first refers to wines matured on the coast at Sanlucar de Barrameda, and they have the aroma and taste of the salt air. Amontillado is the name given to aged finos, but is more often used to describe a number of medium-sweet commercial blends. Sherry is vinified completely dry. The sweetness of ordinary wines is not residual sugar, but is added after the fermentation.

A second unique feature of sherry production is the solera system. The young butts of wine are divided according to type and stored in a nursery or criadera to be incorporated into the solera. Sherry, in common with Champagne and tawny port, is the product of the wine-blender's art. The great merchant houses which dominate the trade aim at a particular style for each of their wines. This is done by blending wines of various ages. When a proportion of the oldest wine is taken from a butt, it is replaced by wine from the next oldest cask. This in turn is replenished from the next cask in line, and so on down to the youngest wines. Some soleras contain wines dating back over one hundred years. These great stores form the backbone of all good sherries and ensure a constant supply of fine wine in a particular style.

The Rioja is Spain's best-known district for fine red wine. These vineyards are near Logroño, the capital of the Rioja Alta region.

Below The harvest is difficult work in the steeply terraced vineyards of the Douro Valley in northern Portugal.

The Market

Sherry has had an unhappy recent history with intense price competition taking precedence over quality. In addition it suffers from a rather old-fashioned image, and has been left behind by consumers in Europe and America seeking lighter style white wines. There are signs that the industry has learned from the recent past and recognizes that the only future for sherry is as a fine wine. Certainly there are more high-quality sherries available in Britain and America than there were four or five years ago, and though they are more expensive than the dubious wines which flooded the market in the seventies they are good value for wines so well made.

Christie's can claim a share of the credit for this. Their sales of sherry organized in June 1982, and in November 1985, brought large quantities of very fine wine into the British market for the first time. More importantly such sales have helped bolster trade and consumer confidence in sherry as a fine wine.

The November 1985 sale at Christie's featured a large stock of almacenista sherries which had never before been shipped to the United Kingdom. The almacenistas are stockholders rather than shippers and many have other full-time occupations. Their wines are generally bought by the large merchants to improve the quality of their commercial blends. Some of these wines now appear unblended in the United Kingdom and, less often, in America. They represent some of the finest sherries available, and anyone who has dismissed sherry based on experiences with poor commercial blends should try these wines.

Recommended Producers

Domecq (La Ina, Rio Viejo, Double Century)
Gonzalez Byass (Tio Pepe, La Concha, Apostoles)
Williams and Humbert (Pando, Dry Sack)
Sandeman (Don Fino, Dry Don, Apitiv, Corregidor)
Garvey (La Guita, San Patricio, Tio Guillermo)
Harvey (Bristol Dry, Luncheon Dry, Bristol Cream)
Croft (Original, Particular)
Duff Gordon (El Cid, Fiesta)
Emilio Lustau (Almacenista Sherries)

PORTUGAL

VINTAGE PORT

Vintage port represents a small proportion of total port production, perhaps 4 or 5 per cent in a declared year. Most port is bottled young and intended for early consumption. In the best years shippers set aside production from their finest sites, age the wine in wood for eighteen to twenty-four months, and then bottle it as a vintage. The wine matures slowly in bottle, taking ten to twenty-five years to reach its peak, and good examples will last another twenty years.

TAWNY PORTS

Fine tawny ports are aged in wood for much longer periods and bottled when ready to drink. Each house has a style which remains consistent through careful blending. Fine tawnies, with an average age of ten or twenty years, have not the resale or appreciation value that vintage port has. There is another port which is growing in popularity, confusingly labelled 'late bottled vintage'. These are wines from a selected year, aged for four or five years in wood and bottled ready to drink. Basically, they have more in common with a tawny than with a vintage port. Some are good, and they are attractively priced, but only a few shippers, Taylor and Smith Woodhouse, for example, are making late bottled vintage in a true vintage style.

The Market

Vintage port is thought of as the Englishman's wine, but the market is changing rapidly. Americans have developed a taste for fine port and are prepared to pay for it. Interest is growing in other countries as well, with Germany, Scandinavia, Australia, and New Zealand all expanding markets. The United States will receive about 20 per cent of shipments of the 1983s, and because American merchants will also buy in the British market, the final figure will be higher. This contrasts with twenty years ago when over 95 per cent of vintage port was shipped to Britain, much of it in cask. Historically, the major shippers have declared vintages roughly three times a decade. So far in the eighties, there have been vintages in three of the first four years. Shippers say the quality of the wine dictates vintages, but the present buoyant market must have contributed to declarations in three years out of four.

Vintage Assessment

1983: Very early for these. Concentrated wines with more body than either 1982 or 1980. Probably the best vintage since 1977.

1982: Recently bottled. Good colour and fruit behind the tannin. Not a heavyweight vintage.

1980: Widely declared. A good but not exciting vintage which should be drinking well in the early 1990s.

1977: A great and widely declared vintage. Concentrated, ripe, tannic wines, still opaque. The best vintage since 1963, these wines will need the full twenty years.

1975: Lightish vintage, ideal for drinking now. Currently good value.

1970: A very good and underrated vintage. The wines are delicious now but will improve. Good value for the medium term.

1966: Widely declared though Cockburn preferred 1967. Good, full-bodied wines that are perfect now.

Madeira, a fortified wine from the Portuguese island, is usually sold as a blend like sherry. Vintages are declared in the finest years, and such wines are aged in wood for 20 years or more. Once bottled they live almost indefinitely.

1963: Widely declared. The best vintage since 1945 and the wines to drink for the next two decades. Concentrated, rich, balanced. Great.

1960: A good vintage for current drinking but looking overpriced compared to 1966 and 1970.

1955: A very fine heavyweight vintage now in its prime. Expensive.

1945: One of the greatest ever vintages, included as an example of how long fine port lasts. Taylor and Graham tasted in 1985 were still in top condition. Scarce and very expensive.

Recommended Producers

The port trade is dominated by large merchant houses rather like Champagne. They own vineyards but buy a substantial proportion of their needs from farmers in the Douro Valley. Each blends wines to a house style, whether it be the inexpensive ruby ports which make up the bulk of sales, or fine old tawnies and vintage wines.

Cockburn: One of the biggest and best known of the great lodges, but their performance has been a bit erratic of late. They did not declare 1977 and preferred 1967 to 1966. However, they made a superb 1983. Their fine tawny is called Directors' Reserve.

Croft: A great favourite in Britain, Croft's vintage wines assembled around the Quinta da Roeda are among the most charming of ports.

Dow: Part of the Symington group, Dow's vintage wines are concentrated and hard, taking a long time to mature. The 1977 is especially fine.

Fonseca: The Guimaraens family business, now a part of the Taylor organization. Though not well known twenty-five years ago, their vintage port is now recognized as one of the very best.

W. & J. Graham: Another Symington enterprise, Graham produces a sweet, rich and immensely likeable vintage wine. The range includes some fine tawnies, and a single-vineyard vintage, Quinta de Malvedos, which is excellent value.

Quinta do Noval: The most famous single-vineyard wine, Quinta do Noval attracted attention in Britain with the great 1931 vintage. Usually not a blockbuster, but a soft, sweet wine. Good old tawnies.

Sandeman: Perhaps the biggest port company, now owned by Seagram, Sandeman make a good vintage and a range of old tawnies.

Taylor, Fladgate & Yeatman: The Château Latour of vintage port, Taylor produce the biggest and longest-lived of vintage ports. They also make excellent ten- and twenty-year-old tawnies, and the superb single-vineyard Quinta de Vargellas, which is always sold with a vintage date.

Warre: Another of the Symington enterprises, Warre produces a fine vintage wine, drier than Graham and more charming than Dow. Their very good tawny is called Nimrod.

Other shippers whose names will appear more frequently if demand for vintage port continues to rise are Offley, Delaforce, Feuerheerd, Quarles Harris, Smith Woodhouse, and Rebello Valente.

8　USA

CALIFORNIA

1 Napa-Sonoma
2 Central Coast

0　　　　200 km

OREGON

GEYSERVILLE
HEALDSBURG
SANTA ROSA
OAKVILLE
SONOMA　NAPA　●SACRAMENTO
●SAN FRANCISCO
SAN JOSE
STA
CRUZ　SANTA CLARA
CO　COUNTY
NEVADA

●HOLLISTER
MONTEREY
●SOLEDAD
MONTEREY
COUNTY　San Joaquin
CALIFORNIA

●LOS ANGELES

ARIZONA
MEXICO

California

Though viticulture in California extends from Mendocino County in the north all the way to the Mexican border, the principal fine wine regions are the Napa and Sonoma Valleys north of San Francisco and the Central Coast from San José to Monterey. The Napa Valley is home to many of California's greatest wineries and it was from here that California Cabernet Sauvignons strode forth a decade ago to take on the world. The California style of Cabernet Sauvignon is rich, full-bodied, and alcoholic. Recently the wines have shown more polish and balance, while still retaining the massive fruit that is their hallmark.

Chardonnays come in a variety of styles, as winemakers seek a balance of fruit, alcohol and acid. The days of fat, over-oaked Chardonnays are numbered.

Pinot Noir has proved more difficult, though there have been just enough successes to encourage growers to keep trying. Most regions are simply too hot for this grape. It has been used with some success in the production of sparkling wines; California's best are Champagne's closest rivals. Winemakers have had increasing success with two other Bordeaux grapes, Merlot and Sauvignon Blanc.

The Market

Wine producers in California have been going through a difficult time. The strong dollar and weak French franc have meant that wine drinkers in the United States, particularly on the East Coast, have access to excellent wines from France at bargain prices. Many wineries established in the last fifteen years, have had to borrow heavily at high interest rates to start their enterprise. The combination of debt and higher production costs in the United States has meant that they cannot compete on price with the imports. This has been doubly true in export markets, Canada and Great Britain being the most important.

California wines arrived in Britain in the mid-seventies, trailing prizes won at comparative tastings against some of France's greatest names. California's top producers set great store by the British market, because it has a reputation for connoisseurship and fairness. They genuinely wanted their wines to be tasted and judged against the world's best, and have made financial sacrifices to retain a presence in Britain. There are signs, though, that things are changing. Prices in Bordeaux have been rising

Most fine California wines are designated by grape variety and under a federal law adopted in 1983 must contain at least 75 per cent of the named varietal. If a county is named on the label (Sonoma, Monterey, etc.) all of that varietal must come from that county. In addition there are certain recognized 'viticultural areas', of which the Napa Valley is one. If Napa Valley appears on a varietal label at least 85 per cent of the wine must come from the varietal grown within the Napa Valley.

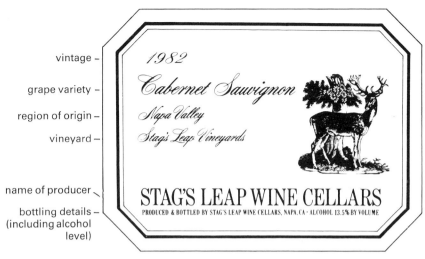

vintage –
grape variety –
region of origin –
vineyard –

name of producer ⟍
bottling details –
(including alcohol
level)

1982
Cabernet Sauvignon
Napa Valley
Stag's Leap Vineyards

STAG'S LEAP WINE CELLARS
PRODUCED & BOTTLED BY STAG'S LEAP WINE CELLARS, NAPA, CA · ALCOHOL 13.5% BY VOLUME

steadily for the past two years. Wines from the fine 1982 and 1983 vintages have become expensive while Californians have kept prices in check. That £10 ($15) bottle of California Cabernet Sauvignon that looked overpriced two years ago is probably still on the market at the same price. Compared with Bordeaux, it now seems a good buy. The same is true of Chardonnays. Prices for 1983 white Burgundy are at record levels, leaving some of California's best, particularly Robert Mondavi, as good buys. Producers in California are learning quickly about export markets, and are looking to the Far East, as well as to Europe. Many see the Pacific nations as the natural market for their wines. Both the 1984 and the 1985 vintages were generally very good. Providing the dollar does not climb in value they should re-establish California wines at home, and perhaps even break through in the competitive European market.

Recommended Producers: The Elite

Chalone Vineyard: This Monterey winery has the best record in California with the grape varieties of Burgundy. They produce a very good Pinot Noir, and great Chardonnay. Small production, very high quality.

Heitz Wine Cellars: Joe Heitz is one of the acknowledged master winemakers of California. His most famous wine, Martha's Vineyard Cabernet Sauvignon, has a deserved international reputation. It is dark, spicy, and concentrated, even by California standards, and ages well. Bella Oaks is another single-vineyard Cabernet, and the cheaper Napa Valley Cabernet is also good.

Mayacamas Vineyard: This small, Mount Veeder winery is the home of one of California's greatest wines. Bob Travers's Cabernet Sauvignon, of which he produces only 2,000 cases, is a dark, chewy, tannic wine that takes years to come around. Travers said in 1985 that his excellent 1974 was still six or seven years from maturity. His Chardonnay is also fine. Difficult wines to find, but worth the effort and price.

The nineteenth-century cellars at Mayacamas high in the hills above the Napa Valley. Mayacamas are one of the most traditional of California wineries.

Robert Mondavi Winery: No one has done more to promote California wine than Robert Mondavi, who combines winemaking skill with the pioneering virtues of courage, perseverance, and daring. Founded in 1966, the Mondavi winery is committed to making outstanding examples of all the important grape varieties. His Cabernet Sauvignon Reserve is probably his best-known wine, and very good it is. His Chardonnay Reserve is regularly among Napa's best, and he is a leading producer of Fumé Blanc. He also makes an outstanding botrytis-affected Sauvignon Blanc. Mondavi and Baron Philippe de Rothschild have launched Opus One Cabernet Sauvignon. The 1979 and 1980 are both excellent, and the only complaints so far have been about the price.

Joseph Phelps Vineyards: Physically impressive and technologically advanced, this Napa winery is a trendsetter in California. Originally known for white wines, they have filled out their list with red wines of real distinction. Their two best Cabernets—the Joseph Eisele and a Cabernet/Merlot blend, Insignia—are regularly among California's best. They make very good Chardonnays and Rieslings and a good Syrah.

Ridge Vineyards: Located in the Santa Cruz mountains south of San Francisco, Ridge are red wine specialists. They are the masters of the Zinfandel, and their Cabernet Sauvignons are always in the top echelons. The Montebello Cabernet is built to last, as are all Ridge's wines. A ten-year-old Zinfandel can taste surprisingly like a fine northern Rhône.

Stag's Leap Wine Cellars: Another of Napa's magic names, Stag's Leap, year in and year out, produces some of California's best and most sought-after Cabernet Sauvignon and Merlot. Their Cask 23 Cabernet Sauvignon is as close in style to a fine Médoc as any California Cabernet. This winery also produces fine Chardonnay and, recently, a well-balanced Sauvignon Blanc.

The Robert Mondavi winery in Oakville, California, built in the local Spanish Mission style.

Other Good Producers

Acacia, Napa: Chardonnay. High quality, high prices.

Alexander Valley Vineyards, Sonoma: Chardonnays.

Beaulieu Vineyard, Napa: Pioneer fine wine producer best known for their Georges de Latour Private Reserve Cabernet Sauvignon.

Beringer Vineyards, Napa: Fumé Blanc and Chardonnay at reasonable prices.

Cakebread Cellars, Napa: Sauvignon Blanc and Chardonnay.

Calera Wine Company, San Benito: Pinot Noir in the best Burgundian style, prices are justifiably high. A good range of Zinfandel.

Carneros Creek Winery, Napa: Big-style Chardonnays and good Pinot Noirs.

Caymus Vineyards, Napa: High-quality Cabernet Sauvignon; deep, very rich in the traditional Napa style.

Chappellet, Napa: Hard, tannic, long-lasting Cabernet Sauvignon. Also Merlot and Chardonnay.

Château Montelena, Napa: Outstanding Chardonnays and good, but variable Cabernet Sauvignons.

Château St Jean, Sonoma: Luscious Chardonnays, good Sauvignon Blanc, and Rieslings, ranging from medium-sweet to very sweet and honeyed.

Clos du Bois, Sonoma: Chardonnay and Merlot.

Clos du Val, Napa: Bordeaux-style Cabernet Sauvignon and Merlot. Surer touch with red than white varietals.

Conn Creek, Napa: Fine, medium-weight Cabernet Sauvignon.

Domaine Chandon, Napa: Owned by Moët & Chandon. First-class sparkling wines.

Diamond Creek, Napa: Tough, long-lasting Cabernet Sauvignon.

Dry Creek Vineyard, Sonoma: Fumé Blanc.

Edna Valley Vineyards, San Luis Obispo: Chardonnay.

Far Niente Winery, Napa: Fine and expensive Chardonnay.

The Firestone Vineyard, Santa Barbara: Cabernet Sauvignon and Merlot. Good value.

Freemark Abbey, Napa: Chardonnay, Cabernet Sauvignon Bosche.

Grgich Hills, Napa: Chardonnay and Riesling. Expensive.

Hanzell Vineyards, Sonoma: Chardonnay; one of the earliest experimenters with Pinot Noir.

William Hill Winery, Napa: Initial releases of Chardonnay and Cabernet promise a bright future.

Iron Horse Vineyard, Sonoma: Chardonnay. Also very good Pinot Noir and sparkling wine.

Jekel Vineyard, Monterey: Chardonnay and Cabernet Sauvignon.

Jordan Vineyard and Winery, Sonoma: Cabernet Sauvignon and Chardonnay.

Kalin Cellars, Marin County: Good Pinot Noir and Chardonnay.

Kenwood Vineyards, Sonoma: Cabernet Sauvignon.

Long, Napa: Outstanding Chardonnay.

Louis M. Martini, Napa: Cabernet Sauvignon.

Matanzas Creek Winery, Sonoma: Excellent Chardonnay and Sauvignon Blanc.

Montevina Wines, Amador County: Zinfandel and Sauvignon Blanc.

Mount Eden Vineyards, Santa Clara: Chardonnay and Cabernet Sauvignon.

Mount Veeder Winery, Napa: Cabernet Sauvignon.

Schramsberg Vineyards, Napa: Outstanding sparkling wines, Blanc de Blancs and Blanc de Noirs.

Sonoma-Cutrer, Sonoma: Outstanding Chardonnays, especially Les Pierres and Cutrer vineyards.

Spring Mountain Vineyards, Napa: Cabernet Sauvignon and Chardonnay.

Sterling Vineyards, Napa: Cabernet Sauvignon Reserve, Chardonnay and Sauvignon Blanc.

Trefethen Vineyards, Napa: Cabernet Sauvignon and Chardonnay. Good value.

Villa Mount Eden, Napa: Very good Cabernet Sauvignon and Chardonnay.

The Pacific Northwest

This region, comprising the states of Oregon, Washington, and Idaho, shows most promise for grape varieties which require relatively cool growing conditions. Early results with Pinot Noir have encouraged many to feel that America's challenge to Burgundy will emanate from here rather than from California. White varieties have also shown promise, and good Chardonnays, Rieslings and Gewürztraminers are now being produced.

The Market

It is too early to determine where these wines will slot into the international wine markets because they are still something of a novelty in the United States. Many of the best examples are available in Britain and the prices are very keen, about a third less than California wines of comparable quality.

Recommended Producers: Oregon

Amity Vineyards: Best early wines have been Pinot Noirs, but Chardonnay and Gewürztraminer are now showing well.
Elk Cove Vineyards: Best for Pinot Noir, but good Chardonnays and Rieslings as well.
The Eyrie Vineyards: Very fine Pinot Noir as far back as 1975 (that is a long time for this region) and, more recently, fine Chardonnay.
Knudsen Erath: A large winery with a reputation for good, reasonably priced Pinot Noir and Riesling.
Tualatin Vineyards: Tualatin's Pinot Noir is one of the region's best wines. The Chardonnay and Riesling are also very good.

Recommended Producers: Washington

Associated Vintners: First attracted attention for white wines, especially Gewürztraminer, but more recently have turned out fine Cabernet Sauvignon.
Château Ste Michelle: A large winery with products in all price ranges. Some good Cabernet Sauvignon and Chardonnay.

Recommended Producers: Idaho

Ste Chapelle Vineyards: Especially notable Chardonnay; good Riesling and Gewürztraminer.

PACIFIC WINE COMPANY

Their catalogues may be tongue-in-cheek, but the Pacific Wine Company are serious wine merchants with especially good selections from Burgundy and California.

Pacific Northwest labels are governed by the same Federal labelling regulation as California wines.

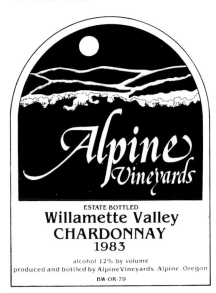

9 Australia and New Zealand

AUSTRALIA

Australia is a country of enormous potential and seemingly boundless enthusiasm for fine wine. The principal regions are in the south-eastern corner in the states of Victoria, New South Wales, and South Australia. Western Australia is also very promising.

It is difficult to define an Australian style. There are new wineries opening all the time and experimentation is the rule. But the wines do have some common characteristics. First of all the reds: these are mainly warm weather vineyards and the style differs from the European archetypes. As in California the problem is not obtaining sufficiently ripe fruit, but rather avoiding overripeness. Australian Cabernets are generally very deep coloured with plenty of fruit and a fair bit of tannin. If they lack anything, it is finesse. The same is true of the Shiraz; these are big, full-flavoured wines.

The Chardonnay produces rich wines, high in alcohol, but, on early evidence, not for long cellaring. The Semillon, which is blended with the Sauvignon Blanc to make the great dry and sweet wines of Bordeaux, is produced as a dry varietal, and there are some fine examples. The Riesling (Rhine Riesling) produces wines in many styles from medium dry to Beerenauslesen sweet. The Muscat is used as a dry varietal, but is also found as a sweet, fortified wine in Victoria. Called Liqueur Muscat, this can be deliciously sweet and nutty: a unique Australian fine wine.

The Market

The main problem for Australia's wine industry is its isolation from the world's major markets, though improved communications and greater interest in fine wines should soon put paid to that. Another difficulty is that many of Australia's best wines never reach overseas markets. Australian wine consumption runs well ahead of either Britain or the United States, and this buoyant home demand has supported the fine wine boom of the seventies. Increased production over the past decade, though, means that some wineries will have to look abroad for new markets. Great Britain, the United States and the burgeoning Asian market are the most likely targets.

Britain, through the Commonwealth connection, seems a natural market, and fine Australian wines have been available for several years. Yet British wine drinkers have been slow to recognize their quality, which is a pity. In the middle price ranges Australian Cabernets, Chardonnays, and Semillons represent very good value.

A good selection of Australian wines is available in Britain. Alexander Findlater in London stocks the most comprehensive range.

The United States presents a different problem. The domestic competition is of roughly similar style and has an established reputation. No Australian producer has made the impact that California wineries such as Heitz and Stag's Leap did in the seventies, but in the Australians' favour, it must be said that the wines are not nearly so expensive.

New South Wales

The Hunter Valley is the cradle of Australia's fine wine industry and home to some of its most reliable producers. Its rejuvenation in the 1960s started Australia's current enthusiasm for fine wine. The Shiraz is the great grape variety here, though the Cabernet Sauvignon is increasingly important. There are also very good Chardonnays, and Semillons so tasty that one wonders why this grape is not cultivated as a dry varietal in Europe. Two other important regions are Mudgee and Cowra.

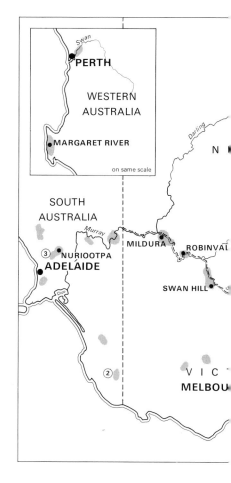

Most new Australian wineries use varietal labels, although they are under no obligation to do so. Generic labels, e.g. 'claret' and 'Hermitage' are still common, as are various vat and bin numbers. Clear and uniform labelling regulations would certainly help Australian producers in export markets.

Recommended Producers

Brokenwood: Fine Cabernet Sauvignon. Also Chardonnay and Semillon.
Lake's Folly: Long-lived Cabernet Sauvignons. Good Chardonnay and Shiraz.
McWilliams: Cabernet Sauvignon from Mount Pleasant vineyards.
Rosemount Estate: Fine, well-priced Chardonnay. Also Semillon and Rhine Riesling.
Rothbury Estate: Very good Semillon and Chardonnay.
Tyrells: Long-established winery. Shiraz, Semillon, and Chardonnay.

Opposite Pruning and training the vines: wintertime activity in the Margaret River, Western Australia.

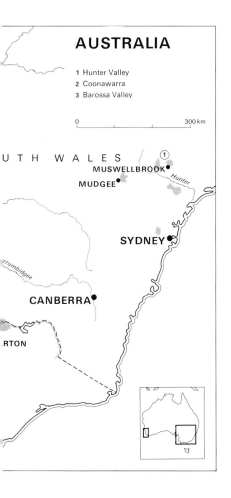

AUSTRALIA

1 Hunter Valley
2 Coonawarra
3 Barossa Valley

0   300 km

U T H   W A L E S

MUSWELLBROOK

MUDGEE

Hunter

SYDNEY

rrumbidgee

CANBERRA

RTON

South Australia

South Australia is most famous for its red varietals, Shiraz and Cabernet Sauvignon, and is the home of Australia's greatest red wine, Penfold's Grange Hermitage. The two most important regions are Coonawarra and the Barossa Valley.

Cabernet Sauvignon is the dominant grape in Coonawarra, and Australia's most elegant and balanced reds are produced here. They have been among the most successful wines in export markets. The Barossa Valley also produces Cabernet Sauvignon, but is better regarded for Shiraz. Australian winemakers frequently blend the two varieties.

Though South Australia is better known for red wines, one winery is producing outstanding whites. Petaluma, near Adelaide, has made prize-winning Chardonnay and Riesling as well as Cabernet Sauvignon and Shiraz. Petaluma's wines are available in both Britain and the United States, and provide solid proof of the region's potential.

Recommended Producers

Brand's Laira: Good reasonably priced Cabernet Sauvignon.
Penfolds: Grange Hermitage. Also St-Henri Cabernet/Shiraz.
Petaluma: Very fine Riesling, Chardonnay, and Cabernet Sauvignon.
Pewsey Vale: Good Rieslings, especially late-harvested bottlings.
Yalumba: Best for reds. Cabernet Sauvignon and Cabernet/Shiraz.

Victoria

The third major wine-growing state in south-eastern Australia, Victoria is a centre for innovation, and produces some of the best new-style white wines. There are some fine reds, too, in the sturdy, 'traditional' Australian style. The most famous wine of the region is the Liqueur Muscat, produced in Rutherglen, though little of it is exported.

Recommended Producers

Balgownie: Rich, full-bodied Chardonnay. Also Cabernet Sauvignon.
Brown Bros: Old-established firm. Riesling, Chardonnay, and Cabernet Sauvignon.
Chateau Tahbilk: Fine Cabernet Sauvignon and Shiraz.
Mildara: Good, reasonably priced Cabernet Sauvignon.
Seville Estate: Fine late-harvested Riesling. Good Cabernet Sauvignon.
Taltarni: Under the same ownership as Clos du Val in California. Good full-bodied Cabernet Sauvignon and Merlot.

Western Australia

In the newest of Australia's fine wine regions, winemakers display the same determination and enthusiasm that won their yachtsmen the Americas Cup. Margaret River is the most important region for both red and white varietals. The Pinot Noir, that trickiest of grapes, has made an encouraging start here.

Recommended Producers

Leeuwin: A winery to watch. Good Riesling, Chardonnay, and Cabernet Sauvignon.
Moss Wood: Cabernet Sauvignon, Chardonnay, and Pinot Noir.
Vasse Felix: Cabernet Sauvignon and Riesling.

NEW ZEALAND

New Zealand is the newest of the New World countries to be producing fine wine. Only ten years ago, over three-quarters of her production was from hybrid grapes and much of this was fortified. Even today there are less than 4,000 hectares of vines in production, but planting is increasing and is based mainly on cépages nobles: Riesling, Chardonnay, Sauvignon for the whites (plus a little Chenin Blanc); Cabernet Sauvignon, Pinot Noir and Syrah for the reds. The particularity of New Zealand lies in the cool climate, which is almost identical to that of France, perhaps even a little cooler. This means that it is the only country in the Southern Hemisphere that can produce wines as light as the equivalent French wines.

Only the big companies, Cooks-McWilliams and Montana, are exporting regularly, but many fine wines are being produced, and technically, thanks to the dairy industry, New Zealand winemakers are the most advanced in the world. This is a country to watch.

The relatively cool climate in New Zealand is especially suitable for white varietals. Many wines from New Zealand are beginning to attract attention in Britain and the United States.

10 Laying Down Wine

First determine your fine wine requirements. Let us assume that you need five cases of red wine per year and five of white. The red might break down further as two cases of Bordeaux, one of Burgundy, and two 'other', which might include Rhône, California, vintage port, and Australia. The white could be three cases of dry dinner wine, one of medium-sweet to sweet, and one of Champagne.

As good vintages are not evenly spread, your purchases will not be either. Assuming that good vintages for red Bordeaux, Rhône and California occur two years out of three, and for Burgundy and vintage port, one out of three or four, you should buy one and a half times your annual requirement of the first three in each good vintage, and three times your annual requirement of the latter two. White wines are easier to buy, because most do not require so much cellarage and, apart from white Burgundy, do not disappear from the market as quickly as the reds.

As money will be the principal obstacle to stocking a cellar, you must also establish priorities. Buy first those wines most likely to sell out or increase sharply in price. The following wines fall into this category: clarets from the top Crus Classés, especially the fifteen or so wines just below the Premiers Grands Crus in quality; Grand and Premier Cru red and white Burgundy from the best domaines; and northern Rhônes from two or three top producers. German Auslesen, Barolos, vintage ports, and Champagnes, good though they are, are not in such great demand. The same is true of most wines from California and Australia.

Here are two cellar plans. One is for the well-heeled and extremely virtuous collector seeking maximum enjoyment from his investment and prepared to delay gratification. The other is for creatures of flesh and blood and more limited means.

London clubs have a reputation for connoisseurship, especially for claret and vintage port. This corner of the wine cellar at Boodle's, St James's, shows that the club's reputation is well founded.

Plan 1: red

Bordeaux

6 bottles Ch. Pichon-Lalande 1983
6 bottles Ch. Léoville-Las-Cases 1983
6 bottles Ch. Léoville-Poyférré 1983
6 bottles Ch. Gruaud-Larose 1982
6 bottles Ch. Grand-Puy-Lacoste 1982
6 bottles Ch. Chasse-Spleen 1982

Burgundy

1 case Mazis-Chambertin 1983, B. Maume
1 case Nuits-St-Georges 'Les Vaucrains' 1983, R. Chevillon
6 bottles Beaune 'Clos des Mouches' 1983, Joseph Drouhin
6 bottles Pommard 'Le Clos Blanc' 1983, Machard de Gramont

Rhône

6 bottles Hermitage 1983, J.-L. Chave
6 bottles Côte-Rôtie 'La Mouline' 1980, E. Guigal

California

6 bottles Cabernet Sauvignon Reserve 1978, Robert Mondavi
6 bottles Cabernet Sauvignon 1981, Stag's Leap

Vintage Port

6 bottles Graham 1977
6 bottles Taylor 1977

Approximate cost red: £1,600 ($2,600)

This is an expensive selection, because it is intended to be the foundation of a fine wine cellar. We have tried to take advantage of the great vintages of 1982 and 1983 in Bordeaux, even though it is too late to buy en primeur. In addition we have included three cases of red Burgundy from the 1983 vintage, because wines of this power and finesse may not appear again for a while. This is really an eighteen-month to two-year plan. What then, should you buy first?

First priority should be the Mazis-Chambertin. Little was produced and it will soon disappear. At the time of writing a few of Burgundy's best producers have not released their 1983s. Although there will be greater choice in 1986–7, none of the best wines will be around long. The next choice would be Chave's Hermitage, although Jaboulet's 'La Chapelle' is equally good. Both will sell out quickly. The 1982 Gruaud-Larose and Grand-Puy-Lacoste would be the next choices. These are two great wines from that extraordinary vintage at a fair price.

As for the other wines, the Nuits-St-Georges is very good; the Côte-Rôtie is outstanding, but it is there as a marker. If you miss it, look out for the 1982. The 1983 clarets will probably go up in price, but they should still be available. The 1977 ports will also rise in price, but more and more will be appearing at auction, so you will still have an opportunity to buy them. The California wines, good though they are, will be followed by even better wines from the 1984 and 1985 vintages.

The 1985 vintage should provide excellent alternatives from Bordeaux, Burgundy, and the Rhône, should the wines listed here become too expensive or sell out completely.

Plan 1: white

Burgundy

6 bottles Bâtard-Montrachet 1983, Domaine Leflaive
6 bottles Meursault 'Perrières' 1982, Domaine des Comtes Lafon
6 bottles Puligny-Montrachet 'Champ Canet' 1981, Etienne Sauzet
6 bottles Chablis 'Les Clos' 1983, René Dauvissat

Alsace

6 bottles Riesling 'Réserve Personnelle' 1983, Hugel
6 bottles Riesling 'Schlossberg' 1983, Domaine Weinbach

California

6 bottles Chardonnay Reserve 1983, Robert Mondavi

Australia

6 bottles Chardonnay Show Reserve 1984, Rosemount

Germany

6 bottles Maximin Grünhäuser Abtsberg Auslese 1983, Count
   von Schubert
6 bottles Graacher Himmelreich Auslese 1983, J. J. Prüm

Sauternes

6 bottles Ch. Rieussec 1983
6 bottles Ch. Coutet 1983

Champagne

6 bottles Laurent Perrier Brut NV
6 bottles Louis Roederer Brut NV
6 bottles Bollinger Special Cuvée NV

Approximate cost white: £900 ($1,500)

Of this list the Burgundies are the wines to buy first, especially the very good 1981 and 1982. The Alsatian Rieslings are very good, but not in such great demand as the Burgundies. German wines have yet to capture the imagination, and even a great vintage like 1983 will probably not sell out quickly. Merchants still have stocks of the outstanding 1976s. The situation for California Chardonnays is the same as for the state's Cabernets: they are not yet accepted as Burgundy's peers. The same is true for the Australian Chardonnay. The two Sauternes are good examples of a very fine vintage, and should be bought while the prices are reasonable. We have preferred non-vintage Champagne, because it is consistently good, ages well, and is more reasonably priced than the vintages, especially the 'luxury cuvées'.

Both white Burgundy and California Chardonnay were successful in 1985 and deserve a place in your cellar. The only problem with the Burgundy might be the price.

The second list is more reasonably priced and includes wines that can be drunk with pleasure within one or two years.

Plan 2: red

Bordeaux

6 bottles Ch. Cantemerle 1983
6 bottles Ch. d'Angludet 1983
6 bottles Ch. Chasse-Spleen 1983
6 bottles Ch. Chasse-Spleen 1982
6 bottles Clos du Marquis 1982
6 bottles Ch. Talbot 1979

Burgundy

1 case Nuits-St-Georges 'Les Vaucrains' 1983, R. Chevillon
6 bottles Aloxe-Corton 1983, Tollot-Beaut
6 bottles Chambolle-Musigny 1980, Domaine G. Roumier
6 bottles Chorey-Lès-Beaune 1983, Tollot-Beaut
6 bottles Bourgogne 'La Digoine' 1983, A. & P. de Villaine

Rhône

6 bottles Ch. de Beaucastel Châteauneuf-du-Pape 1981
6 bottles Côte-Rôtie 1979, E. Guigal

Italy

3 bottles Sassacaia 1980, Tenuta San Guido
3 bottles Barbaresco 1979, Angelo Gaja

California

6 bottles Cabernet Sauvignon 1981, Conn Creek

Vintage Port

6 bottles Graham 1977
6 bottles Fonseca 1970

Approximate cost red: £1,000 ($1,750)

On this list the Nuits-St-Georges is the wine to buy first, followed by the clarets beginning with the Ch. Talbot. Both the Châteauneuf-du-Pape and the Côte-Rôtie are very good, but they come from vintages lacking great reputations. The same is true of the Sassacaia, an Italian Cabernet Sauvignon. The Conn Creek Cabernet is one of the wines for current drinking, as is the 1980 Chambolle-Musigny and the 1983 Bourgogne. The Fonseca 1970 is a beautiful port and just about ready. American port fanciers have so far been most interested in the greatest vintages, for example 1963 and 1977, which means that the very good 1970s are still available at reasonable prices in Britain and America. It might be wise to buy before American drinking habits change.

Plan 2: white

Burgundy

1 case Bourgogne 'Les Clous' 1983, A. & P. de Villaine
6 bottles Chablis 'Les Clos' 1983, René Dauvissat
6 bottles Meursault 'Clos de la Barre' 1982, Domaine des Comtes Lafon

Alsace

6 bottles Riesling 'Réserve Personnelle' 1983, Hugel
6 bottles Riesling 'Schlossberg' 1983, Domaine Weinbach

California

6 bottles Chardonnay Reserve 1983, Robert Mondavi

Australia

6 bottles Chardonnay Show Reserve 1984, Rosemount

Germany

6 bottles Maximin Grünhäuser Herrenberg Auslese 1983, Count von Schubert
6 bottles Schlossböckelheimer Kupfergrube Riesling Kabinett 1983, Staatliche Weinbaudomäne

Sauternes

6 bottles Ch. Rieussec 1983
6 bottles Ch. Liot 1983

Champagne

6 bottles Louis Roederer Brut NV
6 bottles Bollinger Special Cuvée NV

Approximate cost white: £650 ($1,100)

This list is similar to Plan 1, but contains a few more wines for current drinking and twelve rather than eighteen bottles of Champagne. The wines to buy first are the Meursault and the Chablis, followed by the Ch. Rieussec.

WINE STORAGE

Once you have decided to invest in fine wine, it is important to provide proper storage. There is no point in spending money on young fine wines if they are not going to be in good condition when mature.

Wines are living compounds with acids, tannins, sugars and enzymes interacting to shape the smell and taste. Most wines have completed these processes before bottling and can be drunk straight away; fine wines, however, are in the embryonic stage when bottled. Maturation can continue because the cork ensures that oxygen will not enter the bottle. If it did, the wine would quickly oxidize, that is, turn to vinegar. Storing wine on its side keeps the cork moist, so that it will not shrink and let air into the bottle.

Other dangers to wine are heat, sudden changes in temperature, light, odours, and vibration. The last three are easily dealt with. The first two are more of a problem. The ideal place is a cool cellar, and if you have one, it is easy to prepare it for wine. Choose a spot which is well away from a heat source (a central-heating boiler, for example, or a clothes-dryer), clean the walls and floor, and treat them for damp. If you are storing wine in cases and cartons, place them on pallets, so that air can circulate around the base. Even a couple of sturdy damp-treated planks will do.

The ideal temperature is a constant 55°F (12°C), but anything within the range of 45°F (7°C) and 65°F (18°C) is acceptable. The lower the temperature, the longer the wines will take to mature. Some seasonal fluctuations in temperature are to be expected, and a variation of 10 to 15 degrees within the band will not harm the wine, as long as the changes are gradual.

The cellar arrangement can be on any lines you choose; you may wish to divide the wines by colour, region, grape variety or style. To keep track of the inventory, you will need a cellar book. Such books can be bought, but you can make your own with a loose-leaf binder. Enter each purchase with the name of the wine and vintage, the merchant's name, date of purchase, price, quantity, and whether you or your wine merchant are storing it. It is as simple as that. Each time you open a bottle note it in the book. You can also enter comments, including the wine's state of evolvement.

If you do not have a cellar, you may arrange somewhere in your house, but it is best to use it only for short- to medium-term storage. A dark, cool room or cupboard will serve that purpose, but it is no place for fine wines over the long haul. Even in Britain the summer-time temperatures will rise above the safe level, and in the United States, with its more extreme climates, the wines would be in danger most of the year round. Wines that you do not plan to drink within one to three years should be left with a merchant until they mature. If you purchased wine at auction or from a merchant not offering cellarage, you should arrange storage yourself. Your wine merchant can help you with a list of warehouses that provide storage for private clients.

The wines most suitable for long-term ageing are big tannic reds—claret, northern Rhônes, and vintage ports. Some Burgundies need several years, but in general the Pinot Noir needs less time than the Cabernet Sauvignon. California Cabernets do not have a long enough track-record to allow one to judge and most are consumed young in America. It is worth keeping good examples for five to seven years, and if you can afford to experiment, leave a few bottles even longer.

White wines generally evolve faster, but Grands Crus from the Côte de Beaune need six or seven years in good vintages, and the best of them a decade or more. Premiers Crus usually reach their peak after four or five years. California Chardonnays do not have that sort of staying power, and are better consumed after two or three years. Sweeter varieties last much longer, and a fine Sauternes might begin drinking well after six or seven years, but continue to improve for another decade. The same is true of the sweeter German varieties.

BORDEAUX BLANCS

Year	Name	Region		Price
1983	Château Tertre de Launay	Entre deux Mers		86
1983	Château d'Ardennes	Graves		98
1983	Château Respide	Graves		110
1982	Château de Fieuzal	Graves		160
1982	Château Suduiraut	Sauternes	D	240
1982	Château Haut Brion	Graves		780
1981	Château Piada	Barsac	D	160
1981	Château Carbonnieux	Graves		190
1981	Château Laville Haut Brion	Graves		440
1981	Domaine de Chevalier	Graves		440
1981	Pavillon Blanc du Château Margaux	Bordeaux		450
1979	Château Les Justices	Sauternes	D	180
1979	Château Piada	Barsac	D	180
1979	Château Rieussec	Sauternes		260
1976	Château Loubens	Sainte Croix du Mont		140
1976	Château Rayne Vigneau	Sauternes		370
1976	Château Rieussec	Sauternes		410
1976	Château d'Yquem	Sauternes		1300
1975	Château La Rame	Sainte Croix du Mont		170
1975	Château d'Arche	Sauternes		290
1975	Château Rieussec	Sauternes		430
1973	Château Filhot	Sauternes		210
1971	Château Doisy Védrines	Barsac		490
1971	Château Climens	Barsac		550
1970	Château Piada	Barsac		360
1970	Château de Malle	Sauternes		410
1970	Château Filhot	Sauternes		530
1966	Château Suduiraut	Sauternes		620
1961	Château Guiraud	Sauternes	D	680
1953	Château Gilette	Sauternes		780

BORDEAUX ROUGES

Year	Name	Region		Price
1983	Château La Tonnelle	1ers Côtes de Blaye		86
1982	Domaine de Chastelet	1ers Côtes de Bordeaux		86
1982	Château La Grave	Fronsac		96
1982	Château Tour Pibran	Pauillac	M	98
1982	Château du Glana	Saint Julien		110
1981	Château Le Piat	Côtes de Bourg		92
1981	Château Mazeris	Canon Fronsac		98
1981	Château d'Ardennes	Graves		98
1981	Château Beaumont	Haut Médoc	M	110
1981	Château La Tour de By	Médoc		110
1981	Château Fourcas Dupré	Listrac		110
1981	Château de la Dauphine	Fronsac		120
1981	Château Potensac	Médoc		120
1981	Château Bertineau Saint Vincent	Lalande de Pomerol		130
1981	Château Terrey Gros Cailloux	Saint Julien	M	140
1981	Château Labégorce Zédé	Margaux		140
1981	Château du Grand Parc	Saint Julien		150
1981	Château Phélan Ségur	Saint Estèphe		150
1981	Château Croque Michotte	Saint Émilion		160
1981	Château Croizet Bages	Pauillac		180
1980	Château Grand Corbin Despagne	Saint Émilion		120
1980	Château La Lagune	Haut Médoc		160
1980	Château L'Angelus	Saint Émilion		160
1980	Château Lynch Bages	Pauillac		180
1980	Château Nenin	Pomerol		180
1980	Château Palmer	Margaux		190
1980	Château Léoville las Cases	Saint Julien	M D	190
1980	Château Ducru Beaucaillou	Saint Julien		190
1980	Château Cos d'Estournel	Saint Estèphe		190
1980	Château Latour	Pauillac		470
1979	Château Canon La Gaffelière	Saint Émilion		160
1979	Château Chasse Spleen	Moulis		170
1979	Château Larrivet Haut Brion	Graves		180
1979	Château de Sales	Pomerol		200
1979	Château Lynch Moussas	Pauillac		200
1979	Château Lagrange	Saint Julien		210
1979	Château Prieuré Lichine	Margaux	M D	210
1979	Château Grand Puy Lacoste	Pauillac	M	240
1979	Château La Lagune	Haut Médoc	M D	240
1979	Château Montrose	Saint Estèphe	M D	240
1979	Château Pape Clément	Graves		260
1979	Château Pichon Lalande	Pauillac	M D	260
1979	Château Beychevelle	Saint Julien		260
1979	Château La Mission Haut Brion	Graves		590
1979	Château Margaux	Margaux		640
1979	Château Mouton Rothschild	Pauillac		640
1979	Château Latour	Pauillac		640
1979	Château Lafite Rothschild	Pauillac		640
1979	Château Petrus	Pomerol		710
1978	Château Phélan Ségur	Saint Estèphe		210
1978	Château Carbonnieux	Graves	M D	250
1978	Château Croque Michotte	Saint Émilion	M D	250
1978	Château Belgrave	Haut Médoc	M	250
1978	Château Haut Batailley	Pauillac	M D	280
1978	Château Rauzan Gassies	Margaux	M D	280
1978	Château Nenin	Pomerol	M D	350
1978	Domaine de Chevalier	Graves	M D	440
1977	Clos L'Église	Pomerol	M D	190
1977	Château Ducru Beaucaillou	Saint Julien	M D	240

BORDEAUX ROUGES (suite)

Year	Name	Region		Price
1976	Château Phélan Ségur	Saint Estèphe		230
1976	Château Gloria	Saint Julien		250
1976	Château Grand Puy Ducasse	Pauillac		260
1976	Château du Tertre	Margaux		260
1976	Château Haut Batailley	Pauillac		280
1976	Château Léoville Poyferré	Saint Julien	M D	340
1976	Château Montrose	Saint Estèphe	M	360
1976	Château Canon	Saint Émilion	M	370
1976	Château Calon Ségur	Saint Estèphe	M	380
1976	Château Pichon Lalande	Pauillac	D	400
1976	Château Nenin	Pomerol	M D	400
1976	Château Ducru Beaucaillou	Saint Julien	D	420
1976	Château Haut Brion	Graves		840
1976	Château Lafite Rothschild	Pauillac	D	840
1975	Château Roudier	Montagne Saint Émilion	M	180
1975	Château Les Ormes de Pez	Saint Estèphe		260
1975	Château Curé Bon La Madeleine	Saint Émilion	M	260
1975	Château La Pointe	Pomerol	M D	320
1975	Château Montrose	Saint Estèphe	M D	420
1975	Château Lynch Bages	Pauillac		440
1975	Château Brane Cantenac	Margaux	M D	440
1975	Château Beychevelle	Saint Julien		460
1975	Vieux Château Certan	Pomerol		480
1975	Château Léoville las Cases	Saint Julien	M	480
1975	Château Figeac	Saint Émilion	M D	480
1975	Château La Mission Haut Brion	Graves		970
1975	Château Mouton Rothschild	Pauillac		1100
1975	Château Haut Brion	Graves	M D	1100
1975	Château Lafite Rothschild	Pauillac	D	1100
1971	Château Lanessan	Haut Médoc		390
1971	Château Montrose	Saint Estèphe		550
1971	Château Lynch Bages	Pauillac		560
1971	Château Brane Cantenac	Margaux		560
1971	Château Léoville las Cases	Saint Julien		580
1971	Château Nenin	Pomerol		580
1971	Château Mouton Rothschild	Pauillac	D	1600
1971	Château Latour	Pauillac		1600
1971	Château Lafite Rothschild	Pauillac		1600
1970	Château Roudier	Montagne Saint Émilion	M D	220
1970	Château Capbern Gasqueton	Saint Estèphe		280
1970	Château Siran	Margaux		280
1970	Château Duhart Milon	Pauillac		420
1970	Château La Pointe	Pomerol		420
1970	Château Rauzan Gassies	Margaux		470
1970	Château La Lagune	Haut Médoc		590
1970	Château Léoville Poyferré	Saint Julien		590
1970	Château Pichon Lalande	Pauillac		680
1970	Château Léoville las Cases	Saint Julien		710
1970	Château Ducru Beaucaillou	Saint Julien	M	710
1970	Château La Mission Haut Brion	Graves		1600
1970	Château Mouton Rothschild	Pauillac	D	1900
1970	Château Haut Brion	Graves		1900
1966	Château Les Ormes de Pez	Saint Estèphe		490
1966	Château Beauregard	Pomerol		490
1966	Château Duhart Milon	Pauillac		530
1966	Château Belgrave	Haut Médoc		530
1966	Château Haut Batailley	Pauillac		580
1966	Château La Gaffelière	Saint Émilion		690
1966	Château Talbot	Saint Julien		690
1966	Château Brane Cantenac	Margaux		690
1966	Château Giscours	Margaux		690
1966	Château Haut Brion	Graves		2700
1964	Château Margaux	Margaux		2700
1961	Château Greysac	Médoc		540
1961	Château Cap de Mourlin	Saint Émilion		660
1961	Château Calon Ségur	Saint Estèphe		1800
1961	Château Léoville las Cases	Saint Julien		2100
1961	Château Ducru Beaucaillou	Saint Julien		2100
1961	Château Margaux	Margaux		3300
1955	Château Lanessan	Médoc		940
1955	Château Balestard la Tonnelle	Saint Émilion		940
1937	Château Nenin	Pomerol		3800
1937	Château Lafite Rothschild	Pauillac		5500

CHAMPAGNE

Coteaux Champenois				
S.A.	Blanc de Blancs de Chardonnay	Laurent-Perrier		190
S.A.	Bouzy Rouge	P.-L. Martin		210
S.A.	Cramant Brut, Blanc de Blancs	Champagne Larmandier	D	240
1976	Blanc de Blancs, Réserve Taillevent	Champagne Philipponnat	D	260
1976	Clos des Goisses Brut, Blanc de Noirs	Champagne Philipponnat		340

UNE CARTE SPÉCIALE
présente
tous les grands Noms de la Champagne
et les Eaux de Vie de Taillevent

D Vins servis en 1/2 Bouteille   M Vins servis en Magnum
Prix Taxes comprises. Service 15 % en sus

The wine list at Restaurant Taillevent in Paris is a model for others to emulate. All the important regions of France are represented, and a balance is struck between great names and excellent but less well-known wines. The prices, too, are quite reasonable for a restaurant of this class.

BOURGOGNES BLANCS

1982	Bourgogne Aligoté	Domaine Jayer-Gilles	88
1982	Givry	M. Derain	96
1982	Montagny	B. Michel	96
1982	Bourgogne	J.-F. Coche-Dury	110
1982	Mâcon Charnay	Domaine Manciat-Poncet	130
1982	Chablis, Montée de Tonnerre	F. Raveneau	160
1982	Pernand Vergelesses	R. Rapet	180
1982	Santenay, Passe Temps	Domaine Mestre	200
1982	Meursault Poruzot	F. Jobard	260
1982	Puligny Montrachet, Les Pucelles	Domaine Leflaive D	290
1982	Beaune, Clos des Mouches	J. Drouhin	360
1982	Chevalier Montrachet	Domaine Leflaive D	410
1981	Hautes Côtes de Nuits	Domaine Jayer-Gilles	120
1981	Saint Romain	R. Thévenin-Monthelie	140
1981	Chablis, Valmur	J.-M. Raveneau	180
1981	Meursault Narvaux	B. Michelot-Buisson D	260
1981	Chassagne Montrachet, Caillerets	E. Delagrange-Bachelet	270
1981	Puligny Montrachet, Clavoillons	Domaine Leflaive D	320
1981	Nuits Saint Georges, La Perrière	Domaine H. Gouges	320
1981	Batard Montrachet	Domaine Fontaine-Gagnard D	410
1981	Chevalier Montrachet	Domaine Leflaive D	440
1981	Corton Charlemagne	Domaine Tollot-Beaut	460
1980	Puligny Montrachet, Clavoillons	Domaine Leflaive D	220
1980	Corton Charlemagne	Domaine Tollot-Beaut	290
1980	Montrachet	E. Delagrange-Bachelet	680
1979	Chablis, Les Clos	F. Raveneau	220
1979	Meursault Narvaux	B. Michelot-Buisson D	290
1979	Chassagne Montrachet, Caillerets	E. Delagrange-Bachelet	310
1979	Meursault Désirée	Domaine des Comtes Lafon	340
1979	Nuits Saint Georges, La Perrière	Domaine H. Gouges	360
1979	Batard Montrachet	J. Gagnard D	470
1979	Chevalier Montrachet	Domaine Leflaive D	500
1978	Pouilly Fuissé, Clos du Chalet	Domaine H. Plumet	230
1978	Chassagne Montrachet	E. Delagrange-Bachelet	330
1978	Batard Montrachet	L. Gagnard D	510
1978	Corton Charlemagne	Domaine R. Rapet	560
1976	Corton Charlemagne	Domaine Bonneau du Martray	610

BOURGOGNES ROUGES

1982	Hautes Côtes de Nuits	Domaine Jayer-Gilles	98
1982	Rully, Les Clouds	P. et H. Jacqueson	120
1982	Blagny, La Pièce sous le Bois	F. Jobard	160
1982	Beaune, Clos des Mouches	A. Girardin	170
1982	Morey Saint Denis, Les Monts Luisants	A. Pernin-Rossin	190
1982	Gevrey Chambertin	A. Burguet	190
1982	Volnay, Fremiet	Marquis d'Angerville	220
1982	Nuits Saint Georges, Les Chaignots	A. Michelot M D	230
1982	Echezeaux	J. Confuron-Cotetidot	240
1982	Bonnes Mares	G. Roumier	250
1981	Bourgogne, Clos Saint Pierre	M. Derain	98
1981	Santenay, La Comme	A. Belland	140
1981	Monthelie	R. Thévenin-Monthelie	150
1981	Pernand Vergelesses	R. Rapet	160
1981	Savigny lès Beaune, Aux Vergelesses	Domaine S. Bize et Fils	170
1981	Volnay, Clos des Chênes	Domaine M. Lafarge	220
1981	Nuits Saint Georges, Les Meurgers	A. Cathiard	220
1981	Echezeaux	H. Jayer	240
1980	Chorey lès Beaune	Domaine Tollot-Beaut	130
1980	Mercurey, Les Naugues	P. et H. Jacqueson	140
1980	Santenay, Clos Faubard	Domaine Mestre	170
1980	Aloxe Corton	R. Rapet	210
1980	Beaune Grèves	Domaine Tollot-Beaut D	220
1980	Volnay, Santenots	Domaine des Comtes Lafon	220
1980	Corton Bressandes	Domaine Chandon de Briailles	230
1980	Volnay, Clos des Ducs	Marquis d'Angerville	230
1980	Gevrey Chambertin, Les Cazetiers	Domaine A. Rousseau	230
1980	Nuits Saint Georges, Les Chaignots	G. Mugneret	240
1980	Clos de la Roche	Domaine Dujac D	260
1980	Vosne Romanée, Cros Parantoux	H. Jayer	290
1979	Rully, Les Clouds	P. et H. Jacqueson	160
1979	Fixin, Clos du Chapitre	Domaine P. Gelin	170
1979	Santenay, La Comme	A. Belland	190
1979	Savigny lès Beaune, Aux Vergelesses	Domaine S. Bize et Fils M D	220
1979	Beaune	M. Gaunoux	230
1979	Morey Saint Denis	Domaine Dujac	240
1979	Aloxe Corton	Domaine Tollot-Beaut D	240
1979	Volnay, Clos des Ducs	Marquis d'Angerville M D	270
1979	Nuits Saint Georges, Les Saint Georges	Domaine H. Gouges D	270
1979	Echezeaux	Domaine Dujac	330
1979	Bonnes Mares	G. Roumier	350
1979	Pommard, Clos des Epeneaux	Comte Armand	350
1979	Ruchottes Chambertin	G. Mugneret	390
1979	Chambertin, Clos de Bèze	Domaine P. Gelin	550
1979	Romanée Saint Vivant	A. Cathiard	590
1978	Chorey lès Beaune	Domaine Tollot-Beaut	160
1978	Fixin, Clos du Chapitre	Domaine P. Gelin	190
1978	Monthelie	R. Thévenin-Monthelie	210
1978	Pernand Vergelesses	R. Rapet	230
1978	Morey Saint Denis	Domaine Dujac M	270
1978	Beaune Grèves	Domaine Tollot-Beaut D	310
1978	Gevrey Chambertin, Pte Chapelle	Domaine L. Trapet	350

BOURGOGNES ROUGES (suite)

1978	Nuits Saint Georges, Les Vaucrains	Domaine H. Gouges	350
1978	Chambolle Musigny	Domaine P. Rémy	440
1978	Bonnes Mares	G. Roumier	460
1978	Chapelle Chambertin	Domaine L. Trapet	490
1977	Mercurey	J. Maréchal	160
1976	Givry, Clos du Cellier aux Moines	Domaine Joblot	160
1976	Chorey lès Beaune	Domaine Tollot-Beaut	190
1976	Fixin, Clos du Chapitre	Domaine P. Gelin	240
1976	Beaune Grèves	Domaine Tollot-Beaut D	360
1976	Gevrey Chambertin, Les Cazetiers	Domaine A. Rousseau	410
1976	Nuits Saint Georges, Les Pruliers	Domaine H. Gouges	410
1976	Clos de la Roche	Domaine P. Rémy	480
1976	Latricières Chambertin	Domaine L. Trapet	480
1976	Corton Renardes	M. Gaunoux	580
1972	Savigny, Champ Chevrey	Domaine Tollot-Beaut	380
1972	Morey Saint Denis	Domaine Dujac	430
1972	Latricières Chambertin	Domaine L. Trapet	590
1972	Chapelle Chambertin	Domaine L. Trapet	680
1971	Beaune, Les Teurons	Domaine J. Germain	550
1971	Corton Perrières	R. Rapet	720
1969	Beaune, Cent Vignes	Domaine Duchet	770
1966	Beaune	M. Gaunoux	550
1966	Corton Renardes	M. Gaunoux	790
1961	Beaune, Cent Vignes	Domaine Duchet	840

CÔTES DU RHÔNE BLANCS

1983	Châteauneuf du Pape, Château Fortia	P. Le Roy de Boiseaumarié	170
1983	Condrieu, Château du Rozay	P. Multier	310
1982	Muscat, Beaumes de Venise	Domaine Castaud-Maurin	190
1982	Hermitage	J.-L. Chave	270
1982	Château Grillet	Domaine Neyret-Gachet	390
1981	Saint Peray	B. Gripa	130

CÔTES DU RHÔNE ROUGES

1982	Cornas	G. de Barjac	150
1981	Hermitage, Le Méal	H. Sorrel	230
1980	Crozes Hermitage, Les Picaudières	R. Roure	130
1980	Gigondas, Domaine Raspail	F. Ay	130
1980	Côte Rôtie, La Mouline	E. Guigal	290
1979	Saint Joseph	B. Gripa	160
1979	Cornas	A. Clape	170
1979	Châteauneuf du Pape, Château Fortia	P. Le Roy de Boiseaumarié	200
1979	Côte Rôtie	R. Jasmin	320
1976	Hermitage	J.-L. Chave	360
1961	Châteauneuf du Pape, Mont Redon	Domaine Fabre-Plantin	490

JURA

1982	Arbois	J. Puffeney	96
1979	Côtes du Jura	C. Clavelin	98
1979	Arbois Rouge	J. Puffeney	130
1975	Château Chalon	C. Clavelin	290
1973	Château Chalon	L. Florin	330
1969	Château Chalon	Fruitière Vinicole	380
1961	Arbois, Vin Jaune	M. Bouilleret	490

ALSACE

1982	Riesling, Réserve Particulière	T. Faller	160
1981	Tokay	F.-E. Trimbach	150
1981	Gewurztraminer	P. Rolly-Gassmann	160
1979	Pinot Noir	P. Rolly-Gassmann	160
1976	Muscat, Réserve Henny	H. Preiss-Henny	190
1971	Gewurztraminer, Vendange Tardive	L. Beyer	530

LOIRE

1983	Menetou Salon, Saint Cèols	M. Lebrun	98
1983	Quincy	C. Meunier-Lapha	120
1983	Sancerre, Clos La Néore	E. Vatan	140
1983	Pouilly Fumé, Les Loges	J. Pabiot	140
1982	Quarts de Chaume	J. Baumard	170
1981	Savennières, Coulée de Serrant	A. Joly	270
1980	Chinon Rouge, Clos de la Dioterie	C. Joguet	150
1976	Vouvray	B. Courson	210
1975	Bonnezeaux	R. Renou	230
1959	Coteaux du Layon, Chaume	Château de la Guimonière	360

CETTE CARTE
Hommage aux grands Noms de la Viticulture
a reçu le
Visa de l'Académie des Vins de France

D : Vins servis en 1/2 Bouteille   M : Vins servis en Magnum
Prix Taxes comprises, Service 15 % en sus

Glassware and Decanters

When choosing glasses and decanters the first rule is to keep it simple. Plain, uncut glasses allow the wine to be seen properly and the tulip shape directs the bouquet toward the nose. In truth one glass, the ISO tasting glass (left), is suitable for both red and white still wines. The flute is ideal for Champagne, because its small surface area preserves the delicate mousse better than saucer-style glasses.

Decanting Wine

Any wine which has thrown a deposit must be decanted to remove the sediment from the wine. This includes all vintage port and most older red wines. In addition decanting aerates the wine and allows it to be seen at its best.

The wine should be poured slowly in one continuous movement until the sediment appears in the neck of the bottle. Placing a light under the neck makes it easier to see when the sediment appears.

A general rule is that the younger the wine the earlier it should be decanted. Full-bodied wines such as northern Rhônes and Barolos benefit from early decanting. It is best to be careful with older wines and with all Burgundies: decant them only minutes before serving. After all, the wine can open up in the glass, but once lost, its fragile bouquet cannot be recovered.

Neck medallions for decanters are now coming back into fashion.

Further Reading

General

Broadbent, Michael, *The Great Vintage Wine Book*, London and New York, 1980
Broadbent, Michael, *Compleat Winetaster and Cellarman*, London, 1984
Johnson, Hugh, *Wine Companion*, London, 1983, New York (*Modern Encyclopedia of Wine*), 1983
Johnson, Hugh, *The World Atlas of Wine*, 3rd edn., London and New York, 1985
Lichine, Alexis, *Encyclopaedia of Wines and Spirits*, New York, 1974, London, 1975
Schoonmaker, Frank, *Encyclopedia of Wine*, New York, 1978, London, 1979
Spurrier, Steven, *The Wine Cellar Book*, London, 1986
Sutcliffe, Serena, *André Simon's Wines of the World*, 2nd edn., London and New York, 1981
Sutcliffe, Serena, *The Wine Drinkers' Handbook*, London and New York, 1982

France

Arlott, John and Fielden, Christopher, *Burgundy: Vines and Wines*, London, 1976
Coates, Clive, *Claret*, London, 1982
Dovaz, Michel, *Encyclopédie des Crus Classés du Bordelais*, Paris, 1981
Dovaz, Michel, *Encyclopédie des Vins de Champagne*, Paris, 1983
Duijker, Hubrecht, *The Good Wines of Bordeaux*, New York, 1983
Duijker, Hubrecht, *The Great Wine Châteaux of Bordeaux*, New York, 1983
Duijker, Hubrecht, *The Great Wines of Burgundy*, New York, 1983
Duijker, Hubrecht, *The Wines of the Loire, Alsace and Champagne*, New York, 1983
Feret, Claude, *Bordeaux et ses Vins*, 13th edn., Bordeaux, 1982
Forbes, Patrick, *Champagne*, London, 1967
George, Rosemary, *The Wines of Chablis*, London, 1984
Hanson, Anthony, *Burgundy*, London and Boston, 1982
Livingstone-Learmonth, John and Master, Melvyn, C. H., *The Wines of the Rhône*, London and Boston, 1983
Parker, Robert M., Jr., *Bordeaux*, New York, 1985
Penning-Rowsell, Edmund, *The Wines of Bordeaux*, London, 1985
Peppercorn, David, *Bordeaux*, London and Boston, 1982
Peppercorn, David, *The Pocket Guide to Bordeaux*, London, 1986
Spurrier, Steven, *French Fine Wines*, London, 1984
Sutcliffe, Serena, *The Pocket Guide to Burgundy*, London, 1986

Germany

Jamieson, Ian, *The Pocket Guide to German Wine*, London, 1984
Schoonmaker, Frank, *Wines of Germany*, London, 1983

Italy

Anderson, Burton, *Vino: The Wine and Winemakers of Italy*, Boston and London, 1980
Belfrage, Nicolas, *Life Beyond Lambrusco*, London, 1985
Dallas, Philip, *Italian Wines*, London and Boston, 1983
Hazan, Victor, *Italian Wine*, New York, 1982

Spain and Portugal

Bradford, Sarah, *The Story of Port*, London, 1983
Cossart, Noël, *Madeira, The Island Vineyard*, London, 1984
Jeffs, Julian, *Sherry*, 3rd edn., London and Boston, 1982
Read, Jan, *Rioja*, London, 1984
Read, Jan, *The Wines of Portugal*, London and Boston, 1982
Read, Jan, *The Wines of Spain*, London and Boston, 1982
Robertson, George, *Port*, London, 1982, Boston, 1983

USA

Adams, Leon D., *The Wines of America*, 3rd edn., Boston, 1984
Amerine, Maynard A., Muscatine, Doris, and Thompson, Bob, *Book of California Wine*, Berkeley and London, 1984
Dias Blue, Anthony, *The Wines of America*, San Francisco, 1985

Australia

Evans, Len, *The Complete Book of Australian Wine*, 4th edn., Sydney, 1985
Halliday, James, *Australian Wine Compendium*, London, 1986

Wine Merchants

United Kingdom

This list, representative rather than exhaustive, covers all the fine wine regions mentioned in the book. Most of these merchants will ship to any address in the United Kingdom, and many handle overseas inquiries as well. Despite the advances made by supermarkets and off-licences in recent years, when it comes to buying fine wine the first rule remains: choose a good wine merchant. We have singled out three from the list for special mention. Listed alphabetically these are:

Adnams, The Crown, High Street, Southwold, Suffolk. Telephone 0502 724222. An admirable list. Good selection from all of the major regions of France; excellent Italian wines and choice examples from California's best wineries. The list is well written and includes notes on many of the wines.

Lay & Wheeler, 6 Culver Street West, Colchester, Essex. Telephone 0206 67261. In every respect an exemplary wine merchant. The list, with over 1,200 wines, is the most comprehensive in the country, the prices are reasonable and the service is helpful and well-informed.

Henry Townsend & Co., York House, Oxford Road, Beaconsfield, Bucks. Telephone 0494 678291. A smaller operation than Adnams or Lay & Wheeler and without a retail shop, but none the worse for that. Especially notable for claret and German wines, and opening offers at very keen prices.

Averys of Bristol, 11 Park Street, Bristol. Telephone 0272 214141. Burgundy specialists; comprehensive and well-annotated opening offers, especially for claret.

Berry Bros. & Rudd Ltd., 3 St James's Street, London SW1. Telephone 01-839 9033. The great traditionalist. Best for claret and vintage port. Outstanding service.

David Baillie Vintners, The Sign of the Lucky Horseshoe, Longbrook Street, Exeter, Devon. Telephone 0392 31351. Bordeaux and Burgundy.

Ballantynes of Cowbridge, Stallcourt House, Llanblethian, Cowbridge, South Glamorgan. Telephone 044 63 3044. Fine domaine-bottled red and white Burgundies.

Bibendum Wine, 113 Regents Park Road, London NW1. Telephone 01-586 9761. Relatively new. Wide range of fine wines. Opening offers.

G. E. Bromley & Sons, London Street, Leicester. Telephone 0533 768471. Claret and Rhône.

D. Byrne & Co., 12 King Street, Clitheroe, Lancashire. Telephone 0200 23152. German wines and claret.

The Champagne House, 15 Dawson Place, London W2. Telephone 01-221 5538. Large selection of non-vintage and vintage Champagnes including de luxe cuvées.

Chaplin & Son, 35 Rowlands Road, Worthing, West Sussex. Telephone 0903 35888. Wide range of fine wines, sherry, vintage port.

Corney & Barrow, 12 Helmet Row, London EC1. Telephone 01-251 4051. Long-established city merchant. Fine claret, especially the Pomerols of J-P Moueix. Good value opening offers and bin ends.

Domaine Direct, 29 Wilmington Square, London WC1. Telephone 01-837 3521. Large selection of domaine-bottled red and white Burgundy and Chablis.

Eaton Elliot Winebrokers, 15 London Road, Alderley Edge, Cheshire. Telephone 0625 582354. Fine wines of France. Excellent service.

Farr Vintners Ltd., Wheelwrights, 12 Upper Green, Tewin, Hertfordshire. Telephone 043 879 307. Wholesalers. Especially good for fine red and white Burgundies and the hard-to-locate wines of Pomerol.

Alexander Findlater & Co. Ltd., Heveningham High House, near Halesworth, Suffolk. Telephone 098 683 274. Also: 77 Abbey Road, London NW8. Telephone 01-624 7311. Australian wine specialists with the most extensive list in Britain; also a good Burgundy selection.

Great American Food & Wine Co., Haslemere, 8 Silver Lane, Purley, Surrey. Telephone 01-660 6304. California and New York State.

Peter Green & Co., 37A Warrender Park Road, Edinburgh. Telephone 031-229 5925. Most fine wine regions of France. Rioja.

Gerard Harris, 2 Green End Street, Aston Clinton, Aylesbury, Bucks. Telephone 0296 631041. Best for claret. Also northern Rhône.

John Harvey & Sons Ltd., 27 Pall Mall, London SW1. Telephone 01-839 4695. Also: 12 Denmark Street, Bristol. Telephone 0272 23759. Claret, especially Ch. Latour. Sherry and port.

Haynes Hanson & Clark, 36 Kensington Church Street, London W8. Telephone 01-937 4650. Well-chosen list of fine Bordeaux and, especially, Burgundy.

Hicks & Don, 4 The Market Place, Westbury, Wiltshire. Telephone 0373 864723. Also: Park House, Elmham, Dereham, Norfolk. Telephone 036 281 571. Good value opening offers. Sherry. Italian wines.

J. E. Hogg, 61 Cumberland Street, Edinburgh. Telephone 031-556 4025. Good selection from most of Europe's fine wine regions.

The Hungerford Wine Company, 128 High Street, Hungerford, Berks. Telephone 0488 83238. Good value opening offers, especially early-commitment Bordeaux scheme.

Justerini & Brooks, 61 St James's Street, London, SW1. Telephone 01-493 8721. All the classics; a good selection of older wines.

Laymont and Shaw Ltd., The Old Chapel, Millpool, Truro, Cornwall. Telephone 0872 70545. Outstanding list of fine Spanish wines featuring the Bodega La Rioja Alta.

Layton's Wine Merchants, 20 Midland Road, London NW1. Telephone 01-388 5081. Specialists in claret, Burgundy and Rhône, selling mainly to restaurants, institutions and investors. Very wide range of Burgundy chosen by Graham Chidgey.

O. W. Loeb, 15 Jermyn Street, London SW1. Telephone 01-734 5878. No retail premises but this is Britain's premier German wine merchant. They are also agents for Paul Jaboulet and Domaine Weinbach (Faller) of Alsace.

Andrew Mead Wines, Shovelstrode, Presteigne, Radnorshire. Telephone 054 76 268. Small well-chosen selection of fine French wines. Good German list. Helpful service.

Reid Wines, The Mill, Marsh Lane, Hallatrow, Bristol, Avon. Telephone 0761 52645. Fine and rare wines, particularly old clarets.

Tanners Wines Ltd., 26 Wyle Cop, Shrewsbury, Shropshire. Telephone 0743 53421. Comprehensive list from all the fine wine regions of France. Excellent service. Only the unavailability of cellarage keeps Tanners out of the élite group.

T. & W. Wines, 51 King Street, Thetford, Norfolk. Telephone 0842 63855. Fine and rare wines, especially claret.

La Vigneronne, 105 Old Brompton Road, London SW7. Telephone 01-589 6113. An excellent list featuring the finest producers from around the world. Especially notable are Italy, California, Australia and Sauternes. Regular tastings of fine wines.

Willoughby's Ltd., 53 Cross Street, Manchester. Telephone 061-834 0641. Wide range of fine wines from most important regions.

Windrush Wines, The Barracks, Cecily Hill, Cirencester, Gloucestershire. Telephone 0285 67121. Fine selection of American wines, particularly from the Pacific North-west. Good Italian wines and a selection of the best of Bordeaux, Burgundy and Germany.

The Wine Studio, 9 Eccleston Street, London SW1. Telephone 01-730 7596. Now part of Les Amis du Vin. The largest selection of fine California wines in Britain.

Yapp Brothers, The Old Brewery, Mere, Wiltshire. Telephone 0747 860423. Fine Rhône wines such as Chave and Jasmin. Also Loire.

Yorkshire Fine Wines, Nun Monkton, York, North Yorkshire. Telephone 0901 30131. Fine wines of France. Burgundy.

WINE CLUBS

Les Amis du Vin, 7 Ariel Way, Wood Lane, London W12. Telephone 01-740 0053, 01-743 2066. California, Bordeaux, and Rhône. Special offers and regular tastings.

German Wine Club, 7 Linkside Avenue, Oxford. Telephone 0865 58755. Estate-bottled German wines.

Malmaison Wine Club, 28 Midland Road, London, NW1. Telephone 01-388 5086. We must declare an interest, as Steven Spurrier is a director of Malmaison. Bordeaux, Burgundy, Rhône, opening offers.

Le Nez Rouge Wine Club, 12 Brewery Road, London N7. Telephone 01-609 4711. Burgundy, Italy.

The Wine Society, Gunnels Wood Road, Stevenage, Hertfordshire. Telephone 0438 314161. The pioneer wine club. Claret, Burgundy, Rhône, Italy.

The Wine Club, New Aquitaine House, Paddock Road, Reading, Berks. RG4 0JY. Telephone 0734 481713. Originally the Sunday Times Wine Club, founded by Tony Laithwaite with Hugh Johnson as Chairman. Very good for inexpensive wines from the world over.

USA

This list is also representative, though it excludes those areas where the state is the retailer. The listings are in alphabetical order by state.

California (Northern)

David Berkeley, 515 Pavillons Lane, Sacramento, California. Telephone 916 929 4422.

Beltramo's Wine and Spirits, Menlo Park, California. Telephone 415 854 7545.

Conti Bros. Market, 5770 Freeport Boulevard, Sacramento, California. Telephone 916 391 0300. Italian wines a speciality.

Draper and Esquin, 655 Davis Street, San Francisco, California. Telephone 415 397 3797. Long-established wine merchants, best known for Burgundy selection.

Kermit Lynch, 1605 San Pablo Avenue, Berkeley, California 94702. Telephone 415 524 1524. Outstanding selection of small domaines, particularly from Burgundy and Rhône.

Pacific Wine Company, 2999 Washington Street, San Francisco, California 94115. Telephone 415 922 8600. Burgundy, Rhône and California.

California (Southern)

Los Angeles Wine Company, 4935 McConnell Avenue, Mar Vista, California. Telephone 213-306-9463. Best for Bordeaux and white Burgundy.

The Wine House, 2311 Cotner, West Los Angeles, California. Telephone 213-479-3731. Excellent selection from the major wine regions of Europe.

Colorado

Applejack Liquors, Wheat Ridge, Colorado. Telephone 303 233 3331.

District of Columbia

Calvert-Woodley Liquors, 4339 Connecticut Avenue N.W., Washington D.C. Telephone 202 966 4400.

MacArthur Beverages, 4877 MacArthur Boulevard N.W., Washington D.C. Telephone 202 338 1433.

Mayflower Wines & Spirits, 2115 M Street N.W., Washington D.C. Telephone 202 463 7950. Good Italian list.

Florida

Laurenzo's Italian Center, North Miami Beach, Florida. Telephone 305 945 6381.

Georgia

Happy Herman, 2299 Cheshire Bridge Road N.E., Atlanta, Georgia 30324. Telephone 404 321 3012.

Illinois

Connoisseur's, 77 West Chestnut, Chicago, Illinois 60610. Telephone 312 642 2375. Excellent Rhône and Burgundy selections.

Sam's Wine Warehouse, 1000 West North Avenue, Chicago, Illinois 60622. Telephone 312 664 4394.

Louisiana

Martin Wine Cellar, 3827 Barrone Street, New Orleans, Louisiana 70115. Telephone 504 899 7411.

Massachusetts

Berman's of Lexington, 55 Massachusetts Avenue, Lexington, Massachusetts 02173. Telephone 617 862 0515.

Brookline Liquor Mart, 1354 Commonwealth Avenue, Allston, Massachusetts 02134. Telephone 617 734 7700.

Martignetti's Liquors, 1650 Soldier's Field Road, Brighton, Mass. 02135. Telephone 617 782 3700. Good selection, especially from Italy; keen prices.

Wine Cellar of Silene, 320 Bear Hill Road, Waltham, Massachusetts 02154. Telephone 617 890 2121.

Michigan

Merchant of Vino, 29525 Northwestern Highway, Southfield, Michigan 48034. Telephone 313 354 6505.

Village Corner, 601 South Forest, Ann Arbor, Michigan 48104. Telephone 313 995 1818.

Vintage Wine Company, 185 Malow Street, Mount Clemens, Michigan 48043. Telephone 313 463 3800. Fine estate-bottled German wines.

New York

Garnet Liquors, 929 Lexington Avenue, New York, New York 10021. Telephone 212 772 3211. Less comprehensive selection than some other New York merchants, but very keen prices.

Goldstar Wines, 103–5 Queens Boulevard, Forest Hill, New York. Telephone 718 459 0200. America's premier Italian wine merchant.

Morrell & Co. 535 Madison Avenue, New York, New York 10022. Telephone 212 688 9370. Excellent range including rare old clarets.

Premier Center, Kenmore, New York. Telephone 716 873 6688.

Sherry-Lehmann, 679 Madison Avenue, New York, New York 10022. Telephone 212 838 7500. Comprehensive selections of Bordeaux, Burgundy, and vintage port.

D. Sokolin Co., 178 Madison Avenue, New York, New York 10016. Telephone 212 532 5893.

Texas

La Cave, 2019 North Lamar, Dallas, Texas 7520. Telephone 214 871 2073. Particularly good for Bordeaux.

Dan's Cellars, 1327 Congress, Austin, Texas 78704. Telephone 512 444 1089.

Marty's, 3316 Oak Lawn, Dallas, Texas 75219. Telephone 214 526 7796. California and classic wines of France.

Richard's, 1701 Brun Street, Houston, Texas 77019. Telephone 713 529 6262. Houston's carriage trade wine merchant.

Spec's, 2410 Smith Street, Houston, Texas 77006. Telephone 713 526 8787.

Washington

Esquin Wine Merchants, 1516 First Avenue South, Seattle, Washington 98134. Telephone 206 682 7374.

Price Guide

The following are representative 1985 United Kingdom retail prices per bottle including VAT at 15 per cent unless otherwise stated. Auction prices, taken mainly from Christie's 1984–5 season, are per dozen bottles (or equivalent) duty paid. M = magnum; H = half bottle.

Red Bordeaux
Premiers Grands Crus Classés

CH. LAFITE-ROTHSCHILD (Pauillac)

	Retail Price	Auction Price
1983	£475 per dozen ex cellars	
1982	£56	
1981	£39	
1979	£34	£330
1978	£57	£700
1976	£45	£480
1975	£89	£800
1971		£460
1970	£95	£940
1966	£120	£940
1961	£230	£3,200

CH. LATOUR (Pauillac)

	Retail Price	Auction Price
1983	£395 per dozen ex cellars	
1982	£48.50	
1981	£31.25	
1979	£32	M £290
1978	£52	£560
1976	£42	£380
1975	£65	£680
1971	£50	£400
1970	£75	£820
1966	£87	£1,000
1961	£220	£2,600

CH. MARGAUX (Margaux)

	Retail Price	Auction Price
1983		
1982	£44	
1981	£40	
1979	£35	£290
1978	£45	
1976		£460
1975	£54	£600
1971	£33.50	£440
1966	£75	£960
1961		£2,200

CH. MOUTON-ROTHSCHILD (Pauillac)

	Retail Price	Auction Price
1983	£430 per dozen ex cellars	
1982	£56	
1981	£47	
1979	£32	£310
1978	£43.50	£700
1976	£42	£420
1975	£57.50	£700

	Retail Price	Auction Price
1971	£50	£440
1970	£75	£840
1966	£100	£1,000
1961	£212	£3,000

CH. HAUT-BRION (Graves)

	Retail Price	*Auction Price
1983	£430 per dozen ex cellars	
1982	£44	£580
1981	£43	£250
1979	£28	£300
1978	£37	£480
1976	£35	£400
1975	£52	£620
1971	£50	£420
1970	£65	£800
1966	£70	£980
1961	£202	£2,300

*From Haut-Brion Anniversary Sale 16 May 1985

St-Emilion
Premiers Grands Crus Classés

CH. AUSONE

	Retail Price	Auction Price
1983	£395 per dozen ex cellars	
1982		
1981	£32	
1979	£37	
1978	£49	£500
1976	£42	£290
1975		£440
1971		£350
1970	£39	£500
1966		(1983) £390
1961		£1,200

CH. CHEVAL BLANC

	Retail Price	Auction Price
1983	£496 per dozen ex cellars	
1982	£44	
1981	£33	
1979	£30	£250
1978	£45	£360
1976	£46	£340
1975	£57	£560
1971	£50	£425
1970	£70	£660
1966	£80	£880
1961		£1,700

Pomerol

CH. PETRUS

	Retail Price	Auction Price
1983	£1,500 per dozen ex cellars	
1982	£215	
1981	£106	
1979	£98	£780
1978	£103	£1,000
1976	£92	£920
1975	£179	M £1,850
1971	£212	£2,100
1970	£202	£2,300
1966		£2,400
1961		£9,500

St-Estèphe

CH. COS D'ESTOURNEL (2ème Cru)

	Retail Price	Auction Price
1983	£110 per dozen ex cellars	
1982	£17.83	
1981	£11.46	
1979		£150
1978	£15.64	£165
1976	£14.50	£135
1975	£20.30	£210
1971	£38 M	£160
1970		£280
1966	£28	£330
1961		£680

CH. MONTROSE (2ème Cru)

	Retail Price	Auction Price
1982	£14.00	
1981	£11.33	
1979	£11.16	M £145
1978	£14.85	£160
1976	£12.41	£160
1975	£16.00	£270
1971		£180
1970	£30.13	£310
1961	£57.73	£640

Pauillac

CH. PICHON-LALANDE (2ème Cru)

	Retail Price	Auction Price
1983	£150 per dozen ex cellars	
1982	£19	
1981	£11.50	
1979	£15.64	£125
1978	£19	£250
1976	£17.50	£190

Retail Price	Auction Price
1975 £20.40	£220
1971	£220
1970 £27.60	£320
1966 £42	£380
1961	£720

GRAND PUY-LACOSTE (5ème Cru)

Retail Price	Auction Price
1983 £90 per dozen ex cellars	
1982 £15	
1981 £10.30	
1979 £11.16	£70
1978	£185
1976 £13.94	£145
1975 £15.99	£180
1971	£125
1970 £29	£200
1966 £36	£200
1961 £50	£480

St-Julien

CH. DUCRU-BEAUCAILLOU (2ème Cru)

Retail Price 6/85	Auction Price
1983 £159 per dozen ex cellars	
1982 £19	
1981 £14.38	
1979 £13	£150
1978 £18.40	£220
1976 £20	£200
1975 £24.67	£310
1971 £21	£195
1970 £35	£400
1966 £55	£480
1961 £170 M	£840

CH. GRUAUD-LAROSE (2ème Cru)

Retail Price	Auction Price 12/84
1983 £115 per dozen ex cellars	
1982 £14.55	
1981 £12	
1979 £11	£95
1978 £12	£155
1976 £13.33	£125
1975 £16	£155
1971 £18.25	£160
1970 £24	£260
1966 £33.49	£350
1961 £59	£740

CH. LEOVILLE-LAS-CASES (2ème Cru)

Retail Price	Auction Price
1983 £159 per dozen ex cellars	
1982 £22	
1981 £14.38	
1979 £15.64	£145
1978 £18.40	£210
1976 £19.15	£165
1975 £28.33	£280
1971 £23	£230

Retail Price	Auction Price
1970 £32	£360
1966 £45	£460
1961 £66	£640

CH. TALBOT (4ème Cru)

Retail Price	Auction Price
1983 £100 per dozen ex cellars	
1982 £13	
1981 £9.50	
1979 £10	£86
1978 £10	£130
1976 £10	£130
1975 £16	£150
1971 £16	£155
1970 £20	£240
1966 £27	£260
1961 £46	£420

Margaux

CH. PALMER (3ème Cru)

Retail Price	Auction Price
1983 £295 per dozen ex cellars	
1982 £27.83	
1981 £21.79	
1979 £20.70	£260
1978 £35	£400
1976 £28.69	£300
1975 £54.89	£520
1971 £36.08	£350
1970 £56.01	£700
1961 £230	£2,600

Haut-Médoc

CH. LA LAGUNE (3ème Cru)

Retail Price	Auction Price
1983 £87.60 per dozen ex cellars	
1982 £13.90	
1981 £11.16	
1979 £11	£72
1978 £13.19	£150
1976 £17.48	£145
1975 £17.54	£200
1971 £16.78	£185
1970 £27.50	£230
1966 £23	£340
1961	£420

Graves

Grand Cru

LA MISSION-HAUT-BRION

Retail Price	Auction Price
1983 £396 per dozen ex cellars	
1982 £40.48	
1981 £28.41	
1979 £25	£250
1978 £35	£320
1976 £33.60	£290

Retail Price	Auction Price
1975 £110 M	£580
1971	£370
1970 £60	£620
1966	£880
1961	£2,200

Grand Cru

DOMAINE DE CHEVALIER

Retail Price	Auction Price
1983 £150 per dozen ex cellars	
1982 £17.83	
1981 £15.30	
1979 £18.85	£115
1978 £14.95	
1976	£120
1975 £17.10	£200
1970 £42 M	£310
1966	£370
1961 £60	£460

St-Emilion

CH. FIGEAC (Premier Grand Cru Classé)

Retail Price	Auction Price
1983 £200 per dozen ex cellars	
1982 £17.37	
1981 £17	
1979 £13.34	£150
1978	£180
1976 £17.73	£135
1975 £24.67	£280
1971	£310
1970 £35.00	£440
1961	(Sotheby's 1983) £480

Pomerol

CH. LA CONSEILLANTE

Retail Price	Auction Price
1982 £27.30	
1979 £15	£135
1978 £14.95	
1976	£150
1975	£240
1971 £24	£185
1970 £33.10	£350
1966	£400
1961	£790

CH. LATOUR-A-POMEROL

Retail Price	Auction Price
1983 £165 per dozen ex cellars	
1982 £31.60	
1981 £15.80	
1979 £14.80	
1978 £16.22	
1975 £24	
1971 £24	£210
1970 £33.10	(Sotheby's) £250

Moulis

CH. CHASSE-SPLEEN (Cru Grand Bourgeois Exceptionnel)

Retail Price		Auction Price
1983	£61.20 per dozen ex cellars	
1982	£7.48	
1981	£7.33	
1979	£8.49	£56
1978	£9.66	£130
1976	£9.78	£90
1975	£10	
1970	£16.30	£165
1966		£130
1961		£220

Haut-Médoc

CH. CISSAC (Cru Grand Bourgeois Exceptionnel)

Retail Price		Auction Price
1983	£53.40 per dozen ex cellars	
1981	£6.75	
1979	£6.73	£82
1978	£8.17	£110
1976		£80
1975	£11.02	£92
1971	£11.42	£100
1970		£120
1961		£190

White Bordeaux

1983

Dry

		Retail Price
Ch. Carbonnieux	Cru Classé, Graves	£6.32
Domaine de Chevalier	Cru Classé, Graves	£20.70
Ch. Haut-Brion Blanc	Cru Classé, Graves	£43.70

Sweet (all prices per case ex cellars)

Ch. Coutet	1er Cru, Barsac	£128
Ch. Doisy-Daëne	2ème Cru, Barsac	£80.40
Ch. Raymond-Lafon	Sauternes	£140
Ch. Rieussec	1er Cru, Sauternes	£99
Ch. Suduiraut	1er Cru, Sauternes	£138

1982

Dry

Ch. Carbonnieux	Cru Classé, Graves	£7.02
Domaine de Chevalier	Cru Classé, Graves	£22.42
Ch. Haut-Brion Blanc	Cru Classé, Graves	£48.30

Sweet

Ch. Doisy-Daëne	2ème Cru, Barsac	£7.29
Ch. Rieussec	1er Cru, Sauternes	£8.22
Ch. Suduiraut	1er Cru, Sauternes	£16.50

1981

Dry

Domaine de Chevalier	Cru Classé, Graves	£15.64
Ch. Haut-Brion Blanc	Cru Classé, Graves	£44.85
Pavillon Blanc du Château Margaux		£20.70

Sweet

Ch. Bastor-Lamontagne	Sauternes	£6.90
Ch. Doisy-Daëne	2ème Cru, Barsac	£7.42
Ch. Lamothe-Guignard	2ème Cru, Sauternes	£7.79
Ch. de Rayne-Vigneau	1er Cru, Sauternes	£6.90
Ch. d'Yquem	1er Grand Cru, Sauternes	£57.50

1980

Dry

Pavillon Blanc du Château Margaux		£14.51

Sweet

		Retail Price
Ch. Bastor-Lamontagne	Sauternes	£5.50
Ch. Raymond-Lafon	Sauternes	£13.50
Ch. Rieussec	1er Cru, Sauternes	£8.80
Ch. Suduiraut	1er Cru, Sauternes	£10.43
Ch. d'Yquem	1er Grand Cru, Sauternes	£42.49

1979

Dry

Ch. Carbonnieux	Cru Classé, Graves	£8.00

Sweet

Ch. Coutet	1er Cru, Barsac		£11.50
Ch. Filhot	2ème Cru, Sauternes		£7.44
Ch. Raymond-Lafon	Sauternes		£12.45
Ch. Suduiraut	1er Cru, Sauternes	H	£6.59

1978

Sweet

Ch. Lafaurie-Peyraguey	1er Cru, Sauternes	£8.97
Ch. Raymond-Lafon	Sauternes	£12.50
Ch. Rieussec	1er Cru, Sauternes	£9.68
Ch. d'Yquem	1er Grand Cru, Sauternes	£53.00

1976

Sweet

Ch. Filhot	2ème Cru, Sauternes	M	£25.00
Ch. Guiraud	1er Cru, Sauternes	H	£6.89
Ch. d'Yquem	1er Grand Cru, Sauternes		£50.40

1975

Sweet

Ch. Climens	1er Cru, Barsac	£17.25
Ch. Coutet	1er Cru, Barsac	£13.25
Ch. Suduiraut	1er Cru, Sauternes	£18.40
Ch. d'Yquem	1er Grand Cru, Sauternes	£63.25

Red Burgundy

1983

Village		Retail Price
Gevrey-Chambertin	Bernard Maume	£10.01
Chambolle-Musigny	Georges Roumier	ex cellars £7.60
Vosne-Romanée	Jean Grivot	ex cellars £7.55
Aloxe-Corton	Tollot-Beaut	£9.78
Chorey-Lès-Beaune	Tollot-Beaut	£6.04
Volnay	Jean Germain	£9.11

Premiers Crus		
Gevrey-Chambertin, Clos des Varoilles	Domaine des Varoilles	£12.60
Gevrey-Chambertin, Lavaux St-Jacques	Drouhin-Larose	£11.50
Morey-St-Denis, Clos de la Bussière	Georges Roumier	ex cellars £7.25
Chambolle-Musigny, Les Amoureuses	Georges Roumier	ex cellars £12.75
Vosne-Romanée, Les Suchots	Mongeard-Mugneret	£14.47
Vosne-Romanée, Les Chaumes	Jean Grivot	ex cellars £10.75
Nuits-St-Georges, Les Chaignots	Alain Michelot	£13.03
Nuits-St-Georges, Les Perrières	Robert Chevillon	£10.83
Beaune, Clos du Roi	Tollot-Beaut	£10.37
Beaune, Clos des Mouches	Joseph Drouhin	£11.27
Pommard, Le Clos Blanc	Machard de Gramont	£11.73
Volnay, Clos de la Bousse d'Or	Pousse d'Or	£15.81

Grands Crus		
Chapelle-Chambertin	Damoy	£11.75
Charmes-Chambertin	Joseph Roty	£16.30
Griotte-Chambertin	Joseph Drouhin	£16.22
Mazis-Chambertin	Bernard Maume	£14.40
Chambertin	Joseph Drouhin	£22.43
Bonnes Mares	Domaine des Varoilles	£16.95
Bonnes Mares	Georges Roumier	ex cellars £13.35
Clos de la Roche	Georges Lignier	£14.55
Musigny	Joseph Drouhin	£26.57
Musigny	Georges Roumier	ex cellars £16.45
Clos de Vougeot	Jean Grivot	ex cellars £12.30
Clos de Vougeot	Mongeard-Mugneret	£23.38
Echézeaux	Mongeard-Mugneret	£17.05
Grands Echézeaux	Joseph Drouhin	£32.80
Romanée-St-Vivant	Michel Voarick	ex cellars £20.90
Corton	Tollot-Beaut	£13.08
Corton Bressandes	Tollot-Beaut	£13.60
Corton Clos du Roi	Michel Voarick	£11.79

1982

Village		
Gevrey-Chambertin	Armand Rousseau	£8.00
Morey-Saint-Denis	Dujac	£8.94
Chambolle-Musigny	Georges Roumier	£9.87
Vosne-Romanée	Jean Grivot	£9.11
Nuits-St-Georges	Alain Michelot	£9.57
Aloxe-Corton	Tollot-Beaut	£8.88
Savigny-Lès-Beaune	Simon Bize	£7.39
Pommard	Mussy	£9.83
Volnay	Montille	£8.00
Chassagne-Montrachet	Jean-Marc Morey	£6.42

Premiers Crus		
Gevrey-Chambertin, Clos St-Jacques	Armand Rousseau	£15.99
Gevrey-Chambertin, Combottes	Dujac	£12.73

Morey-Saint-Denis, 1er Cru	Dujac	£11.15
Chambolle-Musigny, Les Charmes	Remoissenet	£11.07
Vosne-Romanée, Les Suchots	Mongeard-Mugneret	£11.45
Nuits-St-Georges, Les Pruliers	Jean Grivot	£11.93
Nuits-St-Georges, Les Vaucrains	Alain Michelot	£11.27
Pernand-Vergelesses, Ile des Vergelesses	Rollin Père et Fils	£7.35
Savigny-Lès-Beaune, Guettes	Machard de Gramont	£6.90
Beaune, Epenottes	Domaine Mussy	£9.39
Beaune, Clos des Ursules	Louis Jadot	£8.30
Pommard, Le Clos Blanc	Machard de Gramont	£8.91
Pommard, Les Jarollières	Pousse d'Or	£12.65
Volnay, Clos de la Bousse d'Or	Pousse d'Or	£13.78
Volnay, Champans	Comtes de Lafon	£9.78
Santenay, Gravières	Pousse d'Or	£7.76

Grands Crus		
Charmes-Chambertin	Dujac	£13.98
Mazis-Chambertin	Armand Rousseau	£11.45
Chambertin Clos de Bèze	Armand Rousseau	£19.90
Bonnes Mares	Georges Roumier	£18.69
Clos de la Roche	Dujac	£14.24
Clos Saint-Denis	Dujac	£15.03
Musigny	Comte de Vogüé	£23.95
Clos de Vougeot	Mongeard-Mugneret	£18.11
Grands Echézeaux	Romanée-Conti	£34.50
Richebourg	Henri Jayer	£41.20
La Tâche	Romanée-Conti	£53.67
Corton Bressandes	Tollot-Beaut	£13.15
Corton Renardes	Michel Voarick	£11.55

1981

Village		
Gevrey-Chambertin	Armand Rousseau	£8.21
Nuits-St-Georges	Alain Michelot	£9.13
Aloxe-Corton	Tollot-Beaut	£8.76
Pommard	Domaine Mussy	£9.83

Premiers Crus		
Morey-Saint-Denis, Clos des Ormes	Georges Lignier	£8.38
Nuits-St-Georges, Les Vaucrains	Alain Michelot	£10.30
Pommard, Grands Epenots	Michel Gaunoux	£12.63

Grands Crus		
Charmes-Chambertin	Domaine Dujac	£13.88
Chambertin	Adrien Belland	£16.30
Clos Saint-Denis	Georges Lignier	£12.70
Clos de la Roche	Domaine Ponsot	£13.22
Bonnes Mares	Domaine Georges Roumier	£16.95
Echézeaux	Henri Jayer	£19.38

1980

Village		
Gevrey-Chambertin	Domaine Clos Frantin	£8.24
Morey-Saint-Denis	Domaine Ponsot	£9.20
Chambolle-Musigny	Michel et Georges Clerget	£9.20
Vosne-Romanée	Robert Arnoux	£11.50
Aloxe-Corton	Tollot-Beaut	£11.17
Pommard	Ampeau et Fils	£10.02

Premiers Crus

Gevrey-Chambertin, Clos St-Jacques	Armand Rousseau	£16.62
Gevrey-Chambertin, Aux Combottes	Dujac	£13.65
Morey-Saint-Denis, Clos de la Bussière	Georges Roumier	£10.78
Chambolle-Musigny, Les Amoureuses	Comte de Vogüé	£15.34
Vosne-Romanée, Les Suchots	Henri Lamarche	£13.25
Vosne-Romanée, Les Chaumes	Robert Arnoux	£12.94
Nuits-St-Georges, Les Vaucrains	Robert Chevillon	£10.50
Pernand-Vergelesses, Ile des Vergelesses	Chandon de Briailles	£7.10
Savigny-Lès-Beaune, Les Lavières	Chandon de Briailles	£6.90
Beaune, Clos des Ursules	Louis Jadot	£10.78
Beaune, Clos des Mouches	Joseph Drouhin	£10.35
Pommard, Rugiens	Montille	£13.23
Volnay, Santenots	Comtes Lafon	£9.89
Volnay, Clos de la Bousse d'Or	Pousse d'Or	£13.36
Volnay, Clos des Ducs	Marquis d'Angerville	£16.10

Grands Crus

Charmes-Chambertin	Domaine des Varoilles	£11.06
Latricières-Chambertin	Louis Trapet	£12.08
Ruchottes-Chambertin Clos des Ruchottes	Armand Rousseau	£14.38
Chambertin	Armand Rousseau	£23.70
Chambertin	Louis Trapet	£17.25
Chambertin Clos de Bèze	Armand Rousseau	£20.70
Clos de la Roche	Dujac	£13.75
Clos Saint-Denis	Dujac	£14.60
Bonnes Mares	Georges Roumier	£15.34
Musigny	Comte de Vogüé	£26.45
Musigny	Georges Roumier	£27.80
Clos de Vougeot	Robert Arnoux	£20.12
Richebourg	Romanée-Conti	£40.25
Corton	Bonneau du Martray	£13.80
Corton Bressandes	Tollot-Beaut	£14.95

1979

Village

Gevrey-Chambertin	Armand Rousseau	£11.82
Morey-Saint-Denis	Dujac	£18.87
Chambolle-Musigny	Georges Roumier	£12.54
Aloxe-Corton	Louis Latour	£11.21
Pommard	Ampeau	£11.01
Volnay	Montille	£11.35

Premiers Crus

Gevrey-Chambertin, Clos St-Jacques	Armand Rousseau	£18.70
Nuits-St-Georges, Les Vaucrains	Henri Gouges	£14.24
Nuits-St-Georges, Clos des Porets St-Georges	Henri Gouges	£13.30
Aloxe-Corton, Les Meix	Edouard Delaunay	£11.35
Beaune, Clos des Ursules	Louis Jadot	£13.08
Beaune, Les Boucherottes	Louis Jadot	£11.59
Pommard, Rugiens	Montille	£18.78
Pommard, Grands Epenots	Michel Gaunoux	£14.38
Volnay, Santenots	Comtes Lafon	£11.50
Volnay, Caillerets	Pousse d'Or	£12.50
Santenay, Clos Faubard	Mestre Père et Fils	£7.48

Grands Crus

Chapelle-Chambertin	Louis Trapet	£15.53
Charmes-Chambertin	Armand Rousseau	£18.26
Chambertin	Louis Trapet	£20.70
Clos Saint-Denis	Dujac	£12.59
Clos de la Roche	Dujac	£14.89
Bonnes Mares	Georges Roumier	£21.99
Musigny	Comte de Vogüé	£41.21
Clos de Vougeot	Georges Roumier	£16.85
Grands Echézeaux	Romanée-Conti	£44.00
La Tâche	Romanée-Conti	£64.00
Romanée-Conti	Romanée-Conti	£110.00
Corton	Bonneau du Martray	£14.38
Corton Pougets	Louis Jadot	£13.08

1978

Village

Gevrey-Chambertin	Louis Latour	£13.36
Chambolle-Musigny	Remoissenet	£16.82
Vosne-Romanée	English Bottled (Avery's)	£14.52
Aloxe-Corton	Camille Giroud	£11.06
Volnay	Camille Giroud	£11.06

Premiers Crus

Gevrey-Chambertin, Clos St-Jacques	Armand Rousseau	£30.00
Chambolle-Musigny, Charmes	English Bottled (Avery's)	£13.94
Vougeot, Les Petits Vougeots	Bertagna	£10.97
Nuits-St-Georges, Clos des Porets St-Georges	Henri Gouges	£18.00
Beaune, Vignes Franches	Louis Latour	£12.50
Beaune, Grèves	Remoissenet	£14.52
Pommard, Les Arvelets	Jaffelin	£18.08
Pommard, Le Clos Blanc	Machard de Gramont	£14.15
Volnay, Clos des Ducs	Marquis d'Angerville	£16.00

Grands Crus

Chapelle-Chambertin	Armand Rousseau		£18.21
Chambertin	Louis Trapet		£24.92
Bonnes Mares	Comte de Vogüé	M	£93.92
Musigny	Remoissenet		£36.94
Clos de Vougeot	Remoissenet		£14.22
Grands Echézeaux	Romanée-Conti		£56.00
Richebourg	Romanée-Conti		£66.36

1976

Village

Gevrey-Chambertin	Louis Latour	£17.95
Morey-Saint-Denis	Dujac	£14.23
Chambolle-Musigny	Doudet-Naudin	£14.90
Beaune	Doudet-Naudin	£13.75

Premiers Crus

Gevrey-Chambertin Cazetiers	Armand Rousseau	£16.15
Vougeot, Les Petits Vougeots	Bertagna	£10.97
Savigny-Lès-Beaune, Lavières	Remoissenet	£12.79
Beaune, Clos du Roi	Tollot-Beaut	£18.50
Beaune, Vignes Franches	Louis Latour	£14.37

Grands Crus

Charmes-Chambertin	Moillard	£17.55
Chambertin	Armand Rousseau	£38.20
Chambertin Clos de Bèze	Armand Rousseau	£38.20
Bonnes Mares	Moillard	£24.25
Clos de la Roche	Armand Rousseau	£27.25
Romanée-St-Vivant	Romanée-Conti	£57.50
Echézeaux	Doudet-Naudin	£16.68
Corton Bressandes	Tollot-Beaut	£22.10

1972

Village

Gevrey-Chambertin	English Bottled (Avery's)	£13.94

Premier Cru

Beaune Champimonts	Chanson	£7.29

Grands Crus

Mazis-Chambertin	English Bottled (Avery's)	£23.14
Bonnes Mares	Comte de Vogüé	£29.47
Grands Echézeaux	Romanée-Conti	£57.64

1971

Village

Morey-Saint-Denis	English Bottled (Berry Bros.)	£12.00
Chambolle-Musigny	Remoissenet	£20.07
Aloxe-Corton	English Bottled (Avery's)	£13.94
Santenay	Remoissenet	£12.79

Grands Crus

Mazis-Chambertin	Sichel	£13.42
Corton	Doudet-Naudin	£18.34

Few wine merchants stock older vintages of red Burgundy, though some regularly acquire small parcels of mature wine.

White Burgundy: Côte d'Or

1984		Retail Price
Puligny-Montrachet	Etienne Sauzet	£10.75
Puligny-Montrachet, Champ Canet	Etienne Sauzet	£13.17
Puligny-Montrachet, Truffières	Etienne Sauzet	£13.63
Bâtard-Montrachet	Etienne Sauzet	£19.26

1983

Village

Meursault	Henri Germain	£8.82
Meursault	Chanson	£7.25
Puligny-Montrachet	Leflaive	£10.86
Puligny-Montrachet	Etienne Sauzet	£10.30
Chassagne-Montrachet	Blain-Gagnard	£10.06

Premiers Crus

Meursault, Charmes	Henri Germain	£10.58
Meursault, Premier Cru	Henri Clerc	£14.81

Puligny-Montrachet, Les Combettes	Etienne Sauzet	£14.67
Puligny-Montrachet, Les Pucelles	Leflaive	£15.41
Chassagne-Montrachet, Caillerets	Blain-Gagnard	£12.08

Grands Crus

Corton-Charlemagne	Louis Latour	£29.50
Bienvenue-Bâtard-Montrachet	Leflaive	£17.25
Bâtard-Montrachet	Leflaive	£19.26
Bâtard-Montrachet	Etienne Sauzet	£20.59
Criots-Bâtard-Montrachet	Blain-Gagnard	£23.00
Chevalier-Montrachet	Leflaive	£22.49
Le Montrachet	Remoissenet	£40.97

1982

Village

Pernand-Vergelesses	Dubreuil-Fontaine	£6.96
Meursault	Henri Germain	£7.71
Meursault	Michelot	£8.82
St-Aubin	Henri Prudhon	£6.38
Puligny-Montrachet	Etienne Sauzet	£10.70
Puligny-Montrachet	Leflaive	£11.01
Chassagne-Montrachet	Marquis de Laguiche	£13.00

Premiers Crus

Beaune, Clos des Mouches	Joseph Drouhin	£13.46
Meursault, Charmes	Comtes Lafon	£10.75
Meursault, Charmes	Louis Jadot	£11.07
Meursault, Perrières	Guy Roulot et Fils	£10.93
Puligny-Montrachet, Champ Canet	Etienne Sauzet	£11.85
Puligny-Montrachet, Les Combettes	Leflaive	£14.49
Chassagne-Montrachet, Les Embrazées	Bernard Morey	£12.80

Grands Crus

Corton-Charlemagne	Bonneau du Martray	£17.25
Bienvenue-Bâtard-Montrachet	Etienne Sauzet	£18.40
Bâtard-Montrachet	Etienne Sauzet	£18.98
Criots-Bâtard-Montrachet	Blain-Gagnard	£18.98
Le Montrachet	Comtes Lafon	£48.59

1981

Village

Meursault	Ampeau et Fils	£10.45
Puligny-Montrachet	Leflaive	£10.65
Chassagne-Montrachet	Louis Latour	£12.95
Saint-Romain	René Thévenin-Monthélie	£6.16

Premiers Crus

Beaune, Clos des Mouches	Joseph Drouhin	£14.38
Meursault, Perrières	Jacques Prieur	£10.93
Meursault, Charmes	Louis Jadot	£12.50
Puligny-Montrachet, Les Combettes	Leflaive	£18.00

Puligny-Montrachet, Champ Canet	Etienne Sauzet	£13.80
Chassagne-Montrachet, Les Embrazées	Bernard Morey	£14.62

Grands Crus

Corton-Charlemagne	Jaffelin	£20.07
Corton-Charlemagne	Bonneau du Martray	£20.13
Corton-Charlemagne	Louis Latour	£30.00
Bâtard-Montrachet	Jaffelin	£23.14

1979

Village

Puligny-Montrachet	Leflaive	£13.42
Chassagne-Montrachet	Louis Latour	£12.84

Premiers Crus

Meursault, Perrières	Chanson	£8.45
Meursault, Genevrières	Louis Latour	£14.72
Meursault, Charmes	Comtes Lafon	£20.13

Grands Crus

Corton-Charlemagne	Michel Voarick	£20.13
Corton-Charlemagne	Louis Latour	£26.18
Le Montrachet	Comtes Lafon	£46.00

1978

Village

Meursault-Blagny	Louis Latour	£15.62
Puligny-Montrachet	Louis Latour	£14.57
Chassagne-Montrachet	Albert Morey	£12.98

Premiers Crus

Meursault, Charmes	Comtes de Lafon	£25.88
Puligny-Montrachet, Clos de la Garenne	René Thévenin-Monthélie	£18.50
Chassagne-Montrachet, Les Champs Gains	Albert Morey	£13.03

Grands Crus

Corton-Charlemagne	Remoissenet	£32.34
Corton Charlemagne	Louis Latour	£55.00

White Burgundy: Chablis

1984		Retail Price

Village

Chablis	Albert Pic	£5.81
Chablis	Domaine de Vauroux	£5.52

Premiers Crus

Chablis Fourchaume	Albert Pic	£7.61
Chablis Montmains	Louis Michel	£7.21
Chablis Vaillons	Albert Pic	£6.98

Grands Crus

Chablis Blanchots	Albert Pic	£11.18
Chablis Les Clos	Albert Pic	£11.18

1983

Village

Petit Chablis	Jean Durup	£4.37
Chablis	Albert Pic	£5.29
Chablis	Etienne Defaix	£5.18

Premiers Crus

Chablis, Fourchaume	Roger Seguinot	£6.62
Chablis, Montmains	Louis Michel	£6.46
Chablis, Montée-de-Tonnerre	Albert Pic	£6.81
Chablis, Vaillons	René Dauvissat	£6.61

Grands Crus

Chablis Les Clos	René Dauvissat	£8.45
Chablis, Valmur	Albert Pic	£8.48
Chablis, Vaudésir	Louis Michel	£11.50

Vintage Port

Retail price		Auction price per dozen duty paid
Croft		
1982	£86.40 per dozen ex cellars	
1977	£19.25	
1975	£12.73	
1970	£21.74	£175
1966	£27.00	£190
1963		£330
1960	£27.50	£280
1955		£420
1945		£1,000
Dow		
1983	£100 per dozen ex cellars	
1980	£12.00	
1977	£19.25	£160
1975	£11.50	£110
1970	£20.90	£140
1966	£27.00	£220
1963		£330
1960		£230
1945		£1,000
Fonseca		
1983	£110 per dozen ex cellars	
1980	£12.21	
1977	£15.00	£190
1975	£11.50	£120
1970	£22.31	£195
1966	£25.85	£220
1963	£40.48	£380
1955	£51.75	

Retail Price		Auction price per dozen duty paid
Graham		
1983	£105 per dozen ex cellars	
1980	£12.21	
1977	£20.15	£175
1975	£12.20	£125
1970	£21.97	£200
1966	£25.85	£220
1963	£37.00	£370
1960	£28.50	£190
1955	£60.00	£480
1945		£1,250
Taylor		
1983	£120 per dozen ex cellars	
1980	£12.50	£125
1977	£24.38	£220
1975	£13.36	£140
1970	£24.04	£210
1966	£28.98	£230
1963	£48.00	£420
1960	£31.00	£240
1955	£61.18	£560
1945		£1,600
1935		£1,500
Warre		
1983	£105 per dozen ex cellars	
1980	£11.93	
1977	£19.25	£165
1975	£11.90	£120
1970	£20.90	£175
1966		£210
1963	£38.18	£310
1960	£30.13	£240
1945		£880

Index

Photographic Acknowledgements

The authors and publishers are grateful to all those institutions and individuals who have lent illustrative material for reproduction in this book.

Adnams & Co. PLC 20, 50
Marchesi L. & P. Antinori 102
The Australian Trade Commission 117
Bayerische Staatsbibliothek, Munich 96 (top)
Berry Bros. & Rudd Ltd. 10
Boodle's 119
Bouchard Père & Fils 56–7, 72, 73
René Burri/John Hillelson Agency Plates 11, 12
J. Calvet & Co. Plate 15
Christie, Manson & Woods Ltd. 25, 26 (top and bottom), 27, 33
Matthew Clark and Sons Ltd. 106–7
Cordier Wines Ltd. 45
Deinhard & Co. Ltd. 94–5, 96
Domaine Dujac (photo R. Seysses) 63
Alexander Findlater & Co. Ltd. 115, 118
Food and Wine from France 13, 14 (bottom), 17, 18, 41, 53 (bottom), 64, 77 (right), 79, 80, 82, 83, 87, 88, 92, Plates 1, 2, 3, 4, 8, 16
Tom Fraily 28
J. R. Freeman & Co. Ltd. 38

The French Government Tourist Office 14 (top), 38, 67, 74
The German Wine Information Service 97, 98–9
Heitz Wine Cellars, Plate 6
Denis Hughes-Gilbey 53 (top)
Paul Jaboulet Aîné 77 (left)
P. Jones-Griffiths/John Hillelson Agency Plate 5
Pablo Keller 106 (top)
By courtesy of Krug 86, 87
Kurti/Camera Press 9
Lay and Wheeler 37 (left and right)
Phillip Lee 7, 24, 104
Château Margaux Plate 7
Mayacamas Vineyards 111
M. P. Miles 108
Robert Mondavi Wine Cellars 112
Joseph Phelps Vineyards Plate 13
The House of Sandeman Plate 9
Brian Seed/John Hillelson Agency Plate 14
Sherry Lehmann, New York 23
Michele de Silva/Camera Press 41
Stag's Leap Wine Cellars Plate 10
Victoria and Albert Museum, London 21
The Wine Society, frontispiece (photo Hans Edwards) 22

$$\begin{array}{r} 37.4 \\ 5.8\overline{\smash{\big)}\,217.0} \\ \underline{174} \\ 430 \\ \underline{406} \\ 240 \end{array}$$